SWEET CAPTIVITY

JULIA SYKES

PROLOGUE

"You don't want to do this," I choked out past the lump of terror that clogged my throat. I kept a wary eye on the wicked hunting knife Cristian Moreno held naturally at his side, as though it were an innocuous extension of his arm rather than a threat to my life. "Let me go."

He threw back his head and laughed, his perfect white teeth flashing as the booming sound assaulted my eardrums. My hands shook violently, causing the ropes that bound my arms behind me to chafe against my wrists. The burn of the rough fibers against my skin and cold bite of the metal chair beneath me were peripheral; my entire focus was centered on Moreno and the way the gleam of the spare overhead light bulb made his dark eyes glint as sharply as the knife in his hand.

"No, Samantha," he corrected me calmly, his

light Colombian accent making his deep voice almost lyrical when he spoke my name. "You're never leaving this place. Not alive, at least. If you answer my questions, I might be inclined to mercy. Otherwise..." He left the unspoken threat hanging in the air, the implication clear. I would experience agony before he finally disposed of me.

No. Don't think like that.

I gasped in several deep breaths so I could manage to speak again.

"My friends will find me," I asserted, knowing Dex wouldn't leave me to die here. My best friend would do whatever it took to rescue me.

"If they do, they won't find more than what's left of your body."

Ice crystallized in my veins. He took a step toward me, raising the knife. I tried to shrink away, but the unyielding metal chair behind my back kept me immobile.

"You can't hurt me," I said desperately, twisting against my restraints. "If you kill me, my friends will hunt you down."

His dazzling smile illuminated his darkly handsome features with cruel amusement.

"I want them to know what I've done. Your death will be a warning. We're going to send a little message to your friends." He gestured behind him, and for the first time, my gaze darted away from the threat before me.

A man loomed a few feet away, the light on his smart phone indicating that he was recording me. A wicked scar puckered his tanned cheek, deepening his fearsome scowl. His black gaze bored into me, his dark glare penetrating my soul. I shuddered and tore my eyes away, unable to bear looking at him.

Moreno laughed again. "What, you don't like my little brother?" He cocked his head at me. "Maybe I'll give you to him to play with, after I'm finished with you. He has... very *unique* tastes." He reached for me, his long fingers trailing down my cheek. I cringed away, my stomach churning. "I think Andrés will like you. Such pale skin. It will mark up nicely." He shook his head slightly, still smiling. "But I'm getting ahead of myself. He can have you when I'm done. I'm going to extract my answers first."

The cool tip of the knife kissed my throat, and I choked on a scream as horror overwhelmed me.

CHAPTER 1
ONE DAY EARLIER

I sat at my computer, my mind completely absorbed in the task before me. The fact that I was staring at the screen didn't register; I'd fallen into my work, as though I was *inside* the code, surrounded by information. I was in my element. I might not be physically kicking ass, but I was powerful in this technological world.

Truthfully, I wasn't all that good at kicking ass. I'd transferred from tech analyst to field agent a few months ago, and I was coming to realize it hadn't been the best life choice. It had been a reactionary thing, a desperate cry for attention. I'd thought that maybe if I put myself in the line of fire, Dex's protective instincts would kick in and he'd finally realize what had been right in front of him for years: me, hopelessly in love with him.

Despite a very small voice in my mind telling

me I shouldn't, I diverted from my mission and hacked into the webcam on Dex's computer. He was seated only a few desks away from me in the FBI field office, but I couldn't allow myself to be caught shooting furtive glances in his direction. This was much more discrete.

Some people might classify my activity as *stalking*, but I'd never quite been able to wrap my mind around unspoken social boundaries. Besides, how else was I ever supposed to work up the courage to look the man I loved in the eye?

Dex was frowning at something on his computer screen, deep in thought. With his chiseled features and piercing, pale blue eyes, he was painfully perfect. Not to mention his blond hair that made him appear like a fierce avenging angel when he was intent on protecting those closest to him.

But he'd never seen me as more than a buddy. I wasn't even sure if he saw me as a woman at all.

I really shouldn't have been surprised. With my skinny figure, shockingly orange hair, and decidedly tomboy-ish sense of style, my feminine side was all but invisible. Maybe if I'd put in more effort, he'd have noticed me. But *seductress* wasn't exactly my M.O., and I'd probably trip in high heels.

I sighed. I was certainly the polar opposite of the brunette bombshell Dex had fallen for: perfect, gorgeous, sensual Chloe Martin. No wonder he was smitten with her instead of me.

Cruelly familiar pain knifed through my chest at the thought of them together, perfectly gorgeous and perfectly happy. Grimacing, I closed the connection to his webcam and threw myself back into my work.

"What are you doing?" I recognized the masculine voice, but I still jolted at its proximity.

I whirled in my office chair to face Jason Harper, the agent I'd been working for over the last few weeks.

Working with, I internally corrected myself, even though it didn't feel that way. Jason tended to bark orders, and I tended to comply. We were supposed to be equals, even if he did have seniority as a field agent. But Jason had a commanding presence about him, and when his green eyes flashed, I jumped to obey.

"Sam," he prompted me in that stern tone that made my insides quiver with unease. I snapped to attention, my gaze fixing squarely on him rather than darting around the room in my familiar nervous pattern. "What are you doing?" he asked again, somewhat impatient. He peered behind me at my computer, squinting at the code scrolling across the screen. He'd have an easier time reading it if it were Cyrillic script, and Jason didn't know a word of Russian.

"Nothing," I said quickly, knowing he wouldn't approve of my activities. I mean, he wouldn't like the stalking thing, but he'd be more annoyed at my personal distraction from my work. Jason and I were supposed to be working a case together, off the books. We were tracking the shadowy Division 9-C, a branch of a clandestine organization we knew little about. Well, we knew they were bad guys, and they needed to be taken down. That was enough for me.

Jason was the muscle on the ground, and I was the brains behind the operation. Or the tech goddess. I'd take either title, really.

Jason's dark brows rose up to his neatly-styled black hair. "Nothing," he mimicked me in a reproving monotone. "Do you want to try that again? The truth this time, Sam."

I shifted on my chair and cut my eyes away. My gaze landed on the water cooler, the worn navy carpet, the shiny spot where the fluorescent lights caught on Jason's highly polished leather shoes; anywhere but meeting his steady stare.

"You don't want to know," I mumbled. "Anyway, don't we need to get out and run surveillance on Moreno? I can fill you in on the other thing on the way."

The *other thing* was our Division 9-C investigation. Our official assignment with the FBI was hunting notorious drug lord Cristian Moreno, who had moved his business into Chicago in recent months after withdrawing from New York. He'd been pushing the date rape drug Bliss, and he was using it to start a human trafficking ring.

Division 9-C might be bad guys, but Moreno was his own special brand of evil.

The toe of Jason's shoe tapped against the carpet in a condemning, staccato rhythm, but he decided not to press me. "Fine," he allowed. "Let's go. We can talk in the car."

I blew out a relieved breath. I hated having all that alpha male power focused on me. It was bad enough dealing with men on a normal basis, much less working alongside walking testosterone like Jason. He was nice, but that didn't mean he didn't intimidate the hell out of me.

At least he kept a respectful distance while we walked across the field office and toward the elevator that would take us down to the parking garage. Once we were trapped inside the confines of the tiny metal box, I shifted my body into the corner to keep as much space between us as possible. It was a matter of habit. I wasn't afraid of Jason, but I never allowed anyone into my personal space if I could help it. I didn't do *people*. I much preferred to sit behind my computer screen, where I was a safe distance from everyone on the web, not to mention completely anonymous.

Now that I was a field agent, I had to actually

interact with people. Talk to them. Look them in the eye.

Moving into the field had been a stupid idea. Reckless. And my involvement in this secret mission for Jason was even more reckless.

But it was too late to go back now. As the FBI's best tech analyst, I had a special skill set that Jason needed. I might have transferred to field agent six months ago, but that didn't mean I'd forgotten all my hacking skills. There was no one else who could do this job for Jason, so I'd step up and be the hero. Heroine. Whichever. Was it sexist to apply gender to the term? Probably. I couldn't keep track of social norms.

When the elevator finally came to a stop and the doors opened, Jason gestured for me to exit first. I knew he was trying to be a gentleman, but I'd have preferred to follow him. As it was, I had to scoot past him, my body almost making contact with his.

He didn't seem to notice my discomfort. Or if he did, he was accustomed to it and didn't really think much of what most people would term *Sam's odd behavior.* Well, that was the nice term.

Weirdo. Freak.

The derogatory name-calling didn't faze me. Not one bit.

"Talk," Jason ordered when we were safely in the privacy of the car. I hadn't trusted anyone in the field office. Well, no one but Jason. If we were over-heard discussing our secret operation, we could be betrayed.

Dex wouldn't betray us. I knew the truth, but I wasn't willing to pull him into this. For one, I was still struggling with the personal sense of betrayal he'd inflicted when he'd fallen in love with Chloe instead of me. For another, Jason had insisted on keeping our op as under-the-radar as possible. This wasn't an official investigation. That meant limiting our manpower. Womanpower. Person-power.

God, this sexism thing was hard.

"Sam," he said my name sharply, calling my attention back to him. I could tell he was getting impatient with my wayward thoughts.

"Right," I said quickly. "Division 9-C has their own hacker. They set up false identities for Natalie. There's an electronic footprint somewhere. I'm working on tracing it, and that will lead us to more information on the organization they represent. Their hacker is good, but I'm better. I just need a little more time."

"And how do you know you're better?" Jason challenged.

"Because I'm me," I said coolly, utterly confi-dent in my capabilities. "You focus on protecting Natalie, and I'll focus on getting us a new lead."

His hands tightened on the steering wheel, his knuckles going white. No doubt, he was remembering the terrible things that had been done to Natalie, the woman he loved. He might have finally rescued her from the people who had tortured her and twisted her mind, but that didn't mean she was safe. The people who had so ruthlessly used her—the clandestine Division 9-C and the organization they represented—were still out there. There might not be physical leads, but there had to be traces of them buried deep in the web somewhere.

We finished driving to our destination in heavy silence. I wished I knew what to say to alleviate some of Jason's tension, but I didn't really know where to begin. So I twisted my hands in my lap and tried to calm my whirring thoughts. Per usual, they were firing in several directions at once. I had the Division 9-C hacker to consider, Jason's feelings to fret over, and our current investigation into Cristian Moreno.

We pulled up outside a nondescript townhouse, positioning our sedan half a block back from our target. This fieldwork was actually kind of boring a lot of the time. We settled in to wait and watch. I'd so much rather be behind my computer, but at least I wasn't having to interact with anyone but Jason. And he was content to focus on our investigation instead of idle chatter.

We'd gotten a lead that this townhouse was being used by Cristian Moreno in his Bliss trafficking. He seemed to have smaller distribution centers set up all over town. It would have been so much easier to raid a massive warehouse, but Moreno wasn't stupid enough to keep his product all in one place.

Chicago police had arrested a man for dealing Bliss in this neighborhood two days ago, and he'd directed us to this townhouse as the place where he picked up his product. We could have raided the building, but we wanted to monitor the situation for a few days first. Taking out one small distribution center would be a win, but we might be able to find the larger network if we identified Moreno's people coming and going and tracked them from the premises.

Overall, it was a pretty boring day. Watching people and taking notes wasn't all that interesting. By the time Jason dropped me off at my own townhome, I was eager to get back online and do something that was actually mentally stimulating.

I dropped into my ergonomic chair and blew out a long sigh. It felt damn good to be back in front of my personal computer. Away from people.

I was so eager to get back to my coding that I didn't even bother to change out of my work clothes and into comfy sweats before turning on my computer. Unfortunately, a chat box popped up as soon as I logged on.

Dex Scott wants to video chat.

I frowned and hit the *ignore* button. I didn't

have time to talk to Dex. I had to find the Division 9-C hacker.

Besides, I didn't want to talk to Dex. I was too fried, too raw to face him. He'd barely paid attention to me since I'd made the reckless decision to become a field agent. Sure, he still contacted me to play an online game from time to time. When he wasn't fucking Chloe. Otherwise, he barely interacted with me at all. Especially not in the office, where he'd made it clear he didn't approve of my choice to transfer into the field.

He was a damn good agent. Far better than I would ever be. I'd longed to train with him when I'd transferred to field agent, to feel his huge body against mine when we sparred.

But he'd refused to help train me.

My cheeks heated and my sex clenched at the thought of him *training* me. After hacking into his internet search history and tracking his sexual predilections for years, I knew my gentle giant of a friend harbored decidedly darker fantasies: domination, bondage, discipline.

I'd never thought I'd be interested in such depraved acts. Truthfully, before I met Dex, I hadn't thought much about sex at all. The girls in my dorm at college had teased me for being an asexual, socially awkward geek. It hadn't bothered me.

Really. Not one bit.

A part of my brain acknowledged the silent lie in my mind.

I'd also tried to lie to myself about Dex for years: that he would come to care for me; that he'd finally realize I was hopelessly in love with him. I craved to be the object of his darker desires.

The beeping emanating from my speakers became incessant.

Dex Scott wants to chat.

I turned off the chat app. Talking to him hurt too much. I needed space to avoid the pain.

Shoving him from my mind, I threw myself back into my work, sinking into the deep web.

I was so absorbed in my task that I didn't hear the lock click back or the soft sound of my front door rubbing across the carpet as it opened. I was jolted out of my work when the back of my neck tingled, an animal response to a lurking threat. A gloved hand clamped over my mouth, muffling my shocked gasp. A sharp sting penetrated my neck as the needle sank in.

The world turned surreal as the drugs instantly cocooned me in soft, dark clouds, and I floated into nothingness.

CHAPTER 2

The safety of my home had been shattered. Someone had drugged me, taken me. My memories of how I'd fallen into Cristian Moreno's clutches were hazy, but there was no denying my terrifying new reality: I was in the hands of the vicious Colombian drug lord, and his knife was at my throat.

Toxic fear engulfed me, freezing the scream that had escaped me for mere seconds. Cristian stepped behind me so his brother's camera could get clearer footage of the horror I was enduring. His big fist tangled in my hair, jerking my head back so I had no choice but to stare up into his cruel black eyes.

The cold tip of the knife scraped upward from the center of my throat, grazing over my skin as it traced a path under my chin. I stopped breathing when the flat of the blade swiped across the line of my lips. A high whimper slipped through them, the resultant vibration threatening to make the knife pierce my skin. As it was, the tightly packed nerve endings on my lips sparked as the cool metal kissed them.

The knife left my mouth, but I didn't have time to suck in a panting breath before the frigid blade returned to my throat.

"You were in my territory today, watching my people. One of my men followed you home. Who are you working for?" he demanded.

"I'm FBI," I said, my voice barely more than a whisper. With the knife at my throat, I could scarcely draw the breath I needed to speak.

He frowned at me. "A sniper made an attempt on my life a few days ago. The feds wouldn't assassinate me. Who are you really working for?" The blade sliced a thin, stinging line across my throat.

"I really am FBI," I said in a rush, the truth spilling from my lips. If he knew I was a federal agent, he wouldn't dare hurt me. "My name is Samantha Browning. I'm a tech analyst. Well, I was. I'm a field agent now. I'm not trying to kill you. We're investigating you. You have to know you're on our radar. Please, I swear I'm FBI." I was aware that I was babbling, but I couldn't stop pleading for my life.

He considered me for a long, terrifying moment, weighing my fate. "You're a tech analyst?

That means you have access to all the evidence the feds have on me. If you're telling the truth about who you are."

"I am," I said quickly. "You can't hurt me. If you do, my friends will come after you."

"I think I'll give you to my brother, after all," he mused. "He'll make sure you're telling the truth. I'd rather not mutilate you, if you're going to be useful to me. Andrés has more creative ways of breaking women. And I'll keep our little video to ourselves. If you are who you say you are, I'd rather your friends at the FBI didn't know I have you."

The knifepoint pressed against my cheek, just below my left eye. The pressure increased slightly, and I felt warmth bead on my skin. It slid down my cheek like a crimson tear. My eyes watered, and Cristian's handsome face wavered above me.

"Maybe I'll give you a scar to match my brother's first," he mused.

A deep growl sounded from a few feet in front of me, and I knew it came from Andrés. I couldn't so much as glance in his direction; Cristian's long fingers in my hair kept me immobile.

A sharp grin lit his features with amusement. "Apparently, he wants you mostly intact. Should I give him what he wants?"

The fearsome growl sounded again, a wordless warning. I shuddered, equally as frightened of the prospect of his desire to *have me* as I was of the knife piercing my cheek.

"Not the face, then," Cristian said decisively. "But I think I'll let Andrés see what he's getting to work with."

The knife left my face, but the blade instantly hooked beneath the top button of my shirt. It gave way easily as the sharp steel tore through thread. He continued to move the blade downward, trailing a sickening path between my breasts, over my navel, down to the top of my slacks. The fabric fell open with a flick of the knife, leaving me exposed in my white cotton bra.

A plea for mercy locked in my throat. I couldn't speak, could barely breathe. My mind began to shut down, the adrenaline created by fear clouding my brain.

Cristian's fingers tightened in my hair, giving me a bite of pain. "Stay with us, Samantha," he ordered smoothly.

The world sharpened around me with cruel clarity just before pain sliced into me. The tip of the knife grated a torturously slow line along my right collarbone. The cut was shallow, but blood welled up as the blade scraped bone. The scream that had been trapped inside me burst out as pain seared through me. He hooked the blade beneath the little strip of cotton at the middle of my bra, parting the fabric and exposing me.

My scream choked off on a sob as terror mingled with humiliation.

"What do you think, *hermanito?*" Cristian asked with mild interest. "Is she pretty enough for you? She's not a great beauty, but her nipples stand out nicely against her pale skin."

My skin turned frigid, my flesh pebbling as ice sank into my veins. I vaguely recognized that I was going into shock as my entire body began to shake violently.

"And her eyes are quite lovely," he continued in detached observation. "So much fear there. You like when they're frightened, don't you, Andrés?"

His low grunt in reply rolled around my mind, but my capacity for conscious thought had been ripped to shreds. The knife left my breasts to slice through the ropes that bound my wrists behind me. I slumped forward, my watery muscles incapable of holding me upright.

Strong arms closed around my shoulders, bracing me before I slid to the floor. I was dimly aware of my body being lifted. My head lolled back, and the last thing I saw before my mind short-circuited was Andrés' fearsome, scarred face looming over me.

STINGING PAIN ON MY CHEST YANKED ME BACK TO awareness, and I bolted upright with a gasp. Panic blinded me, but firm hands gripped my upper arms, pressing me back down against something soft that cushioned my body. I was no longer sitting on the unyielding metal chair. I recognized the feel of a mattress beneath me, and my torso was pinned down against it by a strong, masculine hold.

I squirmed and kicked, instinctively trying to fight my way free. I became aware of cool air against my breasts, and I realized I was still exposed. My heart hammered against my ribcage, and I doubled my efforts to fight off the man holding me down, my fingers clawing blindly. His hands easily encircled my wrists, trapping them at either side of my hips.

"Calm down, *cosita*, or I'll have to restrain you." I recognized the soft Colombian accent.

Moreno had me. He'd hurt me, stripped me...

Oh god. He'd given me to his terrifying brother. Andrés.

And now I was half-naked and helpless in his steely hold.

I couldn't stop thrashing, my muscles rippling with effort to break free. My stomach twisted, nausea rising as the full horror of my situation came down on me.

A low sound of disapproval grated against my mind. His grip instantly shifted, tugging my arms over my head. He secured them there with one big hand. Something cool and supple encircled my right wrist. Metal jingled against metal as he buckled the cuff into place.

I twisted my entire body, trying to angle myself so I could kick out at him. Desperation clawed at my insides, and all my training left my head as animal terror took hold. My awkward attempts to resist him made no effect, and he quickly secured my other wrist.

Working in silence, he caught my left ankle, pulling it diagonally toward the bottom corner of the bed. My eyes finally focused and I watched in helpless horror as he bound my legs to either side of the four-poster, spreading me wide. I still wore my slacks, but I felt terribly exposed and vulnerable.

I thrashed against the restraints, but he pressed his big palm against my bare abdomen, pinning me down against the mattress and effectively ending my struggles. All I could do was jerk uselessly against the cuffs. Fear coursed through me. My fight-or-flight instincts had settled on flight, but there was nowhere for me to go. That didn't stop my body from twisting like a wild thing, panic beating against the inside of my chest.

His dark eyes watched me with calm certainty as he simply waited. I wasn't sure how long it took for my muscles to burn with exertion, and I finally

22

gave up, my limbs trembling where they were stretched above and below me, laying me out before him.

"Are you done?" he asked coolly.

"Fuck you," I seethed, my acid tongue the only weapon left to me.

Keeping me pinned in place with one hand, his other swiftly came down and cracked across the outer swell of my breasts, one after the other in rapid succession. My sensitive flesh instantly began to burn, and I cried out. I couldn't escape the pain; I was trapped in place for the harsh censure.

Tears leaked from the corners of my eyes, and he finally stopped.

"I won't tolerate insults," he said, still unnervingly calm. It almost would have been less disconcerting if he'd shouted. "You will speak to me with respect. Do you understand?"

"No." The refusal came out as a horrified moan.

"You will understand soon," he said, utterly confident. "You're frightened, but you will learn. For now, I'm warning you not to curse at me again. Tell me you'll obey."

The tears came faster, spilling down my temples and falling into my hair.

His face shifted to a forbidding mask. "Tell me."

I couldn't manage more than a fearful whimper, but I nodded shakily. I didn't want him to slap me again, and I recognized that there was nothing I could do to prevent him from doing it if he decided he wanted to.

His countenance softened, his scar easing so it wasn't as pronounced. "In the future, I will expect a verbal answer. You belong to me now, Samantha. Defiance will lead to punishment. Obedience will be rewarded. You choose whichever you want. I might seem like a harsh Master, but I'm fair. Your behavior has consequences, either painful or pleasurable for you."

"Please," I forced out past the lump in my throat. "I can't... I don't... Don't..." I began to pant out the fragmented words as my breathing turned shallower, until I was gasping but not drawing in air.

His hands bracketed my face, shockingly gentle. "Breathe," he ordered, his accented voice low and soft, as though trying to soothe a frightened animal.

I certainly felt like a panicked, primal thing; trapped and terrified.

His fingers threaded through my hair on either side of my head, massaging gently.

"Breathe with me," he cajoled. He drew in a slow, deep breath and then blew it out on a long exhale. "Again," he commanded, and I vaguely recognized that I'd obeyed and matched his breathing, my lungs too desperate for oxygen to resist. I sucked in another shaky breath, mirroring him. We repeated the process several more times, until I was able to breathe almost normally. I sank down into the mattress as my body went limp, all the fight going out of me as exhaustion sapped my mind.

"Better." He nodded his approval. His gaze finally diverted from my face, and he reached for a damp cloth that he'd placed beside me on the bed. "You're still bleeding," he told me. "I'm going to clean you up. This will sting a little. Stay still."

I couldn't have moved away even if I still possessed any willpower to do so. One of his hands remained bracketed at the side of my face, his thumb hooking beneath my jaw to hold me steady.

The cool cloth gently touched my cheek, and I hissed in pain. Just as he'd warned me, the solution that soaked the cloth stung, and I knew it was more than water.

"Good girl," he said, the warm praise in his tone fucking with my addled mind. I only recognized the comfort in it, unable to process the twisted nature of how he was manipulating me. Anything was preferable to the unrelenting terror that had utterly sapped my will and smothered all thought of resistance.

He continued his gentle ministrations, his dark eyes completely focused on his task as he cleaned the cut on my collarbone. Keening sounds eased up my throat, and he softly shushed me.

When he finished, he sat back and considered me for a long moment, his black eyes searching mine. Instinct urged me to look away, to escape his probing gaze. The intensity with which he watched me made it impossible for me to break eye contact. I shuddered violently, unable to bear his scrutiny.

His grip on my face shifted, and his calloused fingertips smoothed over the furrow in my brow.

"You're hurting," he remarked. "You didn't do anything to deserve this."

He reached for something else on the bed beside me, and I cringed when my gaze fixed on it: a syringe. I didn't want to be unconscious again, helpless and unable to defend myself.

"My brother gave me this in case I needed to subdue you, but it will take away your pain. I told you, I'm a fair Master. I won't hurt you if you don't earn a punishment."

"I don't want it," I managed to whisper.

"I decide what's best for you from now on," he declared calmly.

"Please," I begged uselessly as he carefully slid the needle into my arm.

"Hush now, *cosita*," he murmured. "You'll feel better when you wake up."

"No," I slurred, the drugs making my tongue heavy within seconds.

His long fingers smoothed over my hair, petting me as I fell into darkness.

CHAPTER 3

A pleasant, warm weight pressed against my chest. I snuggled into it, finding comfort in the weighted blanket that helped calm my anxiety. I'd bought it three months ago, and I'd found that it helped soothe my racing thoughts enough so I could actually sleep through the night.

I certainly felt rested, even if my mouth was too dry. Like the time I'd binged on Smirnoff Ice and woken up with a wicked hangover. This time, the headache was mercifully absent.

Although my eyes were still closed, my brow furrowed. I didn't remember drinking last night. What did I...?

My eyes snapped open, and my body jerked bolt upright. Andrés' corded arm fell from my chest, where it had been draped across me. I gasped and scrambled away from him, tumbling over the edge of the mattress to fall on my ass. Terror ripped through me as reality slammed back into place.

I pushed up onto my feet and backed away from the bed, desperate to put distance between us. His dark gaze fixed on me, but he didn't so much as lift his head from the pillow. I expected him to come after me, to attack. But he simply watched me with mild curiosity, as though interested to see what I would do next.

I became very aware of his eyes on me, and I realized cool air kissed every inch of my skin. I instinctively covered my breasts and sex before my mind fully processed the fact that I was completely naked. I remembered the needle sliding beneath my skin while I was bound to his bed, helpless. He'd drugged me, stripped me when I was unconscious.

Then he'd *spooned* me.

And I'd cuddled closer.

Tears burned the corners of my eyes as panic overwhelmed me. I was naked with my captor. He'd touched me while I was drugged and unable to defend myself.

I shuddered at the thought of him *touching* me. He could have done anything to me, and I wouldn't know.

How could I have rested comfortably beside the monster for even a moment?

"I thought you were my blanket," I blurted out,

needing to justify my actions to myself but not meaning to speak the words aloud.

One corner of his lips twitched upward. "Excuse me?" he asked, his accented voice colored with amusement. He propped up on one elbow, his gaze sharpening with interest that had become something more than idle curiosity.

I took a hasty step back, clutching my hands tighter against my most vulnerable areas. Fear spiked, instinct driving me to keep as much space between us as possible while trying to cover myself.

"I have a weighted blanket. At home. It helps with anxiety," I babbled, the words spilling out of me as panic addled my mind. "Your arm was heavy. I thought it was my blanket. That's why I... Stop looking at me!" I shouted the last, unable to bear the intensity of his black eyes studying my naked body.

"I like looking at what's mine," he said, his voice deep and even, as though he wasn't saying something abhorrent.

"I'm not yours," I countered, my voice high and thin.

His eyes darkened to flat black as his pupils dilated. He finally stood, the sheets falling from his powerful form. Every inch of him was sculpted, every muscle defined. He wore only sweatpants slung low on his hips, so I got a clear view of just how hulking and strong he was. More than a dozen raised, pale scars crisscrossed his torso and abs, standing out against his tanned skin. They weren't as deep and puckered as the wicked furrow that had been carved into his cheek, but they were no less intimidating. How many times must he have fought and won to bear so many marks of violence on his skin?

I shrank back, feeling small and horribly vulnerable. I might be a field agent, but I wasn't equipped for this. No one had trained me for this terrifying scenario; where I was naked and outmatched by at least a hundred pounds of muscle, facing off against a man who was clearly a ruthless fighter. A man who'd easily wrestled me down and bound me to his bed. A man who had slapped my bare breasts and said I belonged to him.

My flesh tingled with the memory of his harsh rebuke, and a light tremor raced over my skin, making it pebble.

"My brother was right," he said, still studying me intently. "Your eyes are lovely when you're frightened. Wide and blue. Like a pretty doll." He took a step toward me. "Am I so terrifying, *sirenita?*"

I dodged back, and my bare butt hit cool glass. I glanced behind me at the shock of cold, and my stomach instantly dropped at the view. The Chicago skyline stretched out before me, and the people dotting the sidewalk below were far too small. Familiar fear twisted my gut at the sensation of being too high up, adding a fresh layer of terror to my overloaded system. I tried to push away from the floor-to-ceiling window, the only thin barrier between me and a long fall to my death.

I smacked into a wall of warm, hard muscle. Andrés had closed the distance between us swiftly and soundlessly, trapping his prey with ruthless intent. And just like a small, cornered animal, I lashed out at the threat in an attempt to save myself.

My training kicked in without thought, and I swung my fist at his granite jaw. The blow connected, sending pain radiating through my knuckles. He barely flinched. I didn't pause, intent on inflicting as much damage as possible. I brought my knee up, desperate to hit him where he was most vulnerable.

He shifted, his rock-hard thigh blocking my knee before I could make contact. I had a split second to register his disapproving frown before my entire world tilted and spun. His big hands were on my naked body, taking me down to the plush carpet. My hips hit his thighs, and the air rushed from my chest as his palm pressed down between my shoulder blades, pushing my breasts against the floor to the point of pain. My fingernails scrabbled against the carpet, struggling for purchase as my flight response kicked in again.

A high, feral sound left me when his hand left

my back, only to catch my wrists. He encircled both with his long fingers, pinning my arms behind me so all I could do was thrash wildly, gasping and kicking my legs at nothing. I was trapped again, unable to fight, unable to flee. My heart fluttered against my ribcage, and I gasped for air as panic clogged my throat.

I heard the *crack* resound against the high ceiling just before the shocking sting bloomed on my upper thigh. I shrieked and writhed, trying to escape the burn of his palm. A twin hit landed on my other leg, and my shocked cry turned to a furious scream. Impotent rage seared through my veins alongside white-hot mortification. He was *spanking* me.

"Don't ever try that again," he admonished in even tones as he delivered another cruel blow, just beneath the lower curve of my ass. "You will not fight me." Another burning hit. "You belong to me. You will accept your place."

"Stop fucking saying that!" I shouted, tears of frustration and pain pricking at the corners of my eyes.

"I get to say what I want. I get to do what I want." Each statement was punctuated by a slap. "You will learn to mind your tongue. You will learn to behave. You're mine, *cosita*. Mine to play with. Mine to punish. Just *mine*."

"No." The refusal came out on a low moan. My

flesh was on fire, my mind flooded with fear and humiliation. My naked body was draped over my captor's lap, and he was making it clear that I didn't have a hope of fighting him. I didn't realize that I'd stopped thrashing, but a harsh sob tore from my chest.

The blows stopped, and he smoothed his palm over my heated skin. It prickled with awareness, every nerve ending on fire.

"There," he said, his voice rich with satisfaction. "Isn't that better? Don't try to hurt me again, Samantha."

He continued to stroke my aching ass, and I groaned in relief. The light caress helped soothe away some of the pain.

Fresh shock tore through me when he touched two fingers against the seam of my sex.

"You're wet," he said in a low rumble. "We are going to get along, *sirenita*."

I stiffened in his hold. He was touching me *there*. No one touched me there. Not even me.

Horror washed over me, smothering awareness of what he'd said. I couldn't focus, couldn't think. Fear clouded everything, seeping into my mind like dense fog.

"Don't," I squeaked out, renewing my struggles. I became very aware of the hard rod pressing into my belly. His erection throbbed and jerked as I twisted on his lap.

He hissed out a breath, and his hand tightened around my wrists, holding me securely in place. "Stop grinding against me," he said tightly. "You want me to touch your little clit, greedy girl?"

You want me to touch your secret place again, don't you, dirty little girl? a long-forgotten, phantom voice whispered across my mind. Terror and shame mingled in a sickening cocktail, making my stomach clench and my head spin. I couldn't think; I couldn't think about the voice. All thought blanked out, overtaken by pure, icy panic. The cold sank into my bones, and I shuddered violently.

Warmth enfolded me. Slowly, the ice ebbed away. I became aware of a low, lilting voice saying words I couldn't comprehend. A few seconds later, I realized they were spoken in Spanish, but I still didn't understand more than a word or two dotted within the comforting litany.

"You're okay. Don't be afraid," he finally said in English as he continued to smooth his big hands over my body, warming my frigid skin. I realized I was cradled in Andrés' strong embrace, but I couldn't bring myself to try to fight my way free anymore. I felt wrung-out, weak. Small and helpless.

Tears streamed down my face, and my brain whirred back to life. I was naked and crying into my tormentor's chest. The voice in my head was gone; wiped away, forgotten. All I knew was that my captor had tried to touch me sexually, and I'd freaked out. I didn't want to be raped.

"Let me go," I whispered brokenly.

"That's not going to happen" he told me in that same sure, calming tone.

"Stop touching me," I begged. I couldn't bear the feel of his hands exploring my naked, vulnerable body, stroking me like he was soothing a frightened animal. Or a favorite pet.

"I will touch you whenever and however I want." He paused and sighed. "We will work on this later," he declared ominously, but he released me.

I shoved up onto my feet, willing my shaking knees to support me as I put several feet of space between us. My eyes flicked to the closed door across from the bed, which I presumed was the way out.

"No," he said sternly, noticing the direction of my gaze. "Don't try it, or I'll spank you again. Go wash away those tears." He gestured at an open door to my right, which led into a bathroom.

I became suddenly, acutely aware that my basic needs hadn't been met for long hours, and I darted into the bathroom without any further thoughts of defiance. As I moved, I noticed the slickness between my thighs.

You're wet. We are going to get along, sirenita.

Mortification burned through me at the memory of Andrés' words. I might not have considered myself a sexual person, but I wasn't completely naïve. I knew that a woman got wet when she was aroused, so her body would be prepared to accept a man. It wasn't the first time I'd gotten wet, either. Watching Dex's BDSM porn had aroused me, even though I hadn't been brave enough to act on my desire. Whenever I'd gotten too turned on, I'd thrown myself into a particularly challenging task, usually involving hacking. Using the analytical side of my brain helped cool my animal physical responses.

My stomach roiled. Had my obsession with becoming the object of Dex's darker needs twisted me so thoroughly? I'd just been spanked by an evil man who claimed to own me, who wanted to rape me. And I'd gotten wet, my body responding to his harsh dominance.

My tears spilled faster as shame heated my cheeks, and I hastily finished my essential business so I could wash my hands and face. I pressed my palms against my flaming cheeks, turning the water colder to help chase away the heat of my humiliation. A few broken sobs heaved from my chest, but I gulped in air and forced myself to calm down.

In the calm, a single imperative took over: *escape.*

I couldn't wait around for my friends to find me, for Dex to come to my rescue.

I'm not the damsel in distress, I told myself. *I'm the*

hero. Heroine. Whatever. I'm a badass FBI agent/hacker goddess. I can get out of this.

I couldn't take down Andrés without a weapon —something he had made painfully clear. My bottom still ached and stung from his punishment, but that wasn't enough to deter me. He'd stripped me. He'd touched my sex as though he had every right. I refused to sit around and do nothing to defend myself when he clearly intended to rape me.

So, I'd have to find a weapon. Or make one.

I cast my eyes around the opulent bathroom, searching. There, hanging beneath one of the multiple showerheads: a razor.

I quickly crossed the tiled floor and retrieved it. I glanced at the closed bathroom door, knowing I didn't have long before Andrés would start banging on it. Possibly even breaking it down. I'd locked it behind me, but that wouldn't stop him. He'd already proven how strong he was, how relentless.

Turning my attention back to my task, I tamped down my anxiety and applied pressure to the razor's plastic casing. After a few seconds, it snapped. I gripped the flat of one of the blades between my thumb and forefinger, careful of the wickedly sharp edge. If I bloodied my fingers, I wouldn't be able to hold on to my only weapon.

I went to the bathroom door and turned back the lock, knowing he'd hear the metallic click in the bedroom. I didn't open the door. I needed him to come to me, and then I'd catch him by surprise. He'd seen a broken, frightened woman dart into the bathroom to hide from him. He wouldn't expect me to attack again now.

I'm not broken. And I'm not frightened. Okay, maybe that last part was a lie. My hands trembled, and I focused on steadying the fingers that gripped my blade.

"Samantha?" he asked, his rumbling voice emanating through the closed door. "Come out of there."

I made a little sniffling noise to encourage the illusion that I was crying, weakened. Not a difficult feat, considering my tears still mingled with the water droplets that wet my face.

"Come out here. Now, *cosita*." There was warning in the last, a clear threat that he'd come in to retrieve me if I didn't comply.

Come on, then, I mentally urged him, my body vibrating with anticipation.

A heavy sigh sounded through the door. "You will regret this," he said. "You must learn to obey me, even if you're scared or upset. I'm giving you one last chance. Come," he commanded firmly, like he was speaking to a particularly difficult puppy he was trying to train.

I straightened my spine. I wasn't going to be trained. I wasn't going to obey. And I certainly wasn't going to walk out into his scary, strong arms and allow him to violate me.

The door swung open, and I launched myself at him. I had the barest moment to register his dark eyes widening with surprise as I slashed, aiming for his throat. I'd never killed a man before, but I had to escape before something terrible happened to me. I tried to find a cold, calm place in my mind, but instead, I attacked with a furious, desperate shriek.

Maybe my roiling emotions made me sloppy. Maybe I just didn't have it in me to tear open a man's throat.

Or maybe Andrés was simply accustomed to people trying to kill him, and his instincts kicked in.

He managed to dodge back, and my blade cut a long, shallow furrow into his chest. I paused, shocked at the sight of his blood welling up.

I'd done that. I'd hurt him.

I didn't feel any sense of heroic triumph. Instead, horror washed over me. Violence might be ingrained in him, but it turned out, killing wasn't in my nature.

In my moment of hesitation, he grabbed my wrist. He barely had to squeeze before the razor slipped from my fingers. I'd lost my only weapon, and now I was faced by a hulking, bleeding madman.

Only, he didn't look mad. He looked... disappointed? What kind of man faces an attempt on his life with such mild emotion? He could have attacked me. He could have killed me and eliminated the threat.

But the laughable truth was, I wasn't a threat.

Keeping his hold on my wrist, he took a slow step toward me. I dodged back as far as I could, watching him warily. I didn't understand his calm response.

"I cut you," I blurted, trying to comprehend why he wasn't responding to my violence in kind.

"You did," he said coolly, completely unconcerned by the little rivulet of blood dripping down over his defined abs. "Are you really so eager for another spanking already? Did you enjoy it so much? I'll have to devise more clever punishments for you." The ghost of a smile flickered over the corners of his lips. "We are going to get along very well."

"Stop saying that," I forced out, my voice trembling. His calm was beyond unnerving. "I don't want you to spank me. I don't want you to touch me."

He moved with lightning speed, and his body suddenly pressed against mine. My back bumped against the wall, and he captured both my wrists in his big hand again, pinning them above my head.

He caged me in, his powerful body too close for me to defend myself.

My breath caught in my throat, fear fluttering at the center of my chest.

"Liar," he said smoothly. "I won't tolerate that, either. You enjoyed your spanking." His thigh wedged between mine, forcing my legs apart. He reached between us with his free hand and lightly slapped my sex.

A strange, strangled sound left my chest. It felt... weird, being spanked there. It stung, but the rebuke went deeper than physical discomfort. The punitive touch to my most secret, sensitive area was a causal demonstration of ownership. Something inside me clenched. A shadow of the toxic fear that had overtaken me the last time he'd touched my sex made me shudder.

He stared down into my eyes, his black gaze penetrating my soul. He spanked my sex again. This time, a wet sound accompanied the slap.

I bucked in his hold, struggling to escape. My writhing caused his palm to rub against my bud of sensitive nerve endings. I gasped and shivered, my body alight with sensation that was utterly foreign to me. My toes tingled, and warmth curled low in my belly.

But fear persisted, fogging my brain.

"What are you so afraid of, *cosita*?" he asked, his

voice low and silky smooth. "The pain or the pleasure?"

"What?" I managed. *Pleasure?* Nothing about what was happening was pleasurable in any way. My situation was horrifying, disgusting.

He studied me for long, torturous seconds, his hot palm resting against my sex in an obvious proprietary gesture.

"Do you really not understand?" he finally asked. His long fingers played through my sensitive folds, and I felt the slickness of my flesh under his touch.

I pressed my lips together, refusing to contemplate what was happening to me.

Something like a growl rumbled from his chest, and his dark eyes burned into me. "How innocent are you, Samantha?"

"I... I don't like when you touch me there," I whispered the truth.

"*There?*" he repeated. "You mean, your wet little pussy?" He rotated his palm against me, and something strange crackled through my system, making me cry out.

"Stop," I moaned. "I don't like this."

"Liar," he accused again, delivering another stinging slap against my labia. I tried to close my thighs, but he kept me securely pinned in place.

"I don't want you to touch me," I pleaded. Despite the unfamiliar electric current that was coursing through my body, fear still sapped my mind.

Wrong. Dirty.

Dirty little girl.

You want me to touch your secret place again, don't you, dirty little girl? The low, masculine voice whispered across my mind. I stiffened, my horror creeping up my throat to choke off my air supply.

The heat of his hand left my sex, and his palm came up to cup my cheek, his thumb hooking below my jaw to tilt my face up to his. "Look at me," he ordered in soothing tones.

I blinked, and my eyes focused on his face. His scar was deeply pronounced, drawn downward by the twist of his frown. The sight of his displeasure might have made me flinch with fresh fear, but I detected only concern in his dark eyes. He watched me with such intensity that I was unable to look away.

"You will learn to accept my touch," he said. As though to prove his point, he rubbed his thumb along the line of my lower lip. My sensitive nerve endings crackled and danced, and I sucked in a sharp breath. My body quivered, my skin pebbling. "You will learn to crave it," he continued, imbuing the words with command.

"Please, let me go," I begged, unravelling. All my earlier bravado had been torn away as swiftly and as easily as he'd disarmed me. I was left in a fog of fear and confusion. Trapped by Andrés' powerful body, I had no hope of escape. All I could do was plead with him. I struggled to gather my wits, clinging to the final weapon that remained: my mind.

"You have to let me go," I said, with a little more strength. "You can't... hurt me." I couldn't bring myself to say *rape me*. "My friends will find me. Do you really think the FBI won't do whatever it takes to get one of their own back?"

"My brother isn't so sure of that," he countered, still studying me intently. "It's my job to ensure your honesty. He wants the truth from you, and I will have the truth."

"I'm telling you the truth," I insisted.

He cocked his head at me, then nodded. "Yes, I think you are."

"Then you'll let me go?" I asked, hope swelling in my chest.

His fingers tightened around my wrists, and he scowled, his first true show of anger since Cristian had cut me. "No," he declared. "That's my brother's decision to make. Until he does, I'm keeping you."

I glowered up at him, righteous rage rising. "Dex is going to find me," I warned, an absolute truth. "And if you hurt me before he gets here, he will tear you apart with his bare hands."

"No one will find you," he swore. "You belong to me now."

"You're insane," I flung back at him, twisting against his harsh hold. "I don't belong to you."

He rubbed his fingers over my lips, and I could smell my lingering desire that had coated them. "Your pussy says otherwise," he told me. "You nearly came all over my hand, just from a spanking. Your body knows its Master. Your mind will follow."

I snapped my teeth at his fingers. That was his fucking mistake for putting them so close to my mouth.

I barely managed to nip at him before he pulled back. His hand settled around my throat, applying the barest pressure. My eyes went wide, and my mind blanked. Something primal within me surrendered on instinct, my animal brain recognizing the show of dominance, the subtle threat. I was powerless against him, small and fragile in his grip.

"Good girl," he said with approval. "Don't try to bite me again, or I'll find a better use for your pretty mouth."

I sucked in a small gasp. He couldn't mean... I'd never... I didn't want...

His touch shifted, his hand leaving my throat so he could stroke his fingertips down the column of my neck. "Breathe," he coaxed. "You spook very easily, *cosita*. But you will learn to crave me. All of me. My hand, my mouth, my cock. You will accept me."

"I won't," I forced out on a whisper.

He frowned and opened his mouth to say something else that was probably equally terrifying. But a knock on the bedroom door interrupted whatever he was going to say. A masculine voice penetrated the door, speaking in rapid-fire Spanish. Andrés barked something back that I couldn't understand.

Then his gaze fixed on me again. "I have business to attend to," he told me. "We will work on this later."

Work on this. Not *talk about this.* Whatever Andrés' plan for me entailed, it didn't involve my consent.

CHAPTER 4

He stared down at me, considering. I barely breathed. If I did, I'd inhale his purely masculine, purely intimidating scent. As well as the smell of my own confusing arousal. I didn't understand why my body was reacting to his harsh treatment in this twisted way. Maybe it was a defense mechanism, an instinctive response designed to prevent damage to my sex if he did decide to take me against my will.

But that didn't explain the strange tingling in my flesh, the way the blood pumped faster through my veins as I waited for his next move.

He blew out a sigh. "I need to get dressed," he told me. "Can I trust you not to try to attack me again once my back is turned?"

I scowled at him, lifting my chin in defiance. I'd never stop trying to get away from him, even if I knew that physically besting him was next to impossible. I'd had a slim chance with my puny weapon, and now the delicate razorblade lay useless on the carpet.

But I wasn't about to admit meekly that I'd be a good girl and stop trying to fight my way free.

His full lips twisted in a slight frown, dragging his scar down in a fearsome slash across his face. I dimly noted that he would be handsome, otherwise. Beautiful, even. His stubble-covered square jaw was strong and masculine, his cheekbones high and defined. Heavy dark brows drew together over his onyx eyes, and his black hair curled softly to frame his rugged features.

But the scar that marred his cheek... It was difficult to look at; vicious and violent.

Instinct urged my gaze to flit around the room in its familiar anxious pattern. But his eyes. I couldn't look away. His pupils were dilated, fixed on me. A slender ring of rich chocolate brown surrounded them, nearly swallowed by the darkness of his stare.

A light shiver raced across my skin, but I remained locked in his steady gaze.

His frown eased, one corner of his lips ticking up in a perverse smile. In a shockingly tender gesture, he tucked a stray lock of hair behind my ear. "So frightened, but so defiant. I'm going to have to restrain you, aren't I?"

I jerked against his hold, but his grip remained iron around my wrists. "No."

"So you won't try to attack me as soon as I release you?" he asked, the twist of his smile letting me know the question was purely rhetorical.

I struggled again, and a frustrated noise that sounded a little like a growl slipped between my teeth. He laughed; a low, rumbling chuckle of dark amusement.

"Such an angry *gatita*. Maybe I should keep you in cage. Would that tame you?"

"I don't need to be *tamed*," I shot back, my anger bleeding over fear. "I told you the truth. I'm a federal agent. You said you believe me. If you do, then you know you can't risk hurting me. My friends at the Bureau won't stop looking for me, and if you've..." I couldn't bring myself to say *raped me*. "If you've hurt me when they find me, they won't show you any mercy. You have to let me go."

His frown returned. "That's up to my brother to decide. Until he does, you're mine." His fingers tightened around my wrists as he made the perverse declaration.

"You keep saying that," I hissed out. "You're fucking crazy, you know that, right? You're—"

My next insult didn't make it past my lips. He pressed his hand firmly against my mouth, his frown twisting with disapproval.

"You will learn to mind your language when

you're speaking to me," he said coolly. "I need to get dressed, and you need to be quiet and behave while I'm gone. How comfortable you are while I'm out attending to my business is up to you. I can gag you and cage you, or I can leave you free to move around the suite. Make your choice."

My eyes flew wide, finally leaving his face to search the room. *Cage me?* Surely he couldn't be serious.

I sucked in a sharp breath through my nose. I'd been too distressed to notice before. Beneath the enormous four-poster bed were bars. Cushions and a blanket made it look like a second bunk beneath the big bed, but that was just my mind struggling to comprehend what I was truly looking at.

What kind of man had a cage under his bed? One that was clearly waiting to trap a frightened, unwilling woman?

"Choose," he said, his voice gravelly. "Are you going to be a good girl for me, or am I going to have to cage you beneath my bed like a naughty *gatita?*" His cock jerked against my belly, and I shuddered.

I shook my head as best I could, but my movement was restricted by his firm hand on my mouth.

He studied me for a moment longer, then gave a small nod. The weight of his body finally left mine when he took a step back, and my shaky legs nearly collapsed without his support. He maintained his hold on my wrists above my head, keeping me upright until I managed to find my footing. Once I regained my balance, he lowered my arms, but he didn't release them. He kept them trapped in one of his big hands as he moved back toward the bed, pulling me along in his wake.

"Please," I gasped out, my eyes fixing on the cage as panic churned in my gut. "I don't want to go in there."

"I'm not going to put you in the cage," he told me calmly. "You've already been punished for your transgressions. I told you: I might seem harsh, but I'm fair."

"So you're not going to lock me up?" I asked tentatively, my steps faltering as we reached the bed.

He smirked at me. "I didn't say that." He directed me to sit on the mattress and pressed my hands into my lap. "Put your hands on your knees, and keep them there. If you try to fight me again, I think you understand what the consequence will be."

He finally released my wrists, and I slowly directed my trembling hands to my knees, pressing my palms against them and locking my fingers around my kneecaps. He curled two fingers beneath my chin, applying light pressure. I had no choice but to lift my head and straighten my spine.

"Shoulders back," he ordered.

I complied, too intimidated to do otherwise. I'd been hunched over in a last-ditch attempt to protect my most vulnerable areas, but he demanded that I sit upright. In this position, my small breasts were exposed, and his eyes flared as he studied my naked body.

"*Qué bonita*," he murmured. His fingers left my chin, and I started to slump again. He simply clicked his tongue at me and lightly gripped my jaw, returning me to the position he desired.

"Stay," he commanded firmly, using the puppy-training voice again.

The ire that had burned through my veins earlier in response to that tone was utterly absent. Instead, a light shiver raced across my skin. He released my jaw, but I didn't move. He didn't have to touch me in order to restrain me. He'd thoroughly brought me to heel. He might have spanked me, but it was his unnerving calm and gentle but firm touches that were fucking with my mind. If he'd responded to my violence in kind, I might have maintained the determination to fight. As it was, his iron will kept me trapped as effectively as his strong hands.

He stepped back from me, but he didn't take his eyes off me as he crossed the short distance to a chest of drawers set against the wall a few feet away from the bed. He was right to watch me. If he'd taken his steady gaze off me, I would have bolted for the door. As it was, it took nothing more than his dark, stern stare to keep me locked in place where he'd left me.

He opened the top drawer and retrieved a thin strip of black leather, three small silver padlocks, and a length of delicate chain. My breath stuttered as he slowly withdrew the items, allowing me to clearly see what was in store for me.

"I don't want that," I managed breathlessly, my gaze locking on the collar. I'd longed for Dex to give me a collar, to love me and mark me as his own. I knew what it meant in the context of consensual BDSM: commitment, devotion.

With Andrés, it would be a symbol of subjugation. Everything I'd craved would be perverted the moment the leather touched my throat.

A single dark brow rose, and he lifted the collar for me to examine. "Does this scare you? It won't hurt."

"I know it won't," I began to babble. "But I don't want it. Not from you."

He closed the short distance between us. I didn't budge from the position he'd dictated, even though I wanted to shrink away.

He studied me with renewed curiosity, his gaze sharpening on my features. "Not from me? Someone else has collared you before? Maybe you're not so innocent."

"No. He hasn't. I just wanted... I don't want this

from you," I finally managed to curtail the words that threatened to spill out of me. Andrés didn't need to know about my heartbreak and secret longings for my best friend. No doubt, he'd find some way to use it against me.

His black eyes narrowed. "You lost the right to make demands when you tried to kill me," he told me. "I can't trust you not to attack as soon as my back is turned. So, I'm going to chain you to my bed, where you'll wait for me like a good girl while I attend to my business."

"I don't want this," I begged, still not daring to make a move against him.

"And I don't want to have to punish you more severely than I already have. Not so soon. This is for your own good, Samantha."

With that ominous declaration, he brought the collar up to my throat. I shuddered as the cool leather encircled my neck, but I remained in position, trapped by the looming threat of further punishment.

The collar tightened slightly as he slid the small padlock through the hasp at my nape, and the soft *click* as he secured it in place made my stomach clench. A single tear rolled down my cheek. This was all wrong. I'd fantasized about accepting a collar for years, and now one was being forced on me. I wasn't willingly ceding my trust and promising my obedience; I was being conquered, rebuked.

He tenderly brushed the wetness from my face with his calloused thumb. "It's not so bad, *cosita*," he cooed, tracing the line of the collar with his free hand. "It's very pretty on you."

I closed my eyes, no longer able to look at him. This violation went somehow deeper than the sting of his hand on my sex. He was taking my most closely-guarded fantasies and twisting them into something dark and abhorrent.

I heard him sigh, and his touch left my face. The chain clanked, and a light weight tugged at my neck. Behind my closed lids, I could envision him locking the chain to the metal ring at the front of the collar. I didn't have to see what he was doing to know what was happening to me.

His heat finally receded, but I could still feel his presence bearing down on me.

"Look at me," he commanded softly.

My wet lashes fluttered open.

"This is what's best for you," he told me with that same calm assurance that so unsettled me. "While you're with me, you're my responsibility. I will take care of you, even if that means protecting you from yourself."

"You're not protecting me," I hissed. "You've violated me. You've stripped me. You've *spanked* me."

His lips thinned, and his scar deepened. "And if you knew what my brother had planned for you instead, you'd be worshipping at my feet right now and begging to be mine. But we'll get to that later. For now, know that I'm the merciful alternative."

"Rape isn't merciful," I flung at him.

He stared at me, his black eyes glinting with fury. Despite the ire in his gaze, he didn't move to strike me or even raise his voice. Instead, it came out low and rough with a strange mix of emotions I couldn't quite identify. "I haven't raped you. I won't rape you. You won't be rewarded with my cock until you beg me to fuck you."

"That will never happen," I asserted, my eyes clashing with his. I'd already told him he was insane, but I didn't bother saying it again. He was clearly too far out of his mind to care if I thought he was crazy.

His head canted to the side, considering. "Your pretty little pussy has already wept for me. Your body craves to be touched. To be marked and owned. I think you are innocent, Samantha. You don't know what I'm capable of. What I can make you feel. Has any man ever made you come?"

My cheeks flamed, and my eyes dropped to the carpet. His words were shameful, and they shook me to my core. Because my body *had* reacted to him. The sensations might have been foreign to me, but I had to acknowledge that they'd been... intense. And not all unpleasant.

What is wrong with me?

"I see," he said, reading the truth in my shamed silence. "Your first real orgasm will belong to me."

I shivered, the air suddenly far too cool against my heated skin.

"Later," he said, and I got the sense he was speaking to himself more than to me. His fingers trailed through my hair, but I cringed away, completely overwhelmed and at a loss for words. He withdrew his touch, and I heard his footsteps whispering across the carpet as he moved away. When I heard the bathroom door shut behind him, I gasped in a sharp breath and finally looked up from the floor.

Just as I'd suspected, he'd locked the length of chain to the front of my collar and affixed the other end to a ringbolt set into the bedpost. I again wondered what kind of man had such tools of depravity in his bedroom, waiting to restrain and punish an unwilling woman.

A dangerous man, I reasoned. *A sadistic man.*

Andrés didn't strike me as sadistic, though. He'd spanked me and humiliated me, but he hadn't truly hurt me. Remembering Cristian's knife slicing into my skin, I glanced down at my injured collarbone. The cut had been cleaned and sealed with a clear, shiny substance. I realized Andrés must have glued

57

the shallow wound closed after he'd drugged me. To spare me further pain.

I didn't understand him at all. The way he touched me was sick, perverted. But he wasn't slashing me to ribbons as his brother had intended. Should I be relieved that I'd been saved from torture and a gruesome death at Cristian's cruel hands?

I shook my head sharply. Of course not. Despite Andrés' claim that he wasn't going to rape me, he'd still locked a collar around my throat and chained my naked body to his bed. There was nothing merciful about his promise of punishments if I didn't *behave*.

Dex will find me, I reasoned desperately. *Or Jason. They'll work together. They'll come for me.* Of course they would. My friends wouldn't rest until I was rescued.

But what would I have to endure before they arrived?

The bathroom door opened again, tearing me from my whirring thoughts.

Andrés stepped back into the bedroom, wearing nothing but a white towel slung low on his hips. His body was even more clearly on display than it had been in his sweatpants. I could see the dark trail of hair leading from his navel down to...

I sucked in a breath and tore my eyes away from

the glimpse of his erection, straining against the towel.

"You can look at me," he invited. "There's nothing to be afraid of."

A shrill, maddened giggle bubbled from my throat. "Right. Nothing to be afraid of. Only the huge, scarred, scary man who's chained me to his bed."

"Do my scars bother you so much?" he asked, his voice dropping and becoming rougher. "Am I so terrifying to look at?"

I pressed my lips together, locking in a stream of frightened babbling. Every time I allowed myself to speak in fear, I revealed too much. Better to not say anything at all.

He let out a low, rumbling sound of displeasure. I cringed and kept my eyes trained on the floor, not daring to look at his terrifying arousal.

He didn't speak again. I listened to the soft padding of his feet against the plush carpet as he moved through the room. The whisper of fabric against fabric told me he was getting dressed, but I still didn't glance up in his direction.

After a few minutes, silence stretched between us, and I could feel his eyes on me. It finally ended when he grunted once and started walking again. I glanced through my lowered lashes and watched his shiny black leather shoes retreating across the room. When he opened the door that I'd assumed was the exit, I finally looked up in time to see his suit-clad form filling the threshold. Behind him, I got the brief impression of a lavish sitting room, and I realized there was more to his living quarters than this bedroom. He'd mentioned a *suite*. How many rooms would I have to get through before I reached freedom? What obstacles would stand in my way, once Andrés was gone?

Well, for one, there was the collar around my throat and the chain that locked me to the bed.

My short period of speculation for escape routes abruptly ended when he turned to look at me one last time. One corner of his lips ticked up in a satisfied smirk, and his dark eyes raked over me.

"Good girl," he praised, his tone warm with pleasure and lilting with gentle mockery.

I realized I was still sitting exactly as he'd left me: hands on my knees, back straight, breasts thrust out. My jaw dropped, and he chuckled before closing the door behind him.

Too late, I crossed my arms over my chest and huffed out an angry breath. My show of defiance was wasted; Andrés was no longer there to witness it. And would I have dared to defy him if he were still in the room with me?

With a little exasperated growl, I fisted the chain and jerked at it. My only reward was an aching palm where the metal links bit into my skin.

I reached for the padlock that kept the chain tethered to the ringbolt in the bedpost. I pulled down sharply, trying to break it.

I didn't have a hope of snapping the lock on my own. I might have been able to pick it, but I'd need tools for that. I stood and tested my range of movement. I could walk exactly two steps away from the bed before the collar tightened around my throat. Even if I stretched and reached my arm out to the point of discomfort, I couldn't touch the chest of drawers. There was no guarantee that the keys to the locks were kept in there, but it was my best bet.

After a few minutes, I sat back down on the bed, frustrated. I might as well be in the cage, for all the freedom I had.

I shivered and pushed that thought away. My situation was dire, but at least I hadn't been caged like an animal.

Gatita. Andrés had called me a kitten. I might not be familiar with much Spanish, but I knew that word from elementary classes in the language when I was young.

Did he really see me as some sort of unruly little pet he could train into obedience?

The way he'd touched my body made it very clear that he saw me as a woman.

But I fully suspected he still intended to *train* me. He'd claimed that I belonged to him. At least, I would until Cristian decided to let me go.

He *had* to let me go. He'd given me to Andrés to get the truth out of me, and I'd convinced Andrés that I was a federal agent. He'd said he believed me. Surely he'd talk to his brother, and Cristian wouldn't be so reckless as to keep me captive?

I'll get out of this, I thought desperately. I might not currently be able to escape on my own, but my friends would either locate me, or the Moreno brothers would see reason and release me before the full power of the FBI came down on them.

How had it come to this? Before yesterday, I hadn't really stopped to think about how dangerous the Moreno brothers were. I'd been focused on Division 9-C. They were the big, scary bad guys I was targeting.

I hadn't realized how big and scary Andrés was. I hadn't even considered him at all. I'd known Cristian was dangerous, but I'd only been peripherally aware of his little brother.

But I'd been taken from my home, captured. And given to Andrés.

I shuddered at the thought of his scarred face and hulking body, my heartbeat ticking up as panic rose. He'd return at some point soon. I'd need to be prepared, to either route my escape or reason through how I'd convince him to release me.

I took several deep, calming breaths and continued to assess my prison. Turning to my analytical brain was much easier than facing my animal emotions.

The floor-to-ceiling windows that made up one bedroom wall revealed a stunning view of the Chicago skyline. It was beautiful, but unsettling to be so high up. Even if I somehow got free from the collar, I couldn't escape through a window. No doubt, plenty of Andrés' men stood between the suite and the building's exit. I hadn't been able to fight off the single man who was holding me captive, so the prospect of facing down an unknown number of adversaries didn't exactly sound like a good plan.

That non-plan was pointless, anyway, because I was chained to the fucking bed.

The click of the door latch disengaging made me scramble for cover. I hastily snatched up the tangled bedsheet and barely managed to clutch it to my chest before the bedroom door swung open.

A girl stood at the threshold. No, not a girl. A woman, although barely. The too-thin blonde couldn't be more than twenty, but her dull green eyes belonged to a much older woman. If she gained a few pounds, her body would have been model-perfect, a fact which was made clear by the plunging neckline of her skintight red dress. As it was, her breastbone stood out at the center of her chest, and her cheeks were nearly as hollow as her deadened stare. There was no emotion in her eyes whatsoever. If she'd been afraid, I could have assumed she was a fellow captive here. If she'd been hopeful, maybe she might have been an ally here to rescue me. Even disdain would have indicated something useful; it would have identified her as an enemy.

But there was nothing behind her eyes. They were a lovely, forest green, framed in long, dark lashes. No matter how physically striking she may be, it was difficult to look at her.

"Who are you?" I asked, watching her warily.

"Lauren," she replied, as though her softly-spoken name were all she had to offer in response. She hesitated in the doorway, staring at me. I shifted and pulled the sheet up to my chin.

"What do you want?" I pressed. She wasn't attacking me, but she wasn't helping me, either.

"He told me to bring you breakfast," she said, finally moving. She half-turned and directed a small cart into the bedroom. It looked like fancy room service, only, this wasn't a luxury hotel, and Lauren wasn't dressed for the service industry.

"Who is *he*?" I had a good idea whom she meant, but I needed to know the person responsible for sending the food. I doubted Andrés would poison me. He'd been very clear that he wanted to *keep* me. But I wasn't at all certain of Cristian's intentions.

She finished pushing the cart up to the edge of

the bed, but I didn't move toward the food, even though I could smell the delicious scent of bacon.

"Master Andrés," she explained in the same deadpan voice.

My hand shot out, and I gripped her wrist hard. "So you're captive here, too," I said quickly. She must be, if Andrés had broken her and forced her to call him *Master*. Wasn't that exactly what he wanted from me?

"Help me," I urged, tugging at the chain that bound me to the bed. "Do you know where he keeps the keys? They're probably in that drawer." I nodded in the direction of the piece of furniture that held the literal keys to my freedom. "I'm a federal agent. If you get this collar off me, I can get us both out of here."

She blinked at me, then tugged her wrist free from my desperate grip.

"There's no way out," she said flatly.

"Of course there's a way out," I tried to reason with her. "How do we leave this suite? How many men are guarding the building? You know what, scratch that," I said quickly, noting her nonplussed expression. I might have trained as a field agent, but I couldn't get the two of us past multiple guards without a weapon. "If you could just get me a phone, I can call my friends, and they'll come in and get us," I hastened on.

"I can't do that," she said, her refusal devoid of

any emotion. "I'll get into trouble. Besides, you don't want to leave this room. You're safest in here."

"What?" I spluttered, beginning to question the woman's sanity. "You see what he's done to me. This isn't safe. I have to get out of here."

"Master Andrés won't let them dose you with Bliss and pass you around," she said, something finally flickering in her haunted eyes. "He doesn't like it."

"He's not your Master," I said vehemently, trying to get through to her. She'd clearly been tormented, warped. If she'd been dosed with Bliss, she would have no control over her body while under the influence. She'd do anything she was told, including begging to be violated. My stomach turned at the knowledge of Andrés' involvement in trafficking the sick drug. He was ultimately responsible for Lauren's fractured state of mind.

"All the girls call him *Master*." She shrugged. "He used to take care of us. But that was before the Bliss. He doesn't like it," she repeated, as though that explained everything.

I reached for her again, but she dodged back.

"Please," I begged. "I can tell he hurt you. But it doesn't have to be this way. Give me a phone. I just need—"

"Master Andrés didn't hurt me," she said with shocking fervor. "He's nice to me. And he will be very angry with me if I help you. He told me to bring you food, and I brought it."

With that, she turned on her heel and stormed out of the bedroom.

"Wait!" I called after her as the door slammed shut.

I threaded my fingers through my hair, tugging at the coppery strands as I struggled to curb my mounting panic.

Master Andrés.

He'd claimed he was my *Master* now. And he'd proven how commanding and relentless he could be. Did he want to twist me into the same broken, fucked-up state as Lauren? She clearly felt some sort of perverted affection for him, even though she'd obviously been victimized.

I pressed my palms against my closed eyes and struggled to breathe normally.

I'll get out of this. I have to.

I couldn't end up like Lauren. I wouldn't.

CHAPTER 5

I wasn't sure how much time passed. Hours, surely. There wasn't a clock in the bedroom, so my only concept of time was the sun intermittently peeking through the overcast clouds.

I'd never been forced to sit without mental stimulation for so long. Usually, if I wasn't on my computer at home, I was at work. Even during my short commute, I passed the time on my smart phone. I rarely even watched TV or movies without also playing a game at the same time. My brain fired in too many different directions at once for me to focus on any one thing for long. Only digging deep into a case for the Bureau or a little side hacking just for shits and giggles could fully occupy my mind.

Now that I was forced to think about it, I doubted I'd gone longer than a waking hour without some sort of contact with technology in years. Possibly not since I was nine and got my first Gameboy.

I'd exhausted all avenues of possible escape from the bedroom within a very short time. Without Lauren's help, I was powerless to free myself from the collar that kept me tethered to the bed. Quite literally, on a short leash.

The breakfast—now stone cold—taunted me from the tray. I hadn't been provided with any utensils, likely because I would have devised some way to fashion them into weapons. Or possibly find a way to break my chains.

As it was, I had freaking bacon and breakfast potatoes. Like that would do me any good.

Well, my rumbling stomach told me I certainly could use the food, but I didn't trust it. While I doubted Andrés would poison me, he'd proven he had no qualms about drugging me. I didn't want to be unconscious and helpless again. Especially considering the fact that it had cost me my clothes the last time he'd drugged me. My only semblance of modesty now was the bedsheet, which I'd managed to wrap around me in an awkward toga. Maybe it would've been neater if I'd ever attended those fraternity parties in college, but I hadn't been invited.

I hadn't been interested in going, anyway.

I blew out a long breath and rubbed my forehead. Why was I thinking about college? Those weren't my best memories, and I much preferred to sink into my work and my online persona rather than remembering those difficult years.

All my years before joining the Bureau and meeting Dex had been difficult, really. When I joined the FBI, I found a community where I was valued and respected. And I'd found a best friend who never judged me or pushed me to talk about personal, unpleasant things. Dex and I shared a special companionship, even though I wanted to be more than his *companion*.

But pursuing that path had been a mistake. My obsession with my friend and his darker sexual predilections had obviously fucked me up. I'd spent too many hours watching his kinky porn. I'd even followed him to a BDSM club on one particularly desperate Valentine's Day, but he hadn't noticed me watching him from the bar. He never noticed me, not the way I wanted him to.

My yearning for Dex was the only explanation for why my body reacted to Andrés' twisted treatment with signs of desire. Fear might still grip my mind when he touched me, but my body didn't seem to care that I was afraid.

I jolted when the bedroom door opened again. So annoying that Andrés hadn't even bothered to lock it, but I couldn't get close to it with this damn collar around my neck. It was like he did it to taunt me. Or to demonstrate his absolute power over me.

If that was his intention, I had to admit to myself that he was doing a pretty good job at it.

I scrambled upright from where I'd been laying dejected, staring up at the pretty crystal chandelier. I braced myself for the sight of Andrés' hulking body and scarred face, but a different man appeared at the threshold. He was nearly as tall as my captor —a few inches over six feet—but his frame was wiry. He appeared to be as young as Lauren, a downy attempt at a dark blond beard only making him seem younger rather than more mature.

Also like Lauren, he behaved oddly. He didn't so much as glance in my direction as he wheeled a cart of cleaning supplies into the room and headed for the bathroom.

"Hello," I said tentatively.

He didn't respond in any way; he just kept going about his business, which I assumed was to tidy the suite while Andrés was out.

"Um, hey." I made an awkward wave to catch his attention.

No response. He disappeared into the bathroom. I heard the sounds of scrubbing, but no words.

Was the man mute? Surely, he wasn't blind.

So why was he completely ignoring me?

"Hey," I called out. "I'm Sam." I felt like an idiot

introducing myself when I couldn't even see him from my perch on the bed, but maybe if I made an attempt at normal conversation, he'd pay attention. There was a chance he was frightened, another captive who had been twisted like Lauren. I needed to get through to him.

My efforts were ridiculous and ineffective.

"What's your name?" I asked loudly.

He reappeared in the bedroom, wheeling his cart back toward the exit. He still didn't look at me or respond in any way.

"Wait," I said desperately. "I need your help. Talk to me, please. You don't have to be afraid."

His gray eyes finally riveted on me, narrowed in anger. "Of course I do," he hissed. "Do you know what he'd do to me if I helped you? I have a future to think about. I'm not about to fuck it up by pissing off the boss. Especially not for some whore."

I flinched at the word *whore*, but I plowed on. "I can help you. If he's threatened you, my friends can—"

He barked out a laugh. "You think I'm being threatened into staying here? I'm paying my dues, you stupid bitch. Don't fucking talk to me ever again. And don't you dare tell him I spoke to you, or I'll—"

"You'll what?" Andrés interrupted the man, his voice deadly calm.

My captor had approached far too quietly, appearing in the open doorway out of nowhere. The man paled and swallowed hard before slowly turning to face Andrés.

"She was asking for help," he said quickly, his voice hitching. "I was just saying—"

Andrés took a menacing step toward him. "You were threatening her. You were looking at her. I told you not to look at her. You're lucky she's covered. Do you know what I do to men who look at what's mine?"

The boy shook his head and retreated back into the bedroom, moving toward me. He didn't make it two steps before Andrés' hand closed around his upper arm, vice-like. He jerked the boy's body toward his, getting into his personal space.

"Look at her again, and you'll lose an eye," Andrés said softly. "Threaten her again, and it'll be the last thing you ever do. You're relieved of your duties. Never come into my quarters again."

He nodded, but he couldn't seem to manage to speak. Andrés released him, pushing him away in disgust.

"Leave," he bit out.

The boy hastened to comply, practically tripping over his feet to get to his cart and out of the bedroom. He disappeared further into the suite, Andrés' imposing form blocking my view.

I couldn't have watched him leave, anyway. All

my focus was on the terrifying man who'd just threatened to mutilate and murder one of the men who worked for him. Lauren had said Andrés was *nice*. The woman was obviously even more warped than I'd imagined. My captor radiated cold fury, his scarred face twisted in anger.

I shrank back, scooting across the bed until the chain jerked at my collar.

He sucked in a deep breath, and his fierce countenance eased as his eyes focused on my fearful expression. He took a step toward me, and I tried to move farther away. But all I accomplished was pulling at the leather around my neck. There was nowhere to go, no way to escape.

He reached for me, and I flinched. That didn't seem to concern him. He cupped my cheek in his big hand, hooking his thumb beneath my jaw so I couldn't look away.

"Calm, *cosita*," he murmured, stroking my hair with his free hand. "You're safe. He won't hurt you."

"I'm not worried about *him*," I said shrilly. "You're the one who just calmly threatened to cut out someone's eye. And I'm chained to your bed. Naked. I'm freaking afraid of *you*." I brought my hands up to push him away, but he caught my wrists and pinned them behind me at the small of my back. He held them there with one hand and resumed stroking my hair.

"He's lucky I didn't kill him for threatening

you," Andrés responded. "I ordered him not to speak to you or look at you. He did both. I can't have a man in my organization who thinks he can disobey me."

"So you murder anyone who defies you?" I asked, my voice shaking. *I'd* defied him. I'd tried to kill him.

"I will never harm you, Samantha," he said in reassuring tones as he continued to pet me. "No matter how defiant you may be." A smile ghosted around his lips.

"But you spanked me," I argued. "You said you want to punish me."

"Only to correct your misbehavior," he said, sounding as though it were the most rational response in the world. "I'd never do anything that would damage you. But yes, I won't hesitate to punish you when you deserve it."

"I don't *deserve* any of this," I countered hotly, struggling uselessly against his grip.

His gaze turned inward, his lips thinning. "Maybe not. But you're mine now, and there's no going back. I'm keeping you, and you're my responsibility."

"I'm not yours," I insisted. "And you're not *keeping* me. You said that's your brother's decision. Did you tell him you believe I'm FBI? Have you both seen reason and decided to let me go before the Bureau comes for you?"

"I'll let him discuss this with you," he replied.

He released my wrists and wrapped one hand behind my nape, pulling me toward him. I was forced to scramble across the mattress and get to my feet.

"Behave," he ordered, squeezing my neck slightly in warning. Then he called out in Spanish.

Cristian Moreno appeared in the doorway, flanked by two men who were nearly as massive as Andrés.

My stomach dropped, and a horrible memory of Cristian's knife slicing through my flesh flashed across my mind. I took a small step back, not realizing I was positioning myself closer to Andrés.

His grip on my neck eased, his fingers threading through my hair to massage my scalp. It helped ground me in the present, saving me from being thrust back into panic and choking terror.

Cristian's dark eyes—so like his brother's—watched my movements, coldly calculating. It occurred to me that I'd moved away from one tormentor to find shelter with another, and I eased away from Andrés. His fingers tightened in my hair, holding me firmly in place. He waited a few seconds, then released the tension and resumed massaging me once he was certain that I wasn't going to struggle.

"You are Samantha Browning," Cristian announced. "Andrés is convinced, and I had my people look into your story. You're a fed." He sneered the last.

I lifted my chin. "So you'll let me go?"

"No."

"But you have to," I insisted in a rush. "If you keep me here, my friends—"

"They won't find you here," he cut me off with cool certainty. "One of my shell corporations owns this building. They won't trace it back to me."

"They know I was investigating your organization before you took me," I said. "They'll suspect you're behind my disappearance. They'll follow you until you lead them to me."

"Then it's a good thing I don't come here often. This is my little brother's home."

Home? I thought, baffled. This entire freaking building was Andrés' *home*? How much money did the Moreno family have at their disposal?

"Besides," he continued. "It's not like I'm stupid enough to get out of my car out on the street. And your people don't have surveillance cameras in our private garage for this building. Which, I'll remind you, they have no idea I own. So, Samantha Browning, no one is going to find you."

My heart sank. If anyone could hack into Cristian Moreno's life and trace his financials and properties, it was me. And I was trapped here, isolated from the Bureau and completely cut off from technology.

"You're going to kill me," I surmised, my blood running cold. There was no reason to keep me around anymore. He'd checked into my story, confirmed my identity, and he still didn't care that I was FBI. He wasn't intimidated in the least.

"No," he said again. "You're going to work for me from now on."

"What?" I asked, all the air leaving my lungs.

"You're going to erase all the evidence the FBI has on me. You will protect me and my business from them. If you do, I'll let you live."

A staunch refusal teased at the tip of my tongue, but I held it back. If he wanted me to log into the FBI database, that meant he'd have to give me access to the internet. I could get a message to Dex.

"Okay," I agreed quickly. "I'll need a computer."

Too quickly.

He laughed, a hard, cold sound. "Do you think I'm a fool? You'll contact the feds as soon as you get online. Now, I could just threaten to kill you if you try, but then you'd be useless to me if you're dead. So, I'm going to leave you with my brother for a while longer. I'm sure he'll break you in for me. He's so good at that."

Andrés growled, and his fingers tightened in my hair. He bit out something in Spanish, too fast for me to catch a single word.

Cristian smirked. "All right, *hermanito*," he

drawled. "You can keep this one. Just make sure she's useful to me, and we won't have any problems."

"Give me a month," Andrés replied, resuming the calm, assured demeanor that so unnerved me.

"You can have three weeks," Cristian countered. "I don't have time for you to play with your new toy. Break her, or I'll find another way to ensure her cooperation."

Andrés nodded his agreement, as though their discussion of my fate wasn't horrifying enough to make nausea curl in my stomach.

"You can't do this to me," I managed faintly.

Andrés' fingers hooked through the back of the collar, pulling it tight around my throat. I could still breathe, but I was very aware of his control.

"Quiet, *cosita*," he commanded softly. "It's done."

The world blurred with my tears, and I could barely make out Cristian's suit-clad form retreating from the suite, his guards in tow. When they were out of sight, my tormentor pulled me against his hard body, and I sobbed into his chest.

CHAPTER 6

"You haven't eaten, *sirenita*," he murmured as he stroked his big hand up and down my back.

I sniffled against him, collecting my thoughts as my wits returned. I tried to push away from him, but his arms firmed around me, trapping me against his hard body. He allowed me just enough space so I could lift my face to glower up at him.

"I didn't want to be drugged again," I said hotly, a clear accusation.

"I don't need to drug you to keep you compliant." His lips twisted in distaste. "I wouldn't do that."

"You drugged me last night," I reminded him.

He frowned at me. "You were hurting. I was sparing you more pain. Would you have preferred to suffer?"

"Yes," I defied him. "Then I could have at least kept the dignity of my clothing. You stripped me as soon as I was unconscious."

His brows rose. "Do you really think you'd still be wearing clothes if I didn't want you to? You can't hide from me, Samantha."

His fingers fisted in the sheet at my lower back, and he pulled at the soft fabric until it loosened and slid down my body. I twisted in his hold, struggling to cover myself. But my movements only made the sheet shimmy down my legs, leaving me completely bare against my captor. He still wore his sharply-tailored suit. The dichotomy of power was painfully obvious: he was fully dressed, while I was writhing naked in his arms, a collar still locked around my throat in a sign of his ownership.

"You shouldn't have covered yourself," he reprimanded.

"So you would have paraded me naked in front of everyone? In front of your brother? How fucked up is your family?"

His jaw firmed. "I would have covered you before I invited Cristian in. I don't let other men look at what's mine."

I shoved at his chest, accomplishing nothing. "I'm not your property."

His hand fisted in my hair at my nape, tugging my head back and trapping me beneath his black stare. "You could be," he said smoothly. "I could make you my plaything, my eager little fucktoy. And I think you would be eager, Samantha. Your body aches to be touched."

I squirmed against him, my blood pounding through my veins. "I don't want to be your..." The words died on my tongue. They were so vile and vulgar, I couldn't bear to repeat them. "I don't want you to touch me," I managed.

"You do," he countered coolly. "But you're still afraid. You're so innocent, you're scared for me to touch your little pussy. That ends now. Your innocence is mine. Your pleasure is mine. You will accept my touch."

"I won't," I hissed. "I won't invite you to rape me."

"I will never rape you," he replied calmly. "And I won't fuck you at your invitation. You will beg and weep for my cock before I give you what you want."

I shuddered in his arms, completely overwhelmed. In the space of a day, I'd been stripped of my rights, my dignity. And the way he spoke about breaking me with such calm assurance rocked me to my core. In his mind, my surrender was a foregone conclusion.

Fuck. That. He might spank me, but I could handle it. A little sting on my flesh wasn't going to break me. I glared up at him, defiant.

"Go ahead and *punish* me, then," I challenged.

"You can spank me all you want, but I'll never beg you to violate me."

One corner of his lips ticked up with perverse amusement. "I do enjoy a challenge," he purred, his pupils dilating. I felt his cock stiffen against my belly. He leaned down, his lips skimming across my cheek before tickling the shell of my ear. "You enjoyed your spanking, so it's hardly a punishment," he said, the whispered words threading through my mind, reaching deep inside and revealing the truth that I didn't want to acknowledge. "But that's not what I have planned for you. You owe me an orgasm. Your first. I want it. I'm going to make you come hard, so your body has no doubt that I'm your Master. I can give you pleasure. I can give you pain. Obedience is taught through discipline: punishment and reward. It's time you learned exactly what that means."

I trembled, my heart hammering in my chest. I hadn't realized that I'd stopped struggling. He was too strong, too powerful. And his crass words over-whelmed me more effectively than any physical show of force.

His erection pressed against me, thick and hard. "Do you feel what you do to me, *sirenita*?" he asked, his voice rough with lust. "You are so beautiful when you're like this; your little body shuddering in my arms. Are you frightened? Or aroused?" His teeth nipped at my ear, and I sucked in a sharp breath. "Or both?" His hand slid down the length of my spine, caressed the curve of my bare bottom, and dipped between my thighs. He hummed his approval when I whimpered. "Both," he concluded with dark satisfaction as he found the slickness on my labia.

He pressed a tender kiss against my neck, just below my ear. My nerve endings crackled with awareness, and my skin pebbled.

"Stay," he murmured before finally releasing me.

I remained frozen where he'd left me, my body tingling with fear and something else I didn't want to acknowledge. I watched him with wide eyes as he crossed to the chest of drawers and retrieved a few items. This time, he slipped them into his pocket before I could make out what he'd selected.

When he approached me once again, he held a length of black cloth wrapped around his fist. I took a step back, wariness making the fine hairs on the back of my neck stand on end.

"I like watching your lovely eyes when I'm playing with you, but this will make you more aware of what I'm making you feel," he told me.

"What?" I asked faintly, but I didn't have long to wonder what he meant.

He lifted the cloth to my face and pressed it over my eyes. I closed them automatically, and I felt him knot the material firmly at the back of my head. Panic spiked as soon as the darkness closed

84

around me, and I lifted my hands to rip the blind-fold away.

He caught my wrists immediately, guiding them back down to my sides.

"Settle, *cosita*," he cooed. "This isn't going to hurt."

"I'm scared," I admitted on a shaky whisper, the words leaving me without thought.

A low, rumbling sound rolled over my skin. "If I were a good man, I'd tell you not to be frightened. But I'm not a good man." He pulled one of my hands forward, pressing my palm against his bulging erection. "I like having you at my mercy, Samantha. I like when you tremble and whimper for me."

"Please," I whined, trying to tug my hand away from his hard length.

He held me fast. "Just like that," he said with rough approval. "But soon, you'll be begging me to touch you, not to release you."

He finally, mercifully guided my hand away from his terrifying arousal. He released my wrists and gripped my waist, lifting my body as though I weighed nothing. The dark world spun around me as he moved my body and positioned it where he wanted. My back settled onto the soft mattress, and I instantly tried to roll away, disoriented and frightened. I could hear my blood rushing in my ears, and I was very aware of the heat of his hands

JULIA SYKES

on my flesh. His masculine scent infused the air I desperately breathed, until I thought I would drown in it.

His steady grip kept me pinned to the bed. He grasped my wrists again, tugging them above my head. Cool metal snapped in place around them, a sensation that wasn't entirely unfamiliar to me; we'd trained with handcuffs at the FBI academy. As soon as his grip left my wrists, I tried to pull my arms down to cover my exposed body. They jerked against the unyielding metal, and his hands returned to my forearms, pressing them down into the mattress.

"Don't struggle," he ordered. "You'll only bruise yourself. I'm interested to see how easily your pretty skin marks up, but not like this."

His words made my fear spike, and I twisted beneath him. His palm settled over my throat, his long fingers wrapping around my neck.

"*Cosita*," he said, warning imbuing the word. "I gave you an order. Settle down. I'm not going to hurt you."

"But you want to," I whispered tremulously, going utterly still. "You want to break me."

His hand remained at my throat, but his other stroked my hair. "I won't break you. But I am going to tame you."

"I don't want to be tamed. I want to go home."

Tears sank into the black cloth that covered my eyes.

"You're scared," he said softly, still petting me while holding my neck in a gentle grip. "That's natural. But it will pass. You have to trust me, Samantha."

"Trust you?" I asked on a maddened laugh. It was impossible, insane.

"You will trust me. You will give me everything. Trust that I will take care of you. I will give you pain, but you don't yet understand the pleasure I can offer. Now, be a good girl and don't pull against the cuffs."

"Fuck you," I hissed, my terror morphing into rage. It was too intense to bear, so my mind redirected the fear into anger.

"Mind your language," he rebuked. His hand tightened around my throat. I could still breathe, but he pressed down just hard enough to restrict the blood flow to my brain. I'd trained in how to choke a man out, so I knew what was happening to me. If he squeezed too hard, I'd slip into unconsciousness. Maybe even die.

Just as panic began to sap my mind, he released the pressure. Blood rushed back to my head, and a strange high I'd never experienced soared through me. I let out a long sigh, and my entire body relaxed as a pleasant buzz quieted my mind. All my fear, my conflicting emotions, melted away, and I floated for a few ecstatic seconds.

"That's better," he praised, his fingertips skimming along the line of my vulnerable artery at my neck. My skin felt electric beneath his touch, *alive*. A low moan left my chest, and I arched my head back, further exposing my throat to him in mindless invitation for more.

"Stay just like that," he commanded. His touch left my throat, his heat receding as the mattress shifted beneath me. I was aware of his hands on my ankles, one after the other. He spread my legs wide, and supple leather cuffs wrapped around my ankles to lock them in place. I didn't tug against the restraints this time. I lay perfectly still and relaxed, relishing the quiet in my mind. This was much preferable to unrelenting terror.

Then he touched my sex, and instinctive fear surged back. My entire body jerked, but the restraints he'd used to secure me kept my body stretched out for him.

He gently shushed me, continuing to lightly caress me despite my struggles. "This part will be over soon," he said, his voice almost tender. There was something slick on his fingers, a thicker substance than my own arousal. He carefully coated my labia, his fingers dipping between them before circling around my clit. I gasped and shuddered as he teased around the tightly-packed little bundle of nerves, pleasure lighting up my system despite my mounting fear. The longer his touch lingered directly on my sex, the more intense my terror grew. My entire body was shaking by the time he finally withdrew his hand, leaving a strange heat behind, as though he'd branded my sensitive flesh with his touch.

It wasn't an unpleasant heat. In fact, it tingled rather than burning. I squirmed and tried to press my legs together to stop the sensation. The cuffs held my ankles fast, and I was left quivering and helpless to stop what was happening to my body.

"What are you doing to me?" I asked on a throaty whisper.

His fingers trailed beneath my breasts, spiraling upward and inward until they reached my peaked nipples. The same slick substance coated the tight buds.

"This is arousal cream," he told me. "Not that you need it to feel pleasure. You've already soaked my hand when I've spanked you. This is to help you get past the fear. Soon, you'll be desperate for me to touch your pretty pussy. You'll beg for me to grant you release. Need will outweigh fear. Then we can move forward with your training."

"I don't want to be trained," I protested on a whine. The same tingling had set in around my nipples, making me squirm as my body instinctively sought stimulation.

He chuckled. "Most wild things don't. And you are a wild thing, aren't you? You're innocent, untouched. But your body hungers to feel pleasure. Once we get past your fears, I suspect you'll be a very greedy girl. You'll crave my touch. You've already responded so well to your spankings. You'll learn to respond to positive reinforcement, as well."

"You make it sound like I'm an animal," I forced out, trying to ignore the heat that flared between my legs. "I'm not."

"No, you're not," he agreed, his hands skimming down my sides, tracing the slight flare of my hips. "You're a woman. But you're *mine*. That means you're whatever I want you to be. My plaything, my pet. Your sole purpose is to please me, to serve me. I'm your Master now, and it's time you understood what that means."

"But I—"

"Shhh." He blew a stream of cool air over my nipples as he shushed me, and my protest ended on a soft cry as the tight peaks lit up with sensation. My back arched, offering my breasts up to him. His approving rumble vibrated against my skin as he pressed his lips against the soft swells, leaving feather-light kisses in a random, scorching pattern across my flesh. A strange, strangled sound left my chest, and rational thought evaporated.

"Has any man ever touched your breasts?" he

asked before flicking his hot tongue against my tight, aching nipples.

A rough shout tore from my throat, and I thrust myself toward the delicious heat of his mouth. But my cruel restraints held me in place, and he moved away to blow another torturously cold stream of air over them. I whined and writhed, acting like the wild thing he claimed I was.

"Answer me," he prompted. "Be honest, and I'll kiss your pretty pink nipples."

"No," I said, the confession leaving me in a rapid-fire stream. "Not really. Not like this. I went to a convention once. I dressed up like The Dark Phoenix. From *X-Men*. Cosplay, you know? So this guy was Wolverine. I met him at an after-party. He kissed me and copped a feel. But it was over my costume. So I guess that doesn't really count. Does it? I used to think so. But I—" My lust-addled speech ended on a sharp cry when his lips touched my nipple, his tongue swirling around it before flicking the peak.

Keening, animal sounds left me in a steady stream as he continued to stimulate my breasts, alternating between plucking at my nipples with his fingers and kissing the sting away with his soft lips. My head thrashed against the pillow, and I began to lift my hips up in wanton invitation. My core pulsed to the point of aching, my clit throbbing in time with my heartbeat.

His palm rested on my belly, below my navel and tantalizingly close to my heated sex. His fingers traced little circular patterns just above my clit, teasing.

"And your pretty little pussy," he prompted. "Has any man ever touched you here?"

"No," I whimpered, my mind too far gone to worry over confessing my most embarrassing secrets.

"Poor little virgin," he murmured. "You need to be touched, don't you?"

"I... I want..." I bit my lip, barely holding back.

"Tell your Master what you want," he cajoled. "Tell me how you like to be touched. Do you put your fingers inside your tight pussy? Or do you rub your little clit?"

"I don't. I can't. It's..."

Dirty. Wrong.

Dirty little girl.

Something awful stirred at the edges of my mind. I shied away from it. Instead, I focused on the heat that was consuming me, the tingling in my flesh, the gentle brush of Andrés' fingers against my hypersensitive skin.

"You don't touch yourself?" His deep voice was colored with surprise. "You've never made yourself come?"

"I... No." Shame made my cheeks flame, but the heat in my sex kept me distracted. I couldn't see, couldn't think. All I could do was feel and listen to Andrés' lilting voice as he asked me the most devious questions.

"So you've never had an orgasm at all?"

I shook my head and tried to lift my hips again, but his palm on my belly kept me pinned down.

"Then let me show you what your body is capable of," he said, the words distorted by his hungry growl. "In the future, you will beg me for this."

His hand finally shifted down to where I craved it most. One thick finger parted my wet folds, and my entire body tightened as he slowly slid it inside my channel. He felt huge as my inner muscles gripped him, torn between welcoming him in and pushing him out. Emotion swelled along with sensation, fear and pleasure crackling through my system. A harsh sob tore from my chest, and my tears wet the blindfold.

"Too much," I gasped out, twisting against my restraints. "It's too much. Please—"

"Don't fight it," he commanded, finding a secret spot at the front of my inner walls. He crooked his finger against it. At the same time, he brought his thumb down on my clit and rubbed in a demanding rhythm. "Come for me, *sirenita*."

Pleasure lit up my entire being, tearing through me with the force of a tidal wave. A raw scream echoed through the room as all my muscles tensed and shook. Bliss wracked my body, my mind. The world fell away as unrelenting bliss sang through my veins, sweeping away my lingering fear. All that existed was Andrés: his touch, his scent, his *power.* He'd wrung this unknown ecstasy from my soul, ruthlessly subjugating my being with earth-shattering pleasure.

My sex tingled as he continued stroking me. Little lightning strikes of residual pleasure tormented me, making me tremble. I fully surrendered to sensation and sank back against the mattress, utterly sated and thoroughly conquered.

CHAPTER 7

Andrés pressed tender kisses against my slightly sore wrists when he removed the handcuffs that kept me bound to the bed. I didn't move once I was free, and I didn't stir when he unlocked the collar from around my neck. My eyes remained closed when he unknotted the blindfold; I wasn't ready to face reality yet.

I continued floating in quiet bliss as he unbuckled the cuffs around my ankles and carefully lifted my body up into his strong arms. He cradled me against his chest as he carried me, taking long, sure strides toward an unknown destination. I remained carefully cocooned in warm darkness, clinging to pleasure so I didn't have to face the horror of my defeat.

I noted that his chest was bare against my skin, his dusting of dark hair tickling my cheek. He must have removed his clothes while I lay boneless and mindless in my post-orgasmic haze.

The world tilted, and my eyes fluttered open when my feet touched cool tiles. I watched with detached interest as Andrés reached around me and turned the knob for the shower. Water sprayed from every direction, multiple showerheads raining down. It seemed awfully decadent compared to my low water pressure, single showerhead setup at my shabby townhouse.

My heart squeezed, and I quickly smothered my thoughts before they could start firing again. I didn't want to think about my townhouse. About how far I was from home, even though I was located just across town. I might as well be on another planet.

Andrés gripped my hips and guided me into the glass-fronted shower stall. The water was uncomfortably hot, and my pale skin turned pink almost instantly. He seemed to notice everything about my body, so he immediately turned the temperature to something more bearable.

He stayed positioned behind me, and I was grateful for that. If I didn't have to look at him, I didn't have to process the fact that he was fully naked in the shower with me. I'd felt his erection, and that had been terrifying enough.

He didn't allow me much of a reprieve. His hands closed around my waist, pulling my body back against his so I could feel his hard length pressing into my ass. I tried and failed to swallow a whimper as some of my fear resurfaced, despite my best efforts to remain lost in lingering pleasure.

"You're still afraid of my cock," he surmised, but he didn't move away at the sound of my distress. "But you're not afraid when I touch you anymore, are you?"

To prove his point, he pumped soap into his hand from a dispenser on the wall before returning his touch to my breasts. He massaged them gently, and I moaned as his slick palms grazed my nipples. They were still tender from the arousal cream, and he made sure to tease the tight buds as he washed away the substance that lingered on my skin. My flesh tingled, but not as intensely as it had when he'd first applied the cream.

One hand skimmed down my belly to carefully wash my sex, his other remaining at my breasts to play with my nipples. I shuddered and leaned back against him for support as pleasure flooded my body again, the tension at my core building.

"You are a greedy girl," he said, his voice heavy with satisfaction. "I knew you'd be like this. But you don't deserve a reward. Not yet."

A humiliating whine slipped through my lips when he stopped touching me intimately. He grasped my shoulders and turned me to face him.

My eyes darted around the bathroom, avoiding looking at his imposing body.

He caught my chin between his thumb and forefinger, lifting my face to his. I made the mistake of glancing up, and I found myself trapped in his steady black stare.

"You don't like looking at me," he said, an acknowledgement of fact. "My scars frighten you."

"It's not that," I admitted, the words tumbling out of me in my nervousness. "I mean, you're scary. But your scars aren't why you scare me. Well, kind of, because they mean you're violent. But this is just a tic I have. I don't really like looking at anyone. I have to for work, sometimes. It takes effort. It makes me uncomfortable. I mean..." I finally managed to end my rambling confession. Why was I telling him all this?

Because I babbled when I was nervous, that's why. Especially around alpha males, and especially when they turned their full, potent attention on me to impose their will. I did it with Jason, and I definitely did it with Dex. I could barely look at my best friend under normal circumstances, even when I didn't have a reason to be intimidated. I was always nervous around him, in that butterflies-in-my-stomach kind of way.

Not the way Andrés made me nervous. *Nervous* wasn't an intense enough word to express the enormity of what he made me feel. It was why I couldn't look away once he captured me in his dark gaze. I never maintained eye contact with anyone like I did with him. He didn't give me a choice in the matter.

He considered me for a long, tense moment, his jaw tight. "Would it make you more comfortable if I told you I didn't get these scars in a fight?"

I blinked at him. "What?" That didn't make any sense. "Then how—?"

"That's enough questions," he cut me off. "I am a violent man, but I won't harm you. I'll never let anyone harm you. You're mine, which means you'll be protected. It also means you'll accept my touch and my cock. Look at me." When he said it this time, I knew he wasn't ordering me to look him in the eye. "All of me," he prompted when I hesitated. "Now, *cosita*." The last was dark with warning, and my eyes flicked down his body before I could contemplate further defiance.

Once my gaze landed on his cock, I couldn't look away. I might not have been with a man in real life, but I watched porn. And, despite his scarred body, Andrés could have starred in some of the most depraved videos I'd seen. He was huge, long and thick. His cockhead was purple with arousal, and a feminine part of me marveled that this reaction was for *me*.

"Touch me," he bit out, his control slipping. I gasped when his cock bobbed, straining toward me.

I reached out and tentatively brushed my

fingertips along his shaft. His skin was soft and smooth, but he was hard beneath my touch. He hissed in a sharp breath, and I felt him pulse under my fingers. I stared in fascination. I was doing this to him, affecting him the way he'd affected me. A strange sense of heady power teased at the corners of my mind, and I struggled to resist the perverted satisfaction. I shouldn't enjoy my captor's lustful reaction to me.

But it was undeniable that my body instinctively reacted to him, so the knowledge that the balance of power wasn't entirely stacked against me gave me some courage. I wrapped my hand around his length and stroked him from base to head.

"Good girl," he said, his voice more ragged than I'd ever heard it. He was at the edge of his control. I wanted to push him over that edge, to break him the way he'd broken me.

He reached between us with his soap-slicked hand and applied a liberal amount. When I slid my fist back, it glided across his flesh, and he groaned.

"Do you know how hot it is watching you touch me?" he ground out. "Knowing I'm the first man you've touched. The only man you will ever touch. Your first and only, my sweet virgin." A bead of moisture formed on his cockhead, quickly washed away by the cascading warm water.

Emboldened by his words, I used my free hand

to cup his balls, gently exploring their shape and weight.

He rasped out something in Spanish that I suspected was a very dirty word. A sly smile tugged at the corners of my lips, and I struggled to smother it. He was coming apart beneath my touch, losing control. The heady sense of power that I'd been resisting finally settled over me, and I handled his shaft with greater confidence.

"Naughty *gatita*," he said hoarsely. His hand fisted in my wet hair, tugging hard enough to make my scalp light up with awareness. "Very naughty." He cursed again, and his grip on my coppery strands increased to the edge of pain. It only served to spur me on.

"Make me come, *sirenita*," he ordered in an obvious effort to take back control with a command.

But the way he pumped his hips toward me to increase my pace let me know who truly held the power in this moment. He came apart on a harsh shout, his hot seed lashing out to coat my stomach, the heat of it lingering on my flesh even as the water washed it away.

His body pressed against mine, backing me up to the tiled wall as he braced his hands against either side of me. He leaned his forehead against mine, breathing hard.

"That's enough," he said with a shudder.

I finally moved my hand away, satisfied at the sight of his undoing.

A sharp grin suddenly lit his features. "Time for your reward, *gatita*."

"What?" I asked, disconcerted by his jovial mood. I'd expected his anger at being broken under my inexperienced hands, maybe even shame.

"Good girls get positive reinforcement." He tenderly stroked my cheek. "Remember, my pet?" He leaned in so his hot breath played across my neck as he whispered in my ear. "Your Master is training you to please him. You did very well. You've earned a reward."

"No," I said, shaken. How had this turned against me? I'd been riding high, triumphant. He twisted my victory into yet another defeat.

"You don't get to refuse, pet."

"I'm not your pet."

"Aren't you? You wanted to act like a naughty *gatita*. You will be tamed, Samantha."

"I won't."

"Your little pussy wouldn't get so wet for me if you didn't want this. You wouldn't have come so hard while you were bound and at my mercy."

"That's so fucked up. You're—"

His hand clamped over my mouth, his long fingers pressing into my cheek almost to the point of pain.

"We're going to have to work on that tongue of

yours. I have a pretty gag that I think will suit you well until you can learn to mind your language when you speak to me."

My eyes flew wide, and I tried to shake my head. His hand firmed on my face, stilling the sign of my denial.

"Hush now, *gatita*. It's time for your reward."

I brought my hands up and wrapped them around his forearm, clawing at his flesh with my fingernails in an attempt to free my mouth from his cruel hold.

He growled and released me, but only long enough so he could roughly turn my body to face the wall. His weight pressed against my back, pushing my breasts hard against the cold tiles. I yelped and tried to push back, but my hands slipped uselessly against the slick wall. He wrapped one hand around my throat, squeezing. This time, he applied enough pressure to restrict my airflow. I thrashed on wild instinct, but his weight kept me pinned and powerless.

Please, I tried to beg him to release me, but the word couldn't make it past his hold on my throat, and a strangled sound emerged instead.

"Breathe, *cosita*," he urged, not letting up.

I barely managed to suck in shallow breaths. My head began to spin, and I stopped fighting as the strength seeped out of my body. His free hand dipped between my legs, gathering up the slick arousal that inexplicably coated my inner thighs. He moved his touch farther back, trailing his slick forefinger over a sensitive patch of skin between my sex and asshole, then...

No. My lips formed the word, but I wasn't capable of wasting any air to make a sound of protest.

His finger pressed against my tight ring of muscles. I clenched, resisting. He nipped at my earlobe, and the little jolt of pain sizzled through me, reaching my core and making it throb. As it contracted, his finger slipped inside me. He barely penetrated me, but I felt horribly full and utterly trapped. My knees began to tremble as I continued to struggle for oxygen.

"Are you sorry for scratching me?" he asked calmly, as though he wasn't degrading me in a way I'd never wanted to experience.

I managed a thin whine and nodded slightly.

He kissed the hollow beneath my ear. "Good girl. Don't do it again."

He pressed forward, sealing the rebuke by sliding his long finger all the way inside me. My muscles rippled around him, burning as my body tried to resist the intrusion. Something dark stirred low in my belly, tension coiling at my core.

He finally released my throat, and I gasped in a desperate breath. The rush of oxygen went straight to my head, and the world spun around me.

Remaining seated deep inside my most forbidden area, he caught my falling weight with his other strong arm around my waist. I sagged back against him, sucking in air. His hand splayed beneath my bottom, bracing me as a second finger found my wet channel. He eased inside my sex, and I could feel him filling me everywhere.

It was too much to bear, too humiliating. Too stimulating. Rational thought had been obliterated in the wake of the primal imperative to breathe, to survive. My body could only shake and submit to what he was doing to me. All my sensitive nerve endings lit up, and the tension that had been coiling deep inside me released, leaving me on a ragged shout. My muscles clenched around his fingers as I found shameful ecstasy under his ruthless touch. He gently pumped in and out of me, making my nerve endings crackle and dance. Sparks of pleasure raced up my spine to flood my mind, overwhelming all my senses.

The spinning world flickered around me, darkness sliding across my vision. I surrendered to it, closing my eyes as he continued to hold my weakened body upright.

His fingers finally slid out of me, leaving me feeling strangely empty; hollowed out and utterly defeated. The water stopped falling around us, and he lifted me up in his arms again as though I weighed nothing. He was so strong, so hard and unyielding. A fine tremor raced through my exhausted body, the only movement I was capable of.

He wrapped a warm, fluffy towel around me. I snuggled into it, hiding my face between the soft fabric and his sculpted chest, as though I could simply sink into the warmth and disappear. Anything would be preferable to facing the shame of what he'd just done to me.

I'd thought I'd regained some power over him when I'd made him come, but he'd quickly demonstrated how powerless I truly was. His punitive touch had brought me pleasure, pleasure I hadn't wanted but had been wrought from my body by his masterful hands regardless of my wishes.

He'd claimed he wasn't going to break me, but in that moment, I felt completely shattered.

CHAPTER 8

ndrés carefully dried my body, rubbing the soft towel over every inch of my sensitized skin. My nipples and sex ached, and my bottom burned slightly, a constant, cruel reminder of how he'd subjugated my entire being.

When he was satisfied that I was dry, something tugged at my damp hair. I registered the rhythmic pull of brush bristles through my hair, massaging my scalp. It made my head tingle, a pleasant sensation I tried to deny.

"I'm not a doll," I mumbled, keeping my eyes closed to avoid facing reality. I remained still and compliant where he'd placed me in his lap. I couldn't muster up the will to fight.

"Hmmm," he mused, continuing to run the brush through my hair in methodical strokes.

"You're not a pet. You're not a doll. Is there anything you do want to be, *sirenita*?"

"What does that mean?" I asked instead of answering his question. He was teasing me, and I refused to rise to it. If I did, he'd likely devise another devious way to prove to me that I would be whatever he wanted me to be.

"A literal translation would be *little mermaid*," he said.

I finally opened my eyes to study his face. Was he mocking me?

"You mean, like the Disney princess?" I asked.

He chuckled. "It's an endearment. It means I find you beautiful." He traced the line of my lower lip with his thumb. "Sensual."

I blinked at him. No one had ever called me beautiful. And definitely not sensual. I was the awkward geek who was barely worth noticing, unless it was to make fun of me.

"You don't believe me," he said, reading my confusion. "Do you think my cock would get so hard for you if I didn't want you? You are lovely, *sirenita*."

"You're trying to manipulate me," I accused, not quite believing him. Maybe he got turned on by dominating women, and my physical appearance had nothing to do with it. That made much more sense. "It won't work."

"It already is working. I'm not lying when I say I

find you beautiful. But everything I do to you is a manipulation, and I won't pretend otherwise. You're being very sweet and well behaved right now. If I'd known how obedient you'd become when I played with your ass, I would have filled it sooner. You came so hard for me. I thought you were going to pass out. I think you enjoy being manipulated, being shaped into my good girl."

I scowled at him. "You're a bastard."

"That might be true. But you will learn to speak to me with respect. There's a consequence coming for that, but right now, you need to eat."

I almost said I wasn't hungry, the urge to defy him automatic. But my stomach was very aware that I hadn't eaten in over twenty-four hours. I still didn't know what time it was, but it was now dark outside. That meant I hadn't eaten since dinner the night before, because I hadn't trusted the breakfast Andrés had sent up for me.

"Okay," I agreed, trying to sound resentful and failing. I was far too hungry.

Now that I'd finally opened my eyes, I noted that Andrés was seated on the edge of the bed, with me perched on his lap. He reached around me and tugged at the small food cart. A silver dome covered the plate, and when he removed it, I realized that my wasted breakfast had been removed and replaced with a mouthwatering steak.

My cheeks heated even as my stomach growled.

That meant someone had come into the bedroom while we were in the shower. Had they heard my lustful scream?

I didn't have much time to worry over it, because my basic needs were too insistent. A jug of water sat on the cart beside two empty glasses. I reached for it and filled one, immediately gulping it down.

"You didn't drink anything today, either?" Andrés asked, his voice heavy with disapproval.

"I thought you might drug me again," I reminded him.

"And you believe I won't now?"

I shrugged. "I figured that steak is huge enough for two people. There are two glasses, one water jug. So I'm assuming that you're not going to drug yourself too, you know?" I poured another glass and drank half of it before moving to pick up the utensils. I was so famished, all I could think about was cutting into the steak and getting some food in my system. No wonder I'd been so weak in my attempts to fight my captor.

He caught my hand before I could touch the silverware and guided it back to my lap. He also took the water glass from me and set it down beside the plate.

"Do you really think I'm going to let you handle a fork and knife?" he asked drily.

I glowered at him. "I just want some fucking food. I'm starving."

He frowned, his scar deepening to a disapproving slash. "I will train your tongue later," he warned. "And I'm sure you're hungry, which is more pressing than your punishment. I will always see to your wellbeing, Samantha, but don't continue to test me."

"I wasn't going to use the knife on you," I said honestly. "I just want to eat."

"I'm going to take care of you, *cosita*. Trust me."

I snorted. "You're not really giving me a choice. Is it trust if you don't have a choice? Probably not. No, I don't think it is. Nope. Definitely not."

He studied me for a moment, something like a smile tugging at the corners of his lips. "Do you always speak this way?"

"What way?"

"You talk very fast. Like you're speaking every thought that comes into your head as it comes to you. Are you doing it because you're nervous around me? Is this the same as why you don't like looking at people?"

"I mean, I guess," I admitted. "But I don't talk like this because I'm nervous. Well, I guess it's worse when I'm nervous. I just have a lot of thoughts, and they kind of pop out, like you said. My brain is really busy all the time. Like, my thoughts never slow down. I can't focus on only one thing at a time, unless it's really challenging."

"You focus on me quite intently," he said, grinning with smug satisfaction. "Does that mean you find me *challenging*?"

"It means I find you terrifying," I shot back, but there was less malice in my tone than I'd intended. There was something odd about speaking to him so earnestly. I'd never been able to hold back vocalizing my thoughts when pressed by a domineering male, but this was different. I didn't feel particularly nervous at the moment. I was too concerned with my need to eat, and Andrés' arms were relaxed around me. He wasn't threatening me.

At the moment.

He laughed. "Such a feisty *gatita*. You're not terrified. Not like you should be. Then again, I suppose I haven't shown you what I'm fully capable of yet." His smile somehow seemed to show all of his teeth, and I shrank back a little. That just made him laugh again, a sound of pure, arrogant amusement. "I promised to feed you, and it's getting cold," he effectively ended the disconcerting conversation.

His arms surrounded me on either side as he reached forward and picked up the knife and fork. He cut the steak into several small pieces, then shifted the utensils into one fist. I supposed he was smart not to set them down where I could reach them, but I really was too hungry and weak to try to stab him at the moment.

He picked up a piece of steak between his fingers and lifted it to my lips.

I looked up at him, confused. "What are you doing?"

"Feeding my pet." He was still smiling, but something darker stirred in his black stare. "Aren't you hungry, *gatita*?"

I blew out a sigh. "Fine. But only because I'm hungry, not because I'm your pet."

"Can't you be both?"

"No."

He chuckled, but he didn't argue with me again. "Eat."

Too hungry to continue resisting, I parted my lips and reached for the morsel with my tongue. I probably should have bitten him just for being a bastard, but I really wanted to eat. Besides, he'd mentioned another punishment and warned me not to test him. Biting him probably counted as worse than *testing*.

As soon as the steak hit my tongue, rich flavors exploded in my mouth, and a soft moan of appreciation left my chest. I loved a good steak, and this one was cooked to perfection. I wrapped my lips around his fingers without thinking, sucking the juices from them as I sought more of the delicious flavor.

"You like *carne asada*?" he asked, his voice rougher than the simple question should have called for.

I pulled back from his fingers, and they left my mouth with a small *pop*.

"I like meat," I said. "All kinds of meat. If it used to *moo*, I'll definitely eat it. This is so good. I want more."

"Greedy and savage," he remarked, his voice lilting with laughter. "You can have as much as you want."

"I'm not savage," I grumbled. "I couldn't even kill you properly."

"No, you couldn't," he said calmly, obviously remembering my pathetic attempt to attack him with his razor. "I don't think you have it in you. That doesn't mean I'll give you access to a knife anytime soon, though."

"I'm a trained field agent," I said, feeling defensive, mostly because I *should* have been capable of fighting him more effectively than I'd managed so far.

"Not a very good one." He said it like a simple observation, not an insult.

And honestly, was it an insult if it was the truth?

"I shouldn't have transferred from tech analyst," I lamented aloud. If I hadn't tried to go into the field, I wouldn't be in this shitty situation.

"Probably not," he agreed. "My brother has his

own tech team. They looked into you. By all accounts, they were very impressed. It's why Cristian let you live."

"Because he wants me to protect him from the FBI," I said glumly. "He wants me to save his miserable life." I tensed, suddenly worried that Andrés might not take kindly to me insulting his brother.

"He does," he responded in a monotone. I couldn't read any particular emotion in it. "And you will. It's my job to make sure you do. You won't do it for Cristian, but for me. I want you to stop thinking about my brother and start thinking about pleasing me. And you can start by finishing your meal."

"You're the one who insists on feeding me one tiny piece at a time," I complained.

"If you'd stop sassing me, this would go faster," he drawled.

I narrowed my eyes at him to communicate my lingering displeasure with the entire weird scenario, but I allowed him to continue feeding me. I ended up eating well over half the steak before he actually used a freaking fork to deliver mouthfuls of the most delicious seasoned rice I'd ever tasted. I might have felt a little guilty that I ate most of the food, but he seemed content for me to have as much as I needed. When I finally turned my face away, he ate what was left.

He finished and lifted me off his lap to place me on the mattress.

"Stay."

He didn't have to restrain me to ensure that I didn't follow as he wheeled the cart out of the bedroom and out into what I now assumed was a sitting room. By the time he shut the door and returned to me, I lay back on the mattress, exhaustion and a pleasant sense of finally being well-fed making me sleepy.

"Go brush your teeth and wash your face," he ordered, grasping my hand and pulling me upright.

I made a little grumbling noise, which morphed to a yelp when he swatted my ass.

"Go on," he said sternly.

My feet dragged across the carpet as I crossed to the bathroom. Moving seemed much harder than it should, my body aching in places I'd never imagined could feel tired and sore.

I shut the bathroom door behind me and took care of my essential needs. An unopened toothbrush waited for me on the sink, as well as feminine face wash and moisturizer. I wondered when Andrés had gotten these items for me, and I concluded that the boy who'd come in to clean the bathroom must have stocked the place for me.

I glanced at the shower. I hadn't noticed before, but a brand new razor hung from beneath the showerhead, replacing the one I'd broken this morning.

"You got a new razor," I said when I re-entered the bedroom, puzzled as to why he'd let me near a potential weapon again.

He met me with a level stare. "And you didn't break it apart and attempt to cut my throat. I don't need to worry about you trying that again, do I?"

My cheeks heated, and I dropped my gaze from his. I could still see the angry red line of the shallow cut I'd inflicted across his chest. He was covered only in the towel he'd slung around his hips after our shower, his powerful form clearly on display where he lounged on the bed.

"No," I admitted, my voice small with shame. I wouldn't try it again. Not because I didn't want to get spanked, but because I had to acknowledge that I truly didn't have it in me to rip open a man's throat. Besides, it had been a stupid, reckless plan, anyway. Where did I think I was going to go after I took out Andrés? There had to be dozens of men between me and freedom. And I didn't think they'd like it if they found me with their boss' blood on my hands.

"Smart girl," he said with satisfaction. "Come over here."

He stood and pulled back the covers, gesturing for me to get in.

I didn't move toward him.

"What are you doing?" I asked.

"Putting you to bed," he said, as though this was completely normal.

"I'm not a little girl. I don't need you to tuck me in."

A smile flitted around his lips. "Must you be so difficult about everything? You seem to love contradicting me." He patted the mattress. "Do you want a spanking before bed, or are you going to be a good girl for me?"

I huffed out a frustrated breath and closed the distance between us. The sad reality was, I was too tired to keep fighting. I'd managed to get some much-needed calories back in my system, but my mind had been sapped with terror for most of the day. Not to mention the other new, intense experiences he'd forced upon me.

"Only because I'm tired," I said as I slid beneath the sheets.

"If that's what you need to tell yourself," he allowed. "One way or another, you obeyed me, Samantha. That pleases me."

I rolled onto my side, facing away from him, and curled my knees up close to my chest in a protective position. He didn't comment on my small show of resistance. He simply pulled the covers over me and tucked me in like a child. It was weird. Fucked up.

Warm and soft.

And I was so tired.

"Go to sleep, *sirenita*." His long fingers played through my hair, and my eyes slid closed.

Without meaning to, I obeyed yet another of his commands and surrendered to my exhaustion.

CHAPTER 9

The mattress shifted beneath me, rousing me. For a moment, I panicked. I wasn't accustomed to sleeping with anyone else, so the instinctive knowledge that I wasn't alone in my bed startled me.

Then I remembered that I wasn't in my bed. I was in Andrés' bed. The bed where he'd bound me and made me have my first orgasm.

My cheeks colored in the darkness. Shades had been lowered over the huge windows, hiding the Chicago skyline. But no light peeked around them, so I assumed it wasn't morning yet. I hated not having a fucking clock. This room was absolutely devoid of even that level of technology. I'd go mad in here without access to a computer.

I'm going to get out of here, I promised myself. Maybe it wasn't likely that my friends would find me. Maybe there were dozens of men standing between me and freedom. Not to mention my massive, scary captor.

But that wasn't going to stop me from trying. It was nighttime. Most of the building's inhabitants would likely be asleep.

That included Andrés, who was snoring lightly on the other side of the massive bed. I'd awoken when he'd rolled away from me, and his arm no longer weighed me down. If I could slip out without disturbing him, I might be able to make my way out of the suite and get to the exit before he woke up. Once I was in the street, I could shout for help. I could borrow someone's phone.

It occurred to me that I'd have to go out in public naked, but I couldn't risk taking time to rummage through Andrés' drawers for something to cover myself. That would also make noise, and I couldn't afford that, either.

Naked, it is, I told myself, reasoning that I'd attract help faster this way, once I got out into the street.

If I didn't get killed on the way out.

Summoning up my courage, I carefully eased out of the bed, wincing when the mattress shifted ever so slightly beneath me. I paused, barely breathing.

Andrés continued to snore.

I exhaled and began to tiptoe across the plush

carpet, making my way toward the door that led out into the rest of the suite. I squeezed my fist open and closed a few times to stop my fingers from trembling, then carefully turned the knob. The softest *snick* sounded as the latch disengaged.

Andrés didn't stir.

I slipped out the door and cracked it behind me, not daring to shut it all the way in case it thudded closed.

City lights flooded the adjoining room, shining through another wall of windows. As I'd suspected, it was set up like a lavish sitting room. Finally, I spotted a clock. Of course, it was an ornate grandfather clock rather than something modern. Analog. Ugh.

Still, at least I now knew it was three thirty-five AM. Hopefully everyone really was asleep at this hour.

My gaze swept over the room, looking for the exit. Another closed door was set into the opposite wall from the windows. I started to make my way toward it when the shifting lights caught on something silver: an elevator. My way out.

I raced toward it on tiptoe, trying to move silently even as I rushed to freedom. I pushed the call button, which was illuminated in blue.

I nearly jumped out of my skin when a loud buzzer sounded.

Fuck!

I hadn't heard that sound when anyone else had come and gone from the suite. Why now?

Desperate, I punched the button again, knowing I had precious seconds before Andrés' strong arms closed around me. The angry buzz echoed through the suite.

"It won't work for you," he drawled.

I yelped and spun, backing up until my butt hit the cold silver doors behind me. Andrés stood in the doorway to the bedroom, the city lights reflecting stars across his black eyes. He didn't move toward me.

The doors didn't open behind me. Desperate, I hit the call button again.

Buzz.

His teeth flashed white through the darkness. "That elevator is accessed through thumbprint recognition. The only people who can come and go from this suite are those who have my permission. You don't have permission, my curious *gatita*." He finally began prowling toward me. "Did you want to explore my home?" he asked, the innocuous question made terrifying by the silky smooth tone of his voice. "Were you so eager to see the rest of it? I'm more than happy to show you."

I shook my head wildly. "I didn't... I don't... I just want to go home," I forced out past the lump in my throat. Whatever he was about to show me, I was certain it was terrible. I could read it in the hungry glint of his eyes, the sharpness of his smile. Dark anticipation pulsed around him like a palpable thing. It pressed against me, making me shudder.

"This is your home now," he said when he finally reached me. There was nowhere for me to run, nowhere to hide. All I could do was press my body back against the cold metal doors and tremble.

His hand closed around the back of my neck, his fingers tangling in my hair at my nape as he pulled me against him. He was naked, and his huge cock pressed into my belly.

"You weren't really asleep," I accused, knowing the truth. He was toying with me, testing me.

His grin sharpened. "Clever and curious," he remarked with satisfaction. "No, I wasn't asleep." He leaned in, his cheek whispering against mine as he spoke low in my ear. "You can't escape me, Samantha. There's only one way out of this penthouse, and it's barred to you. I don't have to keep you collared and chained to trap you here. I just like it. I like knowing you're naked in my bed, waiting for me."

"You're sick," I said shakily.

He laughed softly. "You've called me worse already. Do you really think your little insults wound me? I'm going to tame your barbed tongue because I enjoy training you, not because it's capable of hurting me. If you continue to defy me in this, the only time you'll be allowed to use your tongue is when you're worshipping my cock."

My stomach churned, fear clogging my throat. I didn't have any words, anyway. What was there to say in response to such a horrible declaration?

"But you wanted to see the rest of my home," he continued smoothly. "Let me show you."

"I don't want to," I squeaked out. "Please. I'll go back to bed."

He clicked his tongue at me. "The time for being a good girl has passed. You've been a curious *gatita*. You know what happens to curious kittens, don't you?"

Curiosity killed the cat. "You said you wouldn't kill me. Your brother wants me alive."

His hand tightened around my nape. "This is about what *I* want," he growled. "I don't want you dead. I want you crying out and begging for mercy. *My* mercy. Don't talk about my brother. Don't think about him. He's not your concern. I am."

Keeping his grip on my nape, Andrés pulled me along in his wake, moving toward the closed door I'd noticed opposite the wall of windows. Dread settled in my gut, and my feet dragged on the carpet in token resistance. I could have clawed at him, at the very least. But my body remembered the punitive feel of his finger invading my bottom, and I didn't even half-formulate a plan to fight before he'd managed to drag me to the door.

"Please," I begged. "I don't want to go in there."

"You don't even know what you're scared of," he said, his voice colored with amusement.

"Whatever it is, I don't want it. You wouldn't want to take me in there if it were anything good. You're scaring me."

"You should be scared. You've been very naughty, trying to escape from me."

"But you just said I can't escape. I can't use the elevator. You don't have to hurt me to keep me from using it," I babbled on, desperate to stay on this side of that closed door. Even though the words tumbling from my lips made my heart sink as I recognized the truth in them, I had to press on. I didn't want to be punished.

He reached for the knob and pushed. The door swung open into darkness. The city lights shining behind us barely penetrated the blackness, as though refusing to illuminate the ominous space. The light had no place here. The scent of leather and something deeper teased through the air that drifted through the open door.

"Don't," I gasped out as he propelled me forward, into the darkness.

The soft click of a light switch being flipped registered in my ears, just before panic seized my senses.

It was like something out of the scariest corners of the internet. I'd seen some fucked up dungeon porn. Andrés might as well use this room as a set for the most depraved, disturbing videos I'd ever glimpsed before quickly clicking the back button on my browser.

Creepy crimson lights illuminated the space so I could clearly see every object that waited to torment me. It reminded me of the time I'd ventured to the BDSM club Dusk on my particularly misguided Valentine's Day mission to seduce Dex.

"This isn't like Dusk," I told myself softly, not realizing I was speaking the words aloud. "It's not. Dusk is Safe, Sane, Consensual." I knew the tenets of BDSM, even if I'd never practiced it myself. "This isn't. I don't want this. Not like this."

"You've been to a BDSM club?" Andrés' voice penetrated my mounting terror. He kept his grip on my nape, but he stepped in front of me. His angry black eyes filled my vision, botting out the horror that surrounded me. "I thought you were my innocent little virgin. Did you lie to me, Samantha? I wondered when I didn't feel your hymen intact. But those can be broken in other ways, and I thought your surrender was genuine." His scar deepened to a furious slash. "I wasn't the first man to touch you. If you think you've suffered under my hand before, that's nothing compared to what's about to happen to you."

JULIA SYKES

"No!" I half-sobbed. "I wasn't lying. I am a virgin, I swear."

"Then how do you know about Dusk?" he demanded.

"I went there one time," I gasped out. "I was looking for Dex. I followed him there. I wanted to see him. I wanted him to see *me*. But he didn't. He never does. I got drunk and left. I didn't do anything but drink at the bar. I promise, I didn't do anything. I didn't lie to you. Please, don't hurt me."

His eyes softened, his scar easing as the tension left his mouth. He didn't release me, but his grip shifted so his fingers rubbed the back of my neck.

"All right, *sirenita*. I believe you. I don't think you could lie convincingly if you tried. You will explain more about this later. For now, you have a lesson to learn."

"I just want to go back to bed." A tear slid down my cheek, and he wiped it away with his thumb.

"I'll put you to bed when we're finished in here. You must be punished for trying to escape. You need to understand that your behavior has consequences."

I started crying in earnest, harsh sobs wracking my chest as fear seized my system.

"Come here." He pulled me against his hard body, wrapping his arms around me in a firm embrace as he continued to rub the base of my scalp in little circular patterns. "It won't be so bad," he cooed. "I'm not angry with you."

"It will be," I insisted, my voice hitching. "Just because it would be worse if you were angry doesn't mean it won't be bad. This place is... It's not right. I don't want to be in here."

I shuddered against him, and his big hand stroked up and down my back in a reassuring motion.

"You'll get used to it," he said, his voice deep and calm. "We are going to spend a lot of time in here. I think you might even enjoy it, in a way." His soothing tone was so at odds with the horrible things he was saying that my mind couldn't quite process it. I felt comforted, even though my heart hammered against my ribcage.

"Take a deep breath," he said, a softly-spoken order. "Good girl. Another."

I hadn't realized I'd complied, but my addled mind couldn't keep up with what was happening to me. My body obeyed, and my roiling emotions began to subside enough that I was no longer shaking and sobbing against my captor.

"Come with me," he commanded, finally releasing my neck to take my hand in his.

It was a sweet gesture, and he held my fingers so gently that he might have been my caring, kind boyfriend.

A caring, kind boyfriend I'd never had. A caring,

kind boyfriend with a scary, scarred body and wicked gleam in his eye. A caring, kind boyfriend who was leading me toward...

I dug in my heels. "No."

"You don't get to say no," he told me, his voice still calm and even. "This is your punishment."

"You said you wouldn't hurt me," I said, trying in vain to jerk my hand out of his suddenly vice-like grip.

"I said I wouldn't harm you," he corrected me. "This won't leave any permanent marks. Although I'm interested to see how easily your pretty skin bruises. I do like seeing my marks on my pet."

I shook my head in wild denial. "Stop it! Stop. I'm not your pet. I don't want be marked or bruised."

"How else will you learn?" he asked, as though the question were completely reasonable.

"I don't need to learn anything. I just need you to let me go."

"You don't know what you need. I know what's best for you."

"You don't know shit," I railed at him, fear morphing to anger. "You're fucked up. You're so fucking messed up. Fuck you." I continued cursing at him, even as he pulled me inexorably forward. Mostly, I hurled the f-bomb at him. For once, he didn't rebuke me. He didn't say anything at all.

Which scared the shit out of me.

So I cursed at him some more.

He barely looked at me when he gripped my waist and positioned my body over the spanking bench. I knew what it was from years of indulging my perverted curiosity online.

But knowing what it was didn't prepare me for the full blast of terror that slammed into me when he pressed my torso down against the padded surface, forcing me to bend at the waist over the edge so my bottom was thrust up shamefully.

He handled my body with an almost detached air. There were no lingering touches, no reassuring strokes of his fingertips along my skin. He didn't even touch me with violent hands. Even that would have been preferable to the methodical way he captured my wrists and secured them with black leather cuffs.

I tried to push up off the bench, even knowing that I couldn't free my hands. He didn't make a sound as he buckled a thick strap around my waist-line, pinning me down against the padded surface. I almost wished he'd click his tongue at me in disapproval. Now, that seemed like almost an affectionate act. This man who so callously arranged my body for torment made my insides quake.

I couldn't stop cussing. I wasn't sure if I was even insulting him directly anymore. A stream of curse words tumbled from my lips in nonsensical, half-formed sentences.

He grasped my legs and guided them apart, securing them with another set of leather cuffs. I was bent over and spread wide, my sex and asshole fully on display and at his mercy.

But I suspected he didn't have any mercy for me.

"Fu—" My final f-bomb was abruptly smothered when something rubbery pressed deep into my mouth, pushing my tongue down as it settled between my lips. He buckled the ball gag closed at the back of my head. I thrashed, as though I could somehow push it out of my mouth.

He gripped my hair, wrapping it around his fist and pulling back sharply. My shocked cry caught against the rubber ball as pain lit up my scalp, commanding my attention.

My head was bowed back, my neck stretched to the point where breathing was difficult. I focused on sucking in air through my nose, my impotent rage and fear finally muffled by the imperative to obtain enough oxygen.

His black eyes stared down into mine, and my mind went oddly blank. I couldn't fight, I couldn't shout obscenities at him. I couldn't do anything but draw in shallow, careful breaths.

"That's better," he said softly, trailing his fingers over my lips, tracing the line of them where they surrounded the red rubber ball that filled my mouth. "Very pretty," he praised.

A fine tremor raced across my skin as a strange sense of relief settled over me. He was looking at me again, touching me. He wasn't treating me like an object. The impersonal way he'd been handling me had scared me more than Cristian's knife cutting into me. The Andrés who held me and promised to protect me in his own messed up way was back, and I was relieved to see him. Fresh tears pooled in my eyes as my toxic fear leaked out of me.

"You're so beautiful when you cry," he murmured, stroking the wetness on my cheeks almost reverently. "Don't you feel better now? You don't have to yell. You don't have to fight. Your Master is in control, and you don't have to pretend otherwise. Not when you're strapped down and spread wide for me to play with. All you have to do is submit. All you *can* do is submit."

Keeping his grip on my hair, he held my face in place as he leaned down and pressed a tender kiss against my forehead.

"Time for your punishment, *gatita*," he said, his soft lips brushing across my skin. "You've more than earned it."

I shivered, but not entirely out of fear. A shadow of it resurfaced, but I couldn't be terrified anymore. There was no point. As he'd said, I wasn't capable of fighting him in my current predicament.

Surrendering was so much easier than panicking, especially when panicking was pointless.

He won't harm me, I reminded myself, playing it over and over again in my head like a soothing mantra. *He won't harm me*.

I'd survived his spankings, his violations. Whatever he had planned for me, I'd survive this, too.

He finally released my hair, and my head dropped forward, my cheek resting meekly against the padded bench.

His palm skimmed across my lower back, the heat of his body sinking into mine.

"Good girl. I'll be right back." He said it like the sweetest reassurance, almost as though he was reluctant to leave my side.

Or maybe I was just delusional, and I was hearing what I needed to hear in order to cope with what was happening to me.

He disappeared behind me, his heat receding. I tried to crane my head back to watch him, but he had walked outside my range of sight. Bound as I was, I could only move my head so far.

Giving up, I settled my cheek back against the smooth leather and closed my eyes. The darkness behind my lids was peaceful. Far preferable to examining the torture chamber that surrounded me.

Silence enfolded me. I couldn't hear Andrés

moving, but I could practically feel his eyes on me. My skin prickled with awareness, but my body remained limp against the bench. I breathed in deeply through my nose, taking in long draws of oxygen.

I tried not to think, but my brain began firing again, wondering what he was going to do to me. Several horrible possibilities occurred to me at once, terrible images of torment flickering across my mind.

Just as I began to tense with mounting anxiety, something cool and smooth tickled my spine. My shocked yelp was muffled by the gag, and my eyes flew open to assess what was happening to me.

Andrés stood behind me, looming over my help- less form. His black eyes glinted in the eerie crimson light as he studied my reaction. He held a flogger in one hand, allowing its multitude of thin black leather falls to kiss my back.

My eyes widened, and I squirmed in my restraints.

I wasn't entirely trying to get away. I'd been curious to know what it would feel like to be flogged. I'd fantasized about it more than a few times.

But this wasn't the scenario I'd envisioned. For one, Dex had always played the hero in my mind. The man standing behind me was no hero. He was my own personal villain.

And he was staring at me as though I was the most fascinating thing he'd ever seen.

"You know what this is?" he asked, trailing the leather falls down the length of my spine.

A small whimper slipped past the gag as my nerve endings crackled to life. I managed a slight nod in response to his question, never even considering refusing to answer. I couldn't have any secrets from Andrés when I was like this: stripped bare and put on display for him. I couldn't hide from him. He wouldn't allow it.

"But no one has ever flogged you before," he said. It wasn't a question. He already knew how innocent I was.

"Kinky little virgin," he mused. "When I decide to allow you to speak again, you'll tell me every depraved thought you've ever had." He smiled down at me with genuine pleasure. "I knew we'd get along."

He took a step back and swung the flogger down in a slow arc. The falls slapped against my bottom, but it didn't hurt. He was going slow with me, watching me with the careful, focused attention of a predator as he monitored my reactions. The heavy strips of leather slid down over my cheeks. They were cool and smooth against my heated skin.

"This is going to hurt," he warned. "It's

supposed to hurt. One day, I'll show you how good it can feel. But not tonight."

I couldn't do anything but shiver and wait for him to begin. The fantasy I'd harbored for so long—Dex lovingly giving me a hit of pain to drive me into a blissful headspace—faded away. This wouldn't bring me to subspace. That was attained through trust and honest surrender. It was something I'd longed for, and it had never been farther from my grasp.

I had to surrender to Andrés, but he wasn't giving me a choice. The restraints around my body weren't part of a kinky game, designed to help me let go of my inhibitions. They were punitive, a means of subjugating me, just as the collar had been. Everything I'd ever secretly longed for was being twisted. As perverted as it was to fantasize about my best friend tying me down and whipping me, that fantasy was sweet and practically vanilla compared to my horrific reality.

I didn't have a safe word. I couldn't do anything to stop this.

When the first hit landed, I shrieked into the gag, my entire body jerking against my restraints in an instinctive effort to move away. The cuffs held fast, and the belt around my waist kept me trapped against the bench.

I stared back at him, silently pleading.

Don't. Not again. I don't like this.

The initial sting of the falls striking my bottom was morphing into a deeper burn, leaving my skin smarting.

"Your eyes are so lovely," he said, studying me with purely masculine appreciation. My wide, shining eyes did nothing to dissuade him. If anything, he was getting turned on. His cock began to stiffen as I shook my head, my pleas muffled by the gag.

A hash cry tore from my throat when he brought the flogger down twice in rapid succession, hitting one cheek and then the other, leaving a scorching path where the thin leather falls raked across my skin.

He paused as I heaved out a sob, but he wasn't looking at my face anymore. He studied my bottom, lightly running his fingertips over my enflamed skin. The contact tingled and stung, and I whined in protest.

"So pretty and red," he observed. He gripped my cheek hard, his fingers digging into my tender flesh. I tried to wriggle away, but there was nowhere to go. "I want to see my fingerprints on your ass tomorrow," he said, as though explaining his actions made them rational. "The bruises from the flogger will remind you of your punishment, but this marks you as mine." He increased the pressure of his cruel hold, and my breath stuttered as tears began to stream down my face.

Finally, he released my cheek. I didn't have time to sag in relief before he brought the flogger down on me again, swift and merciless.

I threw back my head and screamed into the gag, but I couldn't do anything to stop him. He spread the burn of the stinging falls across my bottom and down my upper thighs, painting my flesh with hot red pain.

My entire body began to quiver as my muscles started to give out. I'd been twisting and tugging against my restraints on animal instinct, but I couldn't keep up even that much resistance. I went limp against the bench, trembling.

"Good girl," he said, his voice deeper than I'd ever heard it. "Accept your punishment. You know you've earned it."

My tears came faster. I didn't deserve it. I didn't deserve anything that was happening to me.

But the gag kept my protest locked inside. I couldn't do anything but surrender.

I drew in a shuddering breath, submitting to the pain. As soon as I did, my mind entered a quiet, resigned space. Each blow still stung, but I noticed the heavy thud permeating deeper into my flesh. It was rhythmic. Hypnotic. My breathing began to even out as I focused solely on the sensation of harsh leather hitting my burning skin, the *whoosh* and *smack* of the flogger moving through the air before making contact. Everything else faded: thought, worry, emotion.

I barely registered when the blows stopped. I'd retreated to a protective place in some deep corner of my mind I'd never found before. My rapid-fire thoughts and volatile emotions couldn't touch me here.

I was dimly aware of Andrés' deep voice murmuring a soothing litany in Spanish as his calloused hands traced the contours of my motion-less body.

The gag slipped from my mouth and the restraints fell away, but I didn't try to get up. I couldn't have moved a muscle, even if I wanted to. And resistance didn't even occur to me. That defiant line of thinking had been thoroughly obliterated.

He lifted me up and tucked me against his chest. My tears wet his skin as he carried me away from the bench where I'd been bound and whipped.

I was too exhausted and wrung-out to even register relief. I passed out in his arms before we made it back to the bed.

CHAPTER 10

I rolled onto my back and jolted awake with a gasp when my bottom throbbed. Wincing, I immediately positioned myself on my side. Something tugged at my neck as I moved. I reached up and touched my throat, finding smooth leather beneath my fingertips. Andrés had collared me again. I must have been totally passed out not to have woken up when he was locking around my neck.

I don't have to keep you collared and chained to trap you here. I just like it. I like knowing you're naked in my bed, waiting for me.

His sick words played through my mind as I remembered our terrifying encounter in the middle of the night. I closed my eyes as the full shame and horror of everything he'd done to me washed over me. He'd toyed with me, allowing me to try to escape just so he could punish me for it. He'd taken me to that awful room, strapped me down, gagged me; he'd rendered me completely powerless and flogged my helpless body.

Gingerly, I touched my bottom and winced again as pain flared. I twisted my head back so I could look down at myself. My breath caught at the sight of mottled purple bruises marring my pale skin. Five smaller marks formed a rough circular pattern on my left cheek.

I want to see my fingerprints on your ass tomorrow, he'd said. *The bruises from the flogger will remind you of your punishment, but this marks you as mine.*

I cringed and tore my eyes away from the brand he'd left behind. I didn't need the physical reminder of the pain for the punishment to be burned into my mind.

I wouldn't try to use the elevator again.

It would be stupid and pointless, anyway. If I had access to a computer, I could hack into the building's security system and override the thumbprint recognition, no problem. But without technology, I was powerless. Andrés had made it painfully clear that I wasn't cut out to be a field agent. Months of training in hand-to-hand combat hadn't helped me at all when it came to facing him.

He hadn't needed to collar me and chain me to his bed to keep me from trying to access the elevator. Even though I was alone in the bedroom, I wouldn't have tried to escape that way in his absence. The security system probably logged failed attempts to press the call button. He'd know if I touched it without him here to witness my transgression. I didn't want to risk another punishment for nothing.

My stomach rumbled, rousing me from my dejected state.

Survive, my body reminded me.

I had to keep going, keep fit. I'd never get out of here if I let myself waste away into weakness. I needed to keep my calorie count up and stay hydrated in case an opportunity to escape did present itself.

I sat up in bed and hissed when my weight settled on my bruises. Even the soft mattress was almost too hard to bear.

Grimacing, I glanced around the room. As I'd hoped, the food cart was waiting for me, the fancy platter covered to keep my meal warm.

I wasn't sure how long I'd been alone, but when I removed the cover, the bacon beneath was still warm, at least. I glanced out the windows and noted that the sun was up pretty high. Was that like, ten AM?

I wasn't sure. I wasn't exactly a nature girl, and surviving in the wild with the sun as my only clock wasn't a skill I'd ever had to acquire.

Even the nearly obsolete grandfather clock in

the sitting room would have been preferable, but the bedroom door was closed again. Hell, I'd settle for a freaking sundial at this point.

Sighing, I bit into a particularly crispy piece of bacon. I nearly moaned at the rich, salty flavor.

Andrés might be a sadistic madman, but he was a sadistic madman with a great chef.

I tore my way through five strips of bacon before moving on to the most delicious spicy sausage I'd ever tasted. The breakfast was protein-heavy, and I wondered if Andrés had remembered what I'd said about being a meat lover.

Or maybe he was just trying to keep me slow and sleepy with all this heavy, salty food, because by the time I'd devoured everything and downed a jug of water, I lay back on the bed and closed my eyes.

I was so tired, my brain weirdly fuzzy and slow. My thoughts were still firing, but not in as many directions as usual. My emotions—which should have been spinning in response to my dire predica-ment—were oddly subdued.

Idly, I wondered if Andrés had decided to drug the food, but I didn't believe he'd do that. No, he much preferred physically demonstrating my help-lessness. As he'd said, he didn't need to use drugs to keep me compliant.

I wasn't sure how long I lay there, stray thoughts gliding across my mind from time to time as I settled into a state on the edge of sleep.

The click of the bedroom door opening roused me, and I sat bolt upright. I let out a little yelp at the sudden weight on my bottom, and I scrambled to cover my body with the sheet when I saw Lauren standing at the threshold.

"I just had breakfast," I said when I saw the cart she was pushing into the room. "I'm not hungry."

"I'm not here to bring you food," she said, her voice a hollow monotone. She was looking right at me, but her deep green eyes didn't spark with any emotion whatsoever. I might as well have been a statue she was talking to rather than another woman. She wasn't here to help me, even if she was a victim. She worked for my captor, regardless of whether or not she'd been brutalized and broken.

"Then what's that?" I asked warily, eyeing the items on the cart. There was a small silver pot and a stack of cloth strips, as well as what looked like cleansing wipes. I had no idea what I was looking at.

"Wax," she replied.

"Wax?" I repeated, still not following. Why would she have wax?

Something sparked in her eyes for the briefest moment. My stomach twisted when I registered it as pity.

"For your pussy," she replied bluntly.

I pulled the sheet all the way up to my chin and

squeezed my thighs together, ignoring the flare of pain as I shifted my weight.

"No," I refused, sharp and immediate.

"I'm really good at it," she said, something like kindness softening her tone. "It will barely hurt. I do it all the time."

"Nope. Uh-uh. Not happening. You can leave now."

Her brow furrowed. "I can't do that."

"You totally can. Because I'm not getting my... I'm not getting waxed down there."

"You mean your pussy," she said, eyeing me strangely.

"I mean my lady parts, yes," I replied, my voice higher than usual. "They're not getting waxed. So you can go now, and take that shit with you." I gestured at the cart.

"Master Andrés doesn't like cussing," she said, setting the cart next to the bed.

"I know," I said bitterly, shifting my weight off my aching bottom. Something awful occurred to me. If Lauren wasn't my ally, was she my enemy? "You won't tell him, will you?" I asked desperately. I didn't want him to take me back into that scary room and hurt me again.

"No," she promised, her gaze softening with sympathy. "Just don't do it again, please."

I nodded, knowing she would probably get into trouble if he ever discovered she was keeping my transgression a secret. He was cruel, insane. What would he do to her if he found out she was showing me the smallest kindness? After my punishment last night, I was beginning to understand why Lauren was so compliant.

"Does he hurt you?" I asked quietly. "I don't want him to hurt you because of me."

She blinked at me, surprised. "Master Andrés is nice," she asserted for the second time.

"Okay," I said slowly, trying to wrap my mind around her warped headspace. "But does he hurt you? You can tell me. He hurt me, too."

"I wish Master Andrés would take care of me like he's taking care of you. You're lucky."

"Are you listening to me?" I demanded, my patience slipping. "I said he hurt me. He's not taking care of me."

She glared at me. "Do you want to be downstairs with the rest of us? Where they dose you with Bliss and make you beg them to rape you? Master Andrés is honest. He's fair. He's kind."

I bit my tongue to hold in a frustrated tirade. Lauren had obviously been driven mad. Through my frustration, guilt and pity twisted my gut. Piecing together what she'd revealed, Lauren was being regularly drugged and violated, but not by Andrés. I knew from my investigation that Cristian Moreno was involved in trafficking Bliss and using the sick drug to capture and sell women.

My stomach roiled. Andrés had claimed I'd beg him to fuck me, but at least he wasn't drugging me. We were locked in a battle of wills, and even though he'd won every round so far, I still had my wits about me to keep fighting. He might have forced me to surrender to punishment and wrung pleasure from my untried body, but I still had my mind.

"I'll help you get out of here, Lauren," I swore. "I'm going to get you out."

She stiffened. "I'm not going to help you escape."

"I didn't expect you to," I replied sadly. She was obviously too far gone to defy Andrés. She'd been broken a long time ago. "But that doesn't mean I'm not going to help you. We'll get out of here."

She started at me, nonplussed. "I have a job to do," she announced after a few seconds of silence, as though I hadn't just made a passionate oath to set her free. "Lie on your back, please."

I blew out a long breath and complied. I could physically resist Lauren, but I didn't know what Andrés would do to her if I prevented her from following his orders. I remembered how he'd frightened the young man who'd defied him yesterday. Andrés had threatened to cut out his eye for looking at me.

I didn't want him to hurt Lauren because of my defiant choices. I'd choose another battle to fight with him, one that only involved the two of us and didn't risk collateral damage.

I stared up at the ceiling as she slid the sheet off my body, leaving me bare. I did my best not to squirm with discomfort at being stripped. I'd always been painfully modest, even around other women. I hadn't grown up with sisters or even female cousins, so I wasn't accustomed to anyone seeing me naked.

My cheeks heated, and I resolutely fisted my fingers into the sheet beneath me, preventing myself from slapping Lauren's hands away as she began to work.

The wax was almost painfully hot, but she was as practiced as she'd claimed. Every time she pulled a wax-covered cloth free, she'd apply pressure to my enflamed skin to alleviate the horrible sting that followed. There was nothing sexual about the way she touched me. She was almost clinical in the way she handled my most secret area, her eyes assessing her work rather than studying my sex.

"Done," she announced after a few uncomfortable minutes. She pulled away from me and started tidying everything on the cart.

"Thanks," I said automatically. "I mean. No, thanks. I mean, I didn't mean to thank you. That was totally fucked up. I mean, fuck. I didn't mean to cuss. Damn it. I just—" I stopped rambling before my social awkwardness could get me into more trouble.

Her hand settled over mine, squeezing gently. "I won't tell," she promised. "But you need to be good for Master Andrés."

"Why?" I challenged. "Because he'll beat me if I'm not?"

"Because he needs it."

I gaped at her. "He needs me to be good for him," I said flatly. "I don't know what kind of psycho world you've been living in, and whatever's happened to you, I really am sorry. And I am going to help you get out of here. But I'm not going to roll over and give up just because you told me to. I'm not going to behave for my sadistic captor who gets off on torturing women, no matter what you say."

She shook her head, her shining blond hair waving around her delicate face. "You don't understand him. You don't know him."

"And you do? Just how well do you know *Master* Andrés? What did he do to you, exactly?" Ugly emotions clawed at my insides: anger, bitterness, fear.

She lifted her chin. "He's nice," she insisted, as though that was the only way she was capable of thinking of Andrés.

Ice crystallized in my veins. What had he done to her to warp her so thoroughly?

"Thank you, Lauren," his accented voice rolled through the room. "You can go now."

I jolted and grabbed the sheet, jerking the fabric over my body. Andrés smirked at me as he stepped into the bedroom.

"You know you're not allowed to cover yourself, *cosita*," he said, more amused than stern. "Show me your pretty pussy. I want to see it."

Lauren hurried out of the room, but I couldn't focus on her retreating form. All my attention was riveted on the threat posed by Andrés. My body became very aware of his proximity, remembering the pain he'd inflicted the night before. My heartbeat picked up, my pulse racing. I wanted to pull the sheet all the way up over my head and hide like a child seeking protection from a monster.

But my bottom throbbed, a cruel reminder of what he was capable of if I disobeyed him. I'd already been naked around him pretty much since I'd gotten here. Why risk another punishment just to cover myself now? He'd look at me, one way or another.

Slowly, I curled my fingers into the sheet and forced myself to drag it off my body. His eyes went straight to my bare sex, and they darkened with hunger.

"Very pretty." He made a little rolling motion with his forefinger. "Turn over. I want to see my marks on you."

I glared at him.

He met me with a steady stare, waiting.

I huffed out an angry breath and rolled onto my front. It felt nice not having my weight on the bruises, anyway.

"On your hands and knees," he commanded. "Spread your thighs. I want to see my marks and my pussy."

My eyes narrowed farther, and I didn't move to comply. That was too much. He couldn't honestly expect me to present myself to him so wantonly. Not without putting up a fight.

Only, I didn't have time to fight. His arm snaked beneath my hips, pulling me up onto my knees.

"Hey!" I cried, indignant.

His hand cracked across my bruised thigh, and I shrieked.

"You will learn to obey me," he said calmly. "Spread your legs. Now," he added, the word imbued with warning.

My cheeks burning hotter than my thigh, I slowly eased my knees apart while he kept me in place with his arm braced beneath my stomach.

"Beautiful," he remarked, his voice a low rumble. He touched his fingers to my labia, stroking over my bare skin. My sensitive flesh danced and quivered. It was strange to feel so smooth down there, his touch gliding over my sex in a gentle caress. His fingertips grazed over my clit as he stroked me, and I couldn't quite manage to smother a small gasp as pleasure crackled through the little bundle of nerves.

He chuckled. "I think my kitten likes when I pet her pretty pink pussy."

"Stop," I begged, not daring to say I didn't like it. That would be a lie. I couldn't deny that it felt good when he touched me like this. But that didn't mean I had to admit it aloud. I didn't want to like his touch, but my body betrayed me.

"But I like petting your pussy, *gatita*," he said, not stopping his tender exploration of my bare flesh. It still stung slightly from the waxing, but my core fluttered as he continued to stroke me. "You were very well behaved for Lauren, weren't you? I think you've earned another reward."

"Is this what you did to her?" I hurled at him, my fury rising at the mention of the broken woman. "Beat her and manipulated her until her mind warped? Did she used to hate you before she started worshipping the ground you walk on? Did you—?"

My tirade ended when he abruptly flipped me over and settled his hand around the front of my throat. He didn't apply any pressure this time, but the warning was clear.

"I've never harmed Lauren," he said, his voice rough with his own anger.

A maddened laugh bubbled from my throat.

"You've never *harmed* her? Just like you didn't harm me when you strapped me down and whipped me after mindfucking me into thinking I had a chance to escape? How crazy are you?"

Something cold and scary settled over him, his features shifting to a blank mask. "I never claimed to be sane. Do you think a normal man wants to take an innocent woman and turn her into his plaything? Do you think a good man wants to bend her will and shape her into his obedient little fucktoy?"

"So you..." I swallowed down the lump of horror in my throat. "You did do this to Lauren."

"No," he said, still frigid. "The Bliss broke Lauren, not me."

Tears burned at the corners of my eyes. "So you do want to break me," I whispered.

A frown tugged at the corners of his lips, and some of the ice melted from his gaze. "I told you, I'm going to tame you. I'm going to make you mine and teach you to obey. I don't want to see you broken."

"You told your brother you'd break me for him," I countered, fear pooling in my gut.

His frown deepened to a scowl. "My brother likes to break things. He likes to take things that aren't his and shatter them. If I left you with him, he'd torture you until he discovered what you love most in the world. Then he'd make you watch while he destroyed it. Is that what you'd prefer? That I hand you back over to him?"

Dex. Dex was the only person left that I cared about. My parents had died in a car crash when I was twenty-three. They'd been the only family I had, until I'd met my best friend.

"No," I said faintly, a vision of Cristian's knife slicing into Dex's throat flashing across my mind. I couldn't let that happen, no matter what it cost me.

Andrés wiped away the horrified tears that had spilled down my cheeks.

"I'm not going to let him break you," he promised. "He'll never touch you again. You're mine now. I will be harsh with you. I will hurt you sometimes. And I will enjoy your pain. But I will never cause you harm, not to your body and not to your heart. Do you understand?"

I closed my eyes and turned my face away from his touch. He was basically telling me that I had to sacrifice myself to save Dex. It was a sacrifice I'd make without a second thought, but that didn't mean despair didn't swallow me up as I chose to do so.

"I can see that you don't understand," he said with a sigh. "But you will. It won't be so bad, *cosita*. I'm not so bad." He murmured the last so softly, I barely heard it.

The mattress shifted, and I listened to him moving away from me. I waited until the door closed behind him before I started crying in earnest. I'd do anything to spare Dex pain, but this? Whoring myself out to a man who admitted he enjoyed hurting me? I wasn't sure my mind wouldn't break in the process, no matter what Andrés said.

I can do this, I told myself. *I can be the hero. Hero-ine. I can keep Dex safe.*

I'd find a way out of here somehow. If I got to safety, Cristian couldn't hurt me. He couldn't threaten Dex. I'd save myself and my best friend. I just had to survive whatever Andrés had in store for me until I was able to devise a way to escape. I had to avoid being turned over to Cristian at all costs. Dex's life depended on it.

CHAPTER 11

"You're sad," Andrés observed, tucking my hair behind my ear in a perversion of affection.

"I'm not sad," I countered. "I'm pissed."

"You're not angry." He cupped my cheek so he could study my expression more carefully. "My angry *gatita* is cute and fierce. You're sad."

I huffed out a breath. "I'm bored," I admitted. I'd spent the entire day alone, with nothing to do but mull over my desperate situation. It hadn't exactly been good for my headspace. Lauren had returned briefly to bring my lunch, but other than that short visit, I'd been on my own. It had been dark outside for ages before Andrés had finally returned.

"You keep me chained up. I can't even use the freaking bathroom. Do you know how fu—" I caught myself before the curse word left my lips "—messed up that is?" I finished.

One corner of his lips tilted in a crooked smile. "There's my angry *gatita*," he said with satisfaction, ignoring my accusations. "I was worried about you."

"If you were worried about me, you wouldn't leave me alone for hours with nothing to do. I'm going crazy here. Solitary confinement drives people crazy, you know that, right? Especially people like me."

He frowned slightly. "What do you mean, *people like you*? The purpose of leaving you like this is so you'll wait for me. You'll depend on me for everything. It helps you feel my control, even when I can't be here with you."

I shoved at his chest, but of course I couldn't push him away. It was more a token show of anger than anything else. I'd already given up on physically besting him.

"Do you know how many thoughts I have? Like, all at one time? If I don't have something to focus on, they overwhelm me. I can't live like this."

"It's only been two days," he pointed out. "You'll adjust."

"I won't," I asserted. "You don't know me at all. I'll go nuts if you keep leaving me like this."

His frown deepened. "If you're trying to manipulate me into letting you walk freely around the suite, it's not going to work. That's a privilege you have to earn."

"I'm not trying to manipulate you," I asserted, although now that he said it, I realized it would have been a good try. "That's what you do, right? Manipulate people. Mindfuck them. Well, I'm not like you. I'm telling you the truth. I can't handle this." I tugged at the collar for emphasis. I was no longer chained to the bed, but he'd left the collar locked around my throat while he held me in his lap for this maddening conversation.

He studied me for a long moment, then his frown finally eased. "No. You're not like me. I'll take this into consideration." He brushed a feather-light kiss across my forehead. "I think I have a way to calm that busy brain of yours. You were so good accepting your punishment last night and behaving for Lauren today. I never did give you your reward."

"I don't want it. Having you touch me is not a reward."

"You're still upset," he noted. "This will help you calm down. And before you keep arguing with me, I'll promise that I won't make you come, unless you ask me to. Does that make you feel better?"

I eyed him warily, not trusting him for a second. "What are you going to do to me? I don't want to go back into that torture room."

"It's not a torture room," he said calmly. "But no, we won't go in there. I want you to relax, not get more worked up. No more questions," he announced before I could come up with another rebuttal. "Come with me."

It wasn't like I really had a choice, because he simply picked me up and carried me. He kept doing that, like I weighed nothing more than a doll. I was a toy he could pick up when he wanted to play with me.

I crossed my arms over my chest and scowled up at him.

The bastard laughed. "You really are cute when you're angry."

"You think I'm cute when I'm angry. You think I'm pretty when I cry. You're messed up, you know that, right?"

"Yes, so you've told me," he said, still amused rather than disturbed by my barbed comments. "I'd like to see you smile, too, but I don't think that will happen for a while yet."

I gaped at him. "You think I'm going to *smile* for you?"

"I think you'll settle down and find a way to be happy with me. Once you adjust and accept your place here."

"*Accept my place?*" I demanded, slapping his chest in a burst of anger.

He clicked his tongue at me. "That wasn't very nice. But you're not trying very hard, either. You're upset, and I'm going to make you feel better."

"Short of releasing me, that's not going to happen," I informed him. "Do you really think I'm going to *feel better* about being trapped with a sadistic psycho?"

"Mind your tongue," he said sharply. "I've indulged you too much. You will speak to me with respect."

"Right," I said, unable to bite back the sarcasm. "You've been so indulgent with me. Beating me, violating me, chaining me up. You're so *nice*," I finished spitefully, using Lauren's description of him.

He set me on my feet and stared down at me, his dark eyes curious rather than reproving. "You really can't stop yourself, can you? You're not capable of holding in your thoughts, even knowing they could get you into trouble. I think a little discipline will be good for you. You can learn some self-control over these tics of yours."

I instantly clapped my hands over my bottom. "I don't want you to punish me again."

He smoothed his hand over my hair, reassuring. "Discipline doesn't necessarily mean punishment. Now, try your best to be quiet and stay right here."

He stepped away from me, and I finally was able to assess where he'd placed me. We were in the sitting room, and he'd positioned me in the farthest corner from the door to the torture room. Relief washed through me, strong enough to make my fingers tremble. I hadn't realized just how much fear was building in my chest until it finally released. He really wasn't going to take me in there.

But what was he going to do to me? He still hadn't said, and I knew he wouldn't. I'd just have to watch and wait and hope it wouldn't be too painful.

He was a few feet away from me, drumming his fingers on the highly polished mahogany desk. On the desk was...

I lunged for the laptop without thinking. I caught sight of his sharp grin just before he caught me around the waist and manhandled me down onto the carpet. He placed one hand between my shoulders, easily pinning me down on my front while he opened one of the desk drawers. I thrashed and cursed, but he quickly secured my arms behind me by locking handcuffs around my wrists.

"Do you just have kinky shit stashed everywhere?" I demanded on a growl. I'd thought I was safe from his perversions in this room, but I'd been wrong.

"Of course," he replied coolly. "Settle down. This won't hurt."

"You think I'm going to *settle down* when you basically just taunted me with a laptop? Do you know how starved I am for the internet? For technology? You don't even have a real clock, for god's sake, and you've been hiding a *laptop* from me?"

His hand curled around my nape, pressing my cheek down against the carpet and stilling my shaking head.

"I need my laptop for work," he said calmly. "I'm going to take care of some business, and you're going to be quiet and look pretty for me while I do."

"Work," I said scornfully. "You mean drug trafficking and selling women."

His fingers tightened around my neck. "Be very careful what you say next, Samantha," he warned. "I know you struggle to control your tongue, but I'm warning you to try very hard. I don't want to punish you now, but I will."

"But it's what you do," I said, truly unable to stop myself. "You and your brother. That's your *business*."

"I take care of a lot of things for my brother," he said, his voice still rough with anger, but his grip on my neck didn't tighten. "I do all the things he'd rather not bother with; I deal with the boring details. I keep things running. And yes, what you've accused me of is part of it."

"But you don't like the Bliss." The words popped out of me as I remembered what Lauren had told me. Now that I thought about it, Andrés had seemed almost regretful when he'd told me Bliss had broken Lauren. And he'd expressed

distaste for drugging me to make me more coop-
erative.

He was silent for a moment, his hands
unmoving on my body.

"What I like or don't like about my business
isn't your concern," he finally said. "I need to work,
and you need to be quiet. Your runaway mouth is
very distracting."

"But—" My rebuttal was smothered when the
now-familiar rubbery taste of the ball gag hit my
tongue. I tried to twist my face away, but that only
pressed it deeper into my mouth as he buckled it in
place.

His hand settled against the side of my head,
pressing my cheek back against the carpet as his
fingers massaged by scalp.

"This isn't to punish you," he said gently, as
though it made a difference. I was still rendered
silent and helpless, no matter what his intentions.
"You can't control your tongue, so I'll control it for
you. You'll be much calmer now."

I tried to tell him there was nothing calming
about being gagged, but my words were nothing but
a garbled growl.

"There's no need to keep arguing with me," he said
in a reassuring tone, running his fingers over my hair.
"There's no point trying to fight. Surrender. You'll feel
much better. We'll calm that busy brain of yours."

I wiggled beneath him, but with my arms bound, there was little I could do to escape.

His touch left me, and he retrieved something else from the desk: a huge coil of rope. "I think you'll like this, my kinky virgin."

He grasped my right thigh and lifted it off the floor, wrapping the rope around it. I tried to kick out at him, but he grabbed my flailing ankle and forced me to bend my knee. He wound more rope around my calf and connected it to the bindings around my thigh, pulling tight so my heel touched my bottom.

When one leg was fully restrained, he grasped my shoulders and pulled me into a kneeling position. I would have tried to push to my feet, but with my leg bound securely beneath me, that was impossible. He continued to bind me, drawing the rope around my waist and looping it between my thighs, framing my sex. I shuddered as he teased around my bare flesh, trying to ignore the growing wetness on my labia.

He tied off his work and moved up my body. More rope wound around me, passing beneath my breasts, wrapping behind my back, and coming back over my chest. He looped it over my neck and back through the lengths that framed my breasts. He pulled it taut, and the rope tightened around my sensitive flesh, squeezing my breasts lightly and

making them stand out from my body on lewd
display.

They rose and fell rapidly as I began to draw
in panting breaths. My skin tingled everywhere
the slightly rough fibers trailed across my flesh,
and my nipples tightened to hard buds as the pressure of the rope made my breasts feel heavy and
full.

He lightly brushed his fingertips across the soft
swells, and electricity danced across my skin. I
groaned, and my head dropped back as I mindlessly
arched into him, pressing toward his touch.

I found myself caught his black stare. He
loomed over me, a darkly amused smirk tilting his
lips.

"You like being bound, don't you, kinky virgin?
Has anyone ever tied you up before? Of course
not," he continued before I could even shake my
head in response. He traced the line of my lower lip
with his thumb, and I shivered as my sensitive
nerve endings jumped to attention. "So innocent,"
he rumbled. "And so beautiful in my ropes."

I blinked hard, struggling to maintain my wits
when my entire body was singing with awareness. I
should be struggling, at the very least. Not leaning
into his hands. I should...

Oh!

He fully cupped my breasts and caught my tight
nipples between his fingers, gently pinching them.

My eyes practically rolled back in my head, and I moaned as pleasure washed through me.

"That's better," he praised. "You don't have to fight me. You don't have to worry or think."

I shook my head, trying to clear it. Of course I had to worry. My captor had me bound and at his mercy again. If he chose to hurt me, there would be nothing I could do to stop him.

But he wasn't hurting me.

God, his hands on my breasts felt so *good*...

I was barely aware that he'd unlocked the handcuffs with one hand while continuing to play with my nipples with the other. The cuffs fell away, and he directed me to bend my arms behind me, so I grasped my elbows. He tied my hands in place, somehow threading the rope around my arms through the chest harness so it drew even tighter around my breasts.

My breathing stuttered, and my clit began to throb in time with my heartbeat.

His hands closed around my shoulders, and I realized I'd been swaying. I felt dizzy and warm, disoriented. It should have been disconcerting, but I was having trouble focusing on anything but the feel of the braided ropes caressing my skin, manipulating my blood flow to the most sensitive parts of my body.

He placed one hand on the top of my head, lightly gripping my hair to steady me. With the other, he pressed a button that was set beneath the desk. A soft whirring sound caught my attention, and I looked up, past Andrés.

A large metal ring slowly lowered from the ceiling, dangling from a thick cable. I put two and two together from my time spent on the darker corners of the internet and recognized it for what it was.

Of course he has a retractable suspension point built into his penthouse. Why wouldn't he? The thought skittered across my mind, and I giggled. I was feeling lightheaded, and everything seemed a little surreal and silly.

"That's a lovely sound," he said, touching my lips again. "I'm almost sorry I gagged you so I can't see that pretty smile." His grin sharpened. "Almost. You're very sweet when you can't do more than moan and whimper."

My brow furrowed. I should be mad. The most I could summon up was frustration, and even that wasn't as strong as it should be. I didn't understand this weird detachment from my thoughts and emotions, but I couldn't muster up enough concern to fully examine it.

He tapped my nose with his forefinger in light reprimand. "Stay just like you are," he ordered. "Focus on me."

What else could I do? I was completely under his power, bound and gagged. Only, where the same sensations had brought me misery while he whipped me, now they felt pleasurable. There was no pain this time. Just the soft, sure touches of his masterful hands and the slightly rough caress of the rope. My core ached, and slickness coated my inner thighs. My breasts were growing heavier, my nipples tingling with awareness.

The metal ring came to a stop, dangling a few feet above my head. Andrés picked out another coil of rope and began looping it through the harnesses he'd created around my chest and hips, focusing on the right side of my body. He then fed the ends through the ring and pulled. He braced one arm beneath me as my body tilted and lifted. A strangled cry left me as the ropes shifted and pressed into me. Andrés had arranged them so they held my weight evenly, cocooning my body as he pulled me higher. When I was fully horizontal, he tied off the rope to secure me in place. He wrapped one final length around my left ankle, causing my knee to bend. Gravity kept that leg dangling beneath me, while the restrictive tie around my right leg kept it lifted. My thighs were spread wide, and cool air teased along my exposed, swollen sex.

I drew in shallow breaths as my entire body pulsed with awareness, my world narrowing to focus on the man who'd so thoroughly bound me. His soft smile was at odds with his hungry eyes. I stared into them, fascinated by the black striations that darkened the chocolate brown of his irises.

His hand cupped my cheek, supporting the weight of my head. I realized it was taking effort to hold it upright in this position. My hair dangled toward the floor, weighing me down.

"I'm going to take care of a few things now," he murmured. "You look very pretty, *sirenita*. I think I'll keep you like this more often."

He finally withdrew his touch and sat at the desk. I was positioned at his side, so I could watch him in profile. My heart gave a little twinge when he opened the laptop, and a high whine slipped past the gag as longing tugged at me. I couldn't formulate concrete ideas about escape, but I knew I wanted to get to that computer.

"Hush now," he commanded, not looking in my direction. "The sooner I finish, the sooner I can play with your wet little pussy."

Lust surged through me, redirecting my longing to other, darker things. I did want him to touch me. My sex pulsed and fluttered, desperate for him to stroke me. I whined again, but he ignored me.

His long, elegant fingers began flying over the keyboard. The light, rapid tapping sounds were comforting, familiar. The room started to go hazy, and my body melted into the ropes that held me aloft. I was floating, euphoria settling over me. The world started fading around the edges. I vaguely realized that my head was lolling forward, my eyes drooping closed. But it was so hard to hold upright, so hard to keep my eyes open. After a while, I surrendered to the velvety darkness, sinking into it. I sighed, relishing the comfort of the pitter-patter of his fingers on the keyboard. I was one of my favorite sounds in the world, and it filled my consciousness, lulling me into a quiet, peaceful headspace.

"Is my pet sleepy?" His low, accented voice rolled over me. "Or horny?" I could feel the heat of his words on my exposed neck as he leaned in.

A pitiful, needy keening reached my ears, but I didn't register that I was the one making the sound.

"I have a few questions for you, kinky virgin," he said, his warm breath teasing across my sensitized skin. "If you're honest with me, I'll let you come."

The tension of the gag eased, and the rubber ball slipped from my mouth. I swallowed several times, my tongue feeling thick and unwieldy.

"I'm the first man to touch you, is that true?" he asked.

"Yes," I answered softly, still cocooned in warm darkness. I could feel his heat pulsing against my body, and I ached for him to touch me. If I answered his questions, he'd grant me the release I so desperately needed.

"But you know about BDSM. You've been to a club. You knew what the flogger was when I used it on you, even though no one has disciplined you before, correct?"

"Yes," I confirmed again.

"I want you to tell me how you know these things."

"Porn," I responded. "I watched Dex's porn."

"And who is Dex? You've mentioned him a few times."

"He's my..." I fumbled to find the right words. "My best friend."

"Why did you watch your friend's porn?"

"I wanted to know what he liked. So I hacked into his browser history."

"Why would you care what kind of porn your friend watches?"

"I love him," I slurred, the words leaving me without thought.

Hard fingers gripped my jaw, lifting my face almost violently. "Look at me," he snarled.

My eyes snapped open, instantly focusing on his burning black glare. Fear stirred in the back of my mind, and I tried to scramble away. The ropes around my body twisted and tugged, and a fresh hit of bliss washed through my system. I moaned softly, and my eyelashes fluttered closed.

His fingers tightened on my face. "No," he said, the command low and rough. "Look at me."

I focused on him again, my entire world centered on his dark gaze.

"You're *mine*," he growled. "From now on, you don't think about other men. You exist to please *me*." He reached between my legs and grabbed my sex, thrusting two fingers into my wet channel and cupping his palm over my clit in a possessive hold. I cried out at the sudden, rough intrusion, but his fingertips curled against the sensitive spot at the front of my inner walls, and his palm ground against my clit. "You're mine," he said, the words almost savage. "Your body, your mind. All of you. Your pain, your pleasure, they belong to me." He twisted my nipple, and I cried out, even as my core contracted around his fingers.

"Come for me," he demanded. "Come for your Master."

He continued to pinch and pull at my nipples as he pumped his fingers in and out of my pussy and rotated his palm against my clit. Pain and pleasure entwined, tormenting me with the cruelest bliss. Tears spilled down my cheeks, and I screamed as my orgasm claimed me.

My scream was abruptly muffled when he crushed his lips against mine in a brutal kiss. His teeth sank into my lower lip, and his fierce growl vibrated into my mouth as his tongue surged inside. I whimpered and opened for him, completely over-whelmed and stripped down to my most basic, animal self. Rational thought was long gone. All I could do was feel the pain of his fingers torturing

JULIA SYKES

my breasts, the pleasure of his hand wringing ecstasy from my pussy, the mind-blowing intensity of his mouth subjugating mine. The kiss was raw, primal; an act of force and dominance. I couldn't do anything but submit to the sensations he inflicted upon me, submit to his power over me.

My orgasm went on and on, ecstasy lashing through me. My body jerked and writhed, making the ropes shift around me. It only increased my pleasure, heightened my sense of helplessness. He continued pumping his fingers in and out of my pussy even as my orgasm began to subside. I became overly sensitive, his touch too much to bear.

I whined into his mouth, and he finally showed mercy. He withdrew his hands from my sex and my breasts, but his lips lingered on mine, the kiss slowing to a deep, thorough claiming of my mouth.

When he finally released me, I gasped for air, my head dropping toward the floor. I didn't have any strength left in my body. The world was surreal, and I was still floating; blissed out and buzzing.

I watched with detached interest as he retrieved a pair of shears from the desk. He braced my body with one strong arm while he used the shears to cut away the ropes that bound me. I sagged against him, boneless. He dropped to his knees and cradled me in his arms, holding me close. I closed my eyes and snuggled into him as he stroked me and murmured in Spanish. I couldn't understand the words, but the lilting cadence and low rumble of his voice were comforting.

Without realizing what I was doing, I pressed my lips against my captor's neck, tasting the salt of my own tears on his skin.

CHAPTER 12

The next morning, I awoke to the feel of leather being wrapped around my throat. I sighed and opened my eyes as Andrés locked the collar in place.

"Do you have to do that?" I complained.

He chuckled. "The fact that you still take that tone with me means yes, I definitely have to." He took my hand and pulled me upright. "Go brush your teeth and come back here."

"And then you won't chain me to the bed?" I asked with asperity.

"With that attitude, of course I will," he laughed. He seemed to be in a very good mood this morning. After he'd cut me down from suspension last night, he'd bathed me and fed me before putting me to bed. I'd been too strung out to think about complaining or resisting, but now my spirit was back in full force after a night of the deepest sleep I'd ever had.

I grumbled under my breath about being kept like an animal, but I went into the bathroom to take care of my daily needs. As I splashed warm water on my face, my mind began piecing together my hazy memories of the night before.

He kissed me.

My captor had actually kissed me. That was a surprise. He'd touched my most intimate areas with propriety, but a kiss was... unexpected. It certainly hadn't been tender and loving. But it hadn't been sloppy and awkward like my few other experiences with men.

From now on, you don't think about other men. You exist to please me.

I gasped and braced my hands on the sink.

I'd told Andrés about my feelings for Dex. That put him at risk. I'd made him a target for the Moreno brothers. They would go after him to make me cooperate. I couldn't let them hurt him.

I stormed back into the bedroom, going straight for Andrés. His brows rose in surprise, but my unexpected ire didn't slow his reaction time when I launched myself at him.

He dodged to one side, catching my fist where it had flown past his face. His other hand caught me in the center of my chest, knocking the air from my lungs as he shoved me away. I fell, my back hitting the mattress. His weight settled over me as he straddled my hips and pinned my arms above my head with one hand. My legs kicked out uselessly as he locked the chain to the front of my collar, tethering me to the bed again.

He gripped my jaw, stilling my wild thrashing. "What's this about?" he demanded.

"You leave Dex alone," I shouted at him, jerking desperately against his hold. "I'll kill you if you do anything to him. I swear, I'll kill you."

His fingers tightened around my face to the point of pain, and he snarled down at me. "I have no interest in this man. And from now on, neither do you."

"But you said Cristian would kill him if he found out," I said, panic seizing my senses. Oh god, I'd betrayed Dex for an orgasm. How could I do that?

"I am *not* my brother," he growled, the words so garbled I could barely discern them. "I won't torture you or threaten the people you care about to get what I want out of you." He leaned in close, so I could feel the heat of his anger slapping against me. "I don't need to torture you to get what I want."

"And what do you call tying me down and whipping me until I scream? Is that not torture?"

"If you knew what torture really was, you wouldn't have to ask," he said roughly.

"And how would you know?" I challenged. "It's not like you'd ever let anyone whip you until you cried."

"You think I don't cry when I'm hurt? You think I don't bleed when I'm cut? You think I don't scream just like any other man in pain? I might not be sane, but I'm still human, Samantha. Don't talk about things you don't understand."

I stared up at him, wide-eyed. "Is that how your face..." I trailed off when he bared his teeth at me in feral rage, his scar twisting into something terrifying.

"Don't talk about things you don't understand," he repeated, enunciating every word. "And don't say your friend's name ever again. I don't want you to even think about him. I'm the only man you should be concerned with, the only one you should think about. Your purpose is to serve me, to please me. No one else."

"Please," I forced out, my eyes watering. "You're hurting me." His fingers were digging into my face, hard enough that I thought I might bruise.

He instantly released me and rolled off me with a curse. He didn't look at me as he stiffly crossed the bedroom to his wardrobe and started getting dressed.

"Andrés?" I asked timidly.

He didn't respond.

I decided I believed him when he said he

wouldn't go after Dex. He seemed furious that I'd even think he'd hurt someone I loved in order to hurt me.

I will never cause you harm, not your body and not your heart. I remembered the promise he'd made me. Maybe he did hurt me when he flogged me. And maybe he did enjoy my pain. But he'd never lied about what kind of monster he was.

Guilt nipped at me. Someone had hurt him. That should have been obvious from the very beginning, given his scars. But I'd been so focused on how scary they were that I hadn't stopped to think about the pain he must have endured when he got them. Not to mention the reminder of it when people cringed away from looking at his ruined face. I hadn't been able to bear looking at him when I'd first seen him. What must it be like to have people flinch at the sight of you?

"I'm sorry," I said quietly.

He stiffened further, and he stopped in his tracks. After a few tense seconds, he spoke, but he still didn't turn to look at me.

"I got something for you," he said. "It's on the tray next to your breakfast."

I glanced at the food cart that must have arrived while I was still sleeping. A large, gift-wrapped box sat beside the covered tray.

"What—?"

"I'll see you tonight," he cut me off and strode out of the room.

Curiosity spiking, I went straight for the gift rather than the bacon. I tore off the iridescent white paper and pretty blue bow to find a plain cardboard box. When I opened it, my jaw dropped.

"Wow," I whispered, running reverent fingers over the laminated, first edition X-Men #101 comic book. The first one featuring The Dark Phoenix. It must have cost a fortune. Not to mention acquiring it so quickly. I'd confessed my geeky cosplay kissing session to Andrés like, two days ago. And only yesterday I'd appealed to him about my boredom. How had he managed to get this for me?

He managed with all his drug money, I reasoned. But that didn't stop me from picking up the comic.

Another first edition of the following book lay beneath it.

And another beneath that.

I carefully, lovingly removed each one and laid them out on the bed beside me so I could stare at them in awe. In all, there were twenty collectable comic books that told the entire Dark Phoenix story arc. It was any nerd's wet dream, including mine.

Okay, maybe I wasn't actually wet from looking at them, but the knowledge that Andrés had been paying such close attention to the little things I'd told him touched me somewhere deep inside. He might be a sadistic psycho, but he could be thoughtful. Kind.

God, I'm going to turn into Lauren, I rebuked myself.

Still, there was no denying that giving me the comics was a small act of mercy. Apparently, Andrés didn't want me to go completely insane from being left alone with nothing but my own racing thoughts.

Even though I was almost hesitant to touch them, I was desperate enough for reading material that I eventually opened them. I knew the stories already, but being able to handle these precious editions in person rather than reading reproductions of them on my computer screen was an entirely new experience.

I barely paused to talk to Lauren when she brought me lunch. She didn't seem keen on talking, anyway. And after hearing her disturbing take on Andrés—how *nice* she thought he was—I didn't really want to discuss it with her any more.

Despite taking my time with them, I'd been finished with the final book for quite a while before Andrés returned for the evening. I'd actually started re-reading #101 and was almost done for the second time when he came into the bedroom.

I beamed at him, high on nerd-endorphins. "Thanks," I said, genuinely grateful.

He blinked at me, momentarily stunned. Then

he grinned. "You are even more beautiful when you smile than I imagined."

My smile faded at the reminder of our real relationship dynamic. He wasn't some nice boyfriend who'd bought me a cool gift. He was my captor.

"You're manipulating me again," I accused.

"So you don't want the comic books?"

"No," I said quickly, clutching #101 to my chest. "I mean, I want them. I um, actually already read all of them. But I'll read them again," I babbled on, not wanting him to take them away if I sounded ungrateful.

His brows rose. "You read all of them today?"

"I tried to go slow, but they're so good," I said. "And I process things really fast. I usually do more than one thing at a time to stay occupied. But this was good," I hurried on. "Way better than staring at the ceiling."

"I'll have to get you more, then," he said, smiling again.

"You don't have to get first editions," I replied. "I like newer stuff, too. Graphic novels are awesome. Works by Frank Miller and Alan Moore are great."

"I'll get those for you, then," he said. "And more first editions."

"But I just said you don't have to. I've read most of them online, anyway."

"But they made you smile. So you're getting

more. Don't argue with me, Samantha," he said sternly before I could protest further. "I'll put in an order tonight, and they'll be here in the morning."

"How did you get them so fast?" I asked. "These had to be really hard to find."

"There was a store in New York that had them in stock. I sent someone to go get them."

"But I just told you I was bored last night."

He shrugged. "It's not a long flight."

I gaped at him. "You flew someone from Chicago to New York and back again overnight to get me some comic books?"

"Yes, and it made you smile. So the fifteen minutes it took me to set it all up was more than worth it."

The full power of what his dirty money could get him came down on me like a hammer, deflating the last of my joy.

"What's wrong?" He sounded a little strained.

"I don't want anything you bought with your Bliss money," I said quietly.

His jaw firmed. "You'll get the books, anyway."

"I won't read them."

"That's your choice. You'll still have them."

I glared at him. "You're trying to manipulate me again. You know I'll go out of my mind and end up reading them if they're in here."

A small smile tugged at the corners of his lips.

"If you already know this, then why bother fighting me on it?"

"Because you're a smug bastard, that's why."

He shook his head at me, but his smile didn't waver. "I'm going to find a better use for that dirty mouth."

He crossed to the bed and unlocked the chain from the bedpost. He kept the length of it attached to my collar.

"Come," he commanded, coiling the chain around his fist and tugging gently. The pressure on my neck forced me to scramble to my feet.

"Where are we going?" I asked, having no choice but to follow him as he walked out of the bedroom.

"What was it you so charmingly called it?" he mused. "Oh, yes." He shot a wicked smirk at me. "My *torture room*."

I tried to stop in my tracks, but he kept walking. The chain pulled taut, and I stumbled forward. I fisted the metal links in both hands and yanked. His arm barely tugged back toward me, but he stopped and turned to face me.

My chest rose and fell rapidly, my breaths coming too fast as my heart raced.

"I don't want to go in there," I said, my voice higher than usual. "I won't cuss at you again. I won't."

He shook his head, but the tilt of his lips was

almost indulgent. "You will. You can't seem to help yourself."

"I'll try really hard," I promised. "Just don't take me in there. Please."

He took a step toward me. I flinched back. He frowned and pulled on the chain, forcing my body to tumble against his. I clutched at his shoulders for balance, but his hands had already closed around my waist to prevent me from falling.

"This is part of your training," he said calmly. "It will feel good. Not everything in that room is meant to cause you pain."

"It scares me," I admitted on a shaky whisper, remembering my helplessness when he'd flogged me.

Shock obliterated my growing fear when he leaned in and softly pressed his lips against mine. I tried to jerk away from him, but his hand curved around the back of my head, holding me in place while he continued the kiss. It was gentle, coaxing. My lips began to shape to his, and he increased the pressure of his mouth on mine, turning more demanding. My body softened against him, even as my fingernails curved into his shoulders, clinging on tight.

He growled and nipped at my lower lip. I opened for him on a gasp, and his tongue invaded my mouth, sweeping in to claim me hard and deep.

This kiss was different than our first. That one

had been punishing, branding. This one wasn't tender, but it was more careful. A slow, thorough seduction.

He didn't stop until I was desperate to draw breath, and when he finally pulled away, I gasped for air, my knees going weak as oxygen hit my system. He held me tightly against him, supporting my sagging weight with one strong arm around my lower back. His erection pressed into my hip, straining against his slacks. He still wore his suit, and I was still naked. The power dynamic should have been disconcerting, but my head was spinning from his scorching kiss.

"Are you still scared?" he asked, running his fingers through my hair.

I leaned into his touch without thought. "No," I said, my voice strangely husky.

"I promise this isn't going to hurt," he swore. "Only pleasure today."

"But I cussed at you." I didn't understand. "I called you a bastard."

"I heard you the first time," he said drily. "We're going to train your mouth. From now on, every time you curse at me, you're going to make it up to me by using your tongue another way."

I trembled against him, knowing exactly what he meant. "I don't... I haven't ever..."

He continued to stroke my hair. "I know you haven't," he said, his tone low and soothing. "I'm going to teach you. And I'll make it feel good for you, so you associate my cock in your mouth with pleasure."

"You're trying to condition me again." My accusation came out more shakily than I'd intended. "I don't like when you do that."

"You'll like this." His arm slipped from my lower back, his hand skimming over my bottom before dipping between my legs. He cupped my sex, his fingers playing through my soft folds. Pleasure began to pulse at my core. I couldn't help but respond to his touch.

"Did you know your body is capable of having multiple orgasms?" he asked as he played with me. "I wonder how many you'll have before you can't take any more."

"Please..." I wanted him to stop, before I couldn't stop myself. Heat coiled in my belly, and my lower lips grew slick with my arousal.

"Please make you come?" he asked, lightly mocking. He sensed my internal struggle, and it seemed to amuse him. "Not yet, *sirenita*. You have to come into my playroom first."

"It's a torture room," I countered breathily.

"It's where I play with my fucktoy. That makes it my playroom."

"I'm not your fucktoy."

"It's not an insult, so there's no need to look so spiteful," he said, still amused. "You're my toy, my plaything, my pet. And you love when I play with you and pet you. See? You're creaming all over my hand."

"Just because my body feels one way about it doesn't mean I like it."

"Don't lie, *cosita*. You wouldn't have watched all that kinky porn if you didn't like it. If you didn't long for it."

"I longed for—" I cut myself off before I said Dex's name. I wouldn't risk that again. "I don't want this with you."

"Then why am I the only man who's ever touched you? You were so skittish at first. Do you really think you would have found pleasure with someone else? They wouldn't have understood how to handle you. Not like I do. You need a firm hand."

"I don't," I protested weakly. I really was getting embarrassingly wet as he spoke, responding to all the twisted, crass things he was saying about me.

He brushed a kiss over my lips. My head tipped back in response.

"No more lies," he murmured against my mouth. "You don't have permission to speak. I'm not going to gag you, but know that there will be other consequences if you defy me. The next time you use your mouth, it will be to suck my cock. Once I come down your throat, you'll be allowed to talk again."

I gaped at him, and he traced the *O* of my lips with his fingertips.

"Just like that," he said with satisfaction. "I'm not going to force your mouth, but you will accept me before we leave the playroom."

I shook my head in denial, not daring to utter another word when I knew he was about to take me into the torture room, whether I wanted it or not. But no way was I going to take his cock in my mouth of my own volition. Just the idea was dirty.

Dirty. Wrong.

Dirty little girl.

"*Cosita*," he said firmly, his fingers threading through my hair. The light pull against my scalp grounded me. "Don't be afraid." It was an order. "This is new for you, but I'll guide you through it. You're safe with me."

Safe.

I felt myself nodding, even though that didn't make any sense. All I knew was the fear that had been creeping at the edges of my mind had subsided, and I was grateful for Andrés' commanding touch.

Inexplicably, I felt secure in his firm arms. When he finally released me and began to walk toward the playroom, I followed him without further protest.

CHAPTER 13

A shudder rolled through me when Andrés flipped on the crimson lights. My gaze went straight to the spanking bench, and I took a small step back toward the sitting room.

"No, *cosita*," he said soothingly, wrapping his arm around my waist and guiding me forward. It might have been a sweet gesture, but the way his fingers curled around my hip communicated his control. "We're not using the bench today," he promised, leading me past it. "Do you know what this is? You have my permission to speak."

I blinked and looked down where he pointed. I recognized the black device that curved up in a half-sphere, the flat side resting on the floor. It was built to be straddled. If I went down on my knees, the curve would fit between my thighs as I lowered my weight onto it.

"A Sybian," I answered breathily, knowing exactly what it was.

"Such a clever, kinky virgin," he said with pleasure.

"But I can't... There's not a dildo attached." In all the porn I'd seen, women rode huge dildos as they bounced up and down on the vibrating machine.

"My fingers and my cock will stretch your tight little pussy before I put anything else inside you." His hand tightened possessively on my hip. "The vibrations will be strong enough that you'll feel it everywhere. Your clit, your pussy, your ass. I don't need to fill you with a fake cock to make you scream in pleasure."

"That... That sounds... intense," I said, fumbling over my words. It certainly didn't sound painful. Quite the opposite. But it also sounded like I'd come unraveled if the pleasure was as intense as he claimed. I'd confessed my deepest secrets to him in exchange for orgasms already. What would I do when subjected to this?

Suck his cock.

That was what he wanted from me.

I glanced at the bulge of his erection, which stood out clearly against his slacks. The knowledge that he wanted me made something warm unfurl in my chest; a pure, feminine satisfaction.

The rational part of my mind noted his size, and

I remembered how big he'd felt in my hand when I'd touched him in the shower for the first time.

"I won't be able to fit... It won't fit," I mumbled, my cheeks flaming. I couldn't say *your cock won't fit in my mouth* aloud. It was far too shameful.

"We'll go slow," he promised. "You can take me. You will learn."

He was talking about it like my surrender was already a foregone conclusion.

"And if I say no?" I asked quietly.

"Are you saying no?"

"I... I'm nervous. I mean, you're so big. And I've never... I don't know..." I was babbling, my sentences unfinished and incoherent.

He leaned in and captured my lips with his, taking my mouth slow and deep, until my mind quieted. The anxiety that had started churning in my stomach subsided, giving way to warmth that spread down between my legs.

"You don't have to talk anymore," he murmured, pressing a sweet kiss against my cheek. "It's okay to be nervous. I'll be right here to tell you what to do."

I nodded, almost grateful that he'd forestalled the words that had started spilling out of me. I didn't like when my mouth ran away with me out of nervousness. It felt... comforting, knowing I didn't have to say anything else. That I wasn't allowed to say anything else. His command for my silence freed me from my nervous tic, and it was kind of nice. Liberating.

His grip shifted to my upper arms, and he applied pressure to guide me down. "On your knees."

I sank down far more gracefully than I ever could have managed on my own. When he moved my body, I didn't have to worry about being awkward or ungainly.

"So beautiful," he praised when I fully lowered myself onto the Sybian, my wet pussy coming to rest against the hard, cool surface.

He leaned down and moved my left ankle closer to the device. Supple leather closed around it, and he buckled the cuff closed to secure me in place.

Why? The word teased at the tip of my tongue, but I swallowed it back. I wasn't supposed to talk. It was so much easier than questioning him, anyway.

He cuffed my right ankle on the other side. Testing my range of movement, I tried to push up on my knees, but I couldn't rise up off the Sybian with my legs bound beneath me.

He wasn't done restraining me. He grasped my wrists and directed them above my head. Another set of cuffs dangled from a chain that hung from the ceiling. I didn't resist as he buckled them around my wrists. There was no point. I was already bound to the Sybian, and fighting would have only earned me a punishment.

I didn't want another one of those, especially not with the reminder of the spanking bench looming in front of me.

He's not going to hurt me, I told myself. *He's not going to—*

"Oh!" I cried out as the machine began to vibrate beneath me. My fingers and toes curled as ecstasy rolled through my entire body in a shockwave.

Andrés smirked down at me and fully removed the small black remote control from his pocket.

"You like your new toy, *gatita*?"

I moaned and nodded, not even thinking about forming a verbal response.

He stroked my cheek, communicating his pleasure with me. "Greedy girl. I want you to keep count of how many orgasms you have. Can you do that for me?"

I swallowed another moan and nodded again. The vibrations rumbled through me, just as he'd promised. I should have been ashamed at the pleasure I was finding in the stimulation, but all I could focus on was how good it felt. I started to roll my hips in wanton abandon. As I did, the vibrations concentrated on my clit, then my pussy, then my ass. I really should have felt ashamed of the particular pleasure I found in that, but I couldn't stop myself once I started.

"You're going to be so beautiful when you're riding my cock like that," he said, his voice rough with need. He traced the line of my lower lip with his thumb before pushing inside. I opened for him, and he rubbed his calloused fingertip over my tongue. The sensation of his rough skin against my sensitive nerve endings was wickedly decadent. I groaned and pressed my tongue against him, licking and exploring the slightly salty taste of his skin. He started to gently pump his thumb in and out, pushing a little farther in each time, until he neared the back of my throat. I had to focus on breathing and suppressing my gag reflex. It felt so good, and I didn't want to ruin it.

"Good girl," he ground out, his own desire riding him hard.

My sense of feminine satisfaction intensified, and my eyes went to his erection. I started rocking faster on the Sybian, moving on instinct as I sought more pleasure. The chains that held my arms above my head clanked as I undulated my body. Even though I was bound, I felt powerful, beautiful, blissful. The need in Andrés' voice and the evidence of his hard cock sent me flying high. He wanted me. And I wanted...

With his free hand, he reached down and

pinched my nipple, rolling and pulling it gently. "Come for me," he commanded.

The little bite of pain sent me over the edge. Heat shot straight from my tormented nipple to my clit, and I ground against the Sybian, rotating my hips as I screamed around his thumb. He continued stroking my tongue as I came undone, and I started licking his finger like it was my favorite candy. I couldn't get enough of the sensation of his firm touch inside my mouth. It made me tingle everywhere: my mouth, my pussy, my ass. Dark ecstasy raced through me, and I shuddered in my chains as my orgasm claimed me.

His thumb popped out of my mouth, and I whimpered at the loss.

"Don't forget to count for me," he said as he turned off the machine, his crooked smile filling my chest with warmth. The expression tugged at his scar, but it didn't scare me anymore. He looked... powerful where he loomed above me in his sharply-tailored suit. Dark and definitely dangerous, but utterly masculine and confident. He wanted me, but he found pleasure in giving me pleasure. It was evident in the hungry way he watched me, the way his cock strained toward me.

He chuckled and touched two fingers beneath my chin, redirecting my gaze to his face. "You were supposed to count your orgasms," he reminded me.

"What? Oh. One," I said faintly.

He tilted his head at me. "That's not nearly enough for my greedy *gatita*, is it? I want more, too."

For a moment, I thought he meant he wanted to come himself, but he turned the Sybian on again, obviously intent on giving me more pleasure.

My gaze riveted back on his erection, and I couldn't help imagining what it would be like to feel his cock with my tongue instead of licking his thumb. My surrender was inevitable. Why fight it? Especially now that I knew how good it felt to have something filling my mouth. I'd never have imagined that it could feel so deliciously sensual.

"You want to see me?" he asked huskily, noting the direction of my gaze.

I nodded and started rolling my hips against the Sybian again, moving without thought. Pleasure was already building at my core, my entire body tingling as little sparks crackled through my system.

A low, feral sound slipped through his teeth, and he quickly freed himself from his slacks.

My eyes widened, and trepidation made my stomach clench. I already knew he was huge, but seeing him from this perspective was much more intimidating. I shrank back slightly, my sensual haze beginning to clear in the face of reality. His thumb had felt good in my mouth. This was something entirely different.

He fisted the base in his hand, squeezing

slightly. "You're going to make me lose control," he growled. "Do you have any idea how delicious you are? So innocent and nervous about pleasing me." His fingers touched my chin again, lifting my face so I was captured in his dark gaze. "You do please me, Samantha. Very much."

Something warm buzzed through my veins, something more than physical pleasure. He trailed his fingers over my heated cheek.

"You're perfect. So pretty with your body bound and shaking for me. Do you want to come again?"

"Yes," I gasped out, rolling my hips against the machine.

"You can come when you kiss my cock. Show me how much you want to come. Show me how much you want me." He ground out the words, and a bead of moisture formed at his cockhead.

He shifted his hips toward me, and I pressed my lips against him in a soft kiss. The salty flavor of his pre-cum hit my tongue, and I whimpered against him as my need began to crest.

"Come," he ordered, pinching my nipples, alternating between them with one hand as he continued to fist his cock in the other.

I shrieked as my second orgasm claimed me, and he rubbed his cockhead around my parted lips, spreading his pre-cum on them. I started to come down, panting against his shaft, but he didn't turn off the machine beneath me.

"Please," I begged, my legs beginning to tremble. "It's too much."

"Count," he reminded me.

"Two," I whined, trying to push away from the torturous vibrations.

His fingers left my nipples to twine in my hair. "You're going to have another one. You're going to cry out in pleasure while your mouth is full of my cock. I want to feel you scream."

A small whimper eased up my throat, but my discomfort eased. My core contracted with fresh need, and the vibrations began to stimulate me again rather than torment.

"Taste me," he commanded. "You can come as many times as you want."

I flicked out my tongue, barely touching the underside of his purple head. He hissed out a breath through clenched teeth.

"More," he demanded.

I obeyed, craving more of his unique flavor. His skin was soft, so different from his thumb. It felt velvety smooth as I glided my tongue down his length, traced the underside, and swirled around his cockhead.

"Very good. Just like that." He was breathing hard, his accent thicker than I'd ever heard it.

I pressed my tongue flat beneath his shaft and cried out as another orgasm wracked my system. It started deep inside me, building until the pressure was impossible to bear. I started licking him in earnest, tasting every inch of him as I reveled in the decadent feel of his hard cock under my sensitive tongue. He bit out a curse, and I moaned in satisfaction. Knowing I had such an effect on him was heady. This powerful man who craved control was struggling to hold back his lust for me. I wanted him to come undone, to feel the same wild abandon that had completely overtaken me.

"How many?" he asked roughly as my orgasm finally started to subside.

"Hmmm?" I hummed against his shaft, and his fingers tightened in my hair.

"You know, *gatita*. Don't toy with me. How many?"

"Three," I sighed, rubbing my cheek against him.

"That's it," he encouraged. "Worship my cock. Just like that."

The vibrations continued to torment me, but I didn't bother begging for him to turn off the machine. I knew he wouldn't, and truthfully, I didn't want him to. I was as greedy as he'd claimed I'd be. I wanted more: more pleasure, more power, more *Andrés*.

"Suck me," he ordered, on the edge of his control.

I opened my mouth and invited him in, stroking him with my tongue as he slid inside. He stopped me with his fist on my hair when I tried to take him all the way to the back of my throat.

"Slowly, *sirenita*," he corrected me, his accent so heavy it took me a moment to discern what he'd said.

Using his grip on my hair, he eased my face back so only his cockhead remained inside my mouth. I rolled my tongue around it and stared up at him. His nostrils flared and his eyes turned flat black. He bared his teeth in an expression that was almost vicious. It made my pussy flutter, and another orgasm shuddered through my body. I screamed around his cock—just as he'd ordered me to do.

He thrust forward, hitting the back of my throat. I gagged, and he immediately pulled back so I could gasp in a breath.

"Relax," he growled, but there was no menace in the word, only desire. "I'm going to come down your throat."

I moaned, the only sound I was capable of with him filling my mouth. He pressed farther back, testing me. I breathed through my nose and focused on suppressing my gag reflex.

"Good girl." His hold eased on my hair, and he massaged my scalp as he pushed into my throat. He threw his head back with a roar and finally released, his cum lashing into me. He pulled back so it coated my tongue, filling my mouth.

"Swallow," he snarled. "Take everything I give you."

As I did so, pleasure claimed me again, the vibrations of the machine beneath me relentless. My entire body twisted against the restraints, mindless with ecstasy. He finally pulled free of my lips, but I continued to lick him, cleaning off the last of his desire.

He started murmuring in Spanish, running his fingers through my hair as he praised me.

Finally, he turned off the Sybian, and I collapsed in exhaustion as all my muscles melted. He freed my wrists from the cuffs and bent to catch me before I could fall. He went down on one knee and captured my lips with his.

Surprise sparked through me that he'd kiss me after coming in my mouth, but he didn't seem to care. If anything, he seemed hungrier for me than ever.

When he finally pulled away, he freed my ankles and lifted my sated body up in his arms.

"How many times did you come?" he murmured as he carried me out of the playroom.

"Oh. Um... Like, five? Maybe?" I was too sleepy to really think about it. I pressed my face against his hard chest, enjoying the way it rumbled as he laughed.

If that was what giving a blowjob was like, I wasn't sure why I'd waited so long.

Because I needed Andrés, I realized, recognizing the truth in what he'd said to me earlier. I'd needed him to push past my fears and my weird tics and show me what my body was capable of.

I should be upset at the realization that I needed my scary captor in order to experience intimacy with a man, but he wasn't all that scary, really. His scars might look mean, but he hadn't forced me to suck his cock. He could have beaten me until I broke down and did anything he wanted, but he'd ensured that I enjoyed the experience, possibly even more than he did. He'd come once. I'd come... How many times?

I decided I was too tired to worry about it. Sighing in post-orgasmic contentment, I snuggled against Andrés' chest and drifted in warm bliss.

CHAPTER 14

S omehow, everything started feeling routine. Andrés fed me, bathed me, teased me, and gave me the most mind-blowing orgasms. With the occasional spanking if I got too sassy. He still kept me chained to his bed while he was gone, but the stacks of comics he brought me every morning helped me pass the time.

It had been a week since he'd taken me into his playroom and taught me how to give him a blowjob. I'd had to suck him off several times since due to my penchant for cursing, but I didn't hate the experience, so it wasn't much of a deterrent, really.

For long stretches of time in the evenings, he'd tie me in various positions from the suspension point next to his desk. He claimed that he liked having something pretty to look at while he worked.

Pretty. I'd never thought of myself that way. Despite my fucked up situation, Andrés made me feel beautiful, desirable. And that made me feel powerful in a way I'd never known before. I'd always been confident in my hacking abilities, in the sharpness of my mind. But physically, I'd always felt out of place. Awkward and weird.

I didn't have to worry about being awkward with Andrés. He simply moved my body where he wished, and with his guidance and instruction, I didn't trip all over myself. I couldn't get stuck in my own head and in my own insecurities when he handled me. His strong arms and dark eyes grounded me, keeping me focused on him rather than getting swept up in my racing thoughts.

But I wasn't a fool, and no matter how much Andrés tried to condition me to want to be his pet, I wouldn't cave. Maybe I did like the way he touched me, but that didn't mean I wasn't still intent on escaping him. I had a life to get back to, and I refused to spend my days as the plaything for an evil drug lord.

Evil. I often had to remind myself of what Andrés did for his *business*. He petted me and doted on me, and it would have been much easier on my psyche if I'd just allowed myself to fall into a fantasy of being his cossetted, kinky girlfriend.

But I couldn't forget that all the expensive nerdy gifts he brought me had been purchased with drug money. Money that came from trafficking Bliss and selling innocent women like Lauren.

Not to mention that all of it was a manipulation to *tame* me. To make me docile and obedient so I'd work for his brother without trying to get a message back to my friends at the Bureau the second I had access to a computer.

I'd certainly become docile, despite my best efforts. He kept me drunk on pleasure, and if I did start getting too bold, a sound spanking or his cock in my mouth would subdue me.

For a few days, I'd internally railed at myself that I should have been stronger than this. But beating myself up about enjoying Andrés' kinky games wasn't going to help me escape. I needed my full wits about me, and self-loathing was a distraction I couldn't afford. I could give him my body, as long as I kept my mind. Submitting kept me safe from being punished again. It was the smart thing to do, not weakness.

I didn't bother to look up from reading *Watchmen* when the door opened. Most days, I tried my best not to look at Lauren directly. Her eyes were so disturbing, and the only time anything sparked in them, it was resentment. She clearly would have preferred to be *Master* Andrés' pet to being drugged and whored out to dozens of men.

After facing the reality of captivity with Andrés, I suspected I'd prefer my situation, too.

And that realization was so disturbing, I'd rather ignore Lauren than face it head-on.

I gasped when strong fingers fisted around the collar at my nape, pulling me up off the pillows.

"Andrés," I forced out, struggling to speak with the collar tight around my throat. "What are you doing here?"

Lauren hadn't brought me lunch yet, so it couldn't be past midday. He never returned this early.

I looked up at him, alarmed at the almost violent way he was handling me. His dark eyes were fixed on his task: unlocking the chain from my collar. As soon as it fell away, he lifted me up and tossed me over his shoulder, knocking the air from my chest.

"Put me down!" I demanded, twisting in his hold as panic spiked.

He hadn't spoken to me, he wouldn't look at me. Anger was evident in the stiff way he held me, the too-sharp smack of his hand against my upper thigh.

Fear fluttered in my chest, my heartbeat picking up speed. This wasn't my indulgent captor who cradled me against his chest and kissed me. This man who held me so dispassionately scared the shit out of me. It reminded me of his cold detachment the night he'd strapped me to the spanking bench and flogged me.

"I didn't do anything wrong," I protested, squirming against him as we entered the playroom.

No. *Torture room*.

Because we were headed straight for the spanking bench.

I beat my fists against his lower back, thrashing like a wild thing. "No! Please."

He ignored me, handling me roughly as he pinned my body down on the bench and strapped me in place. Tears dropped down my cheeks as the false image of him I'd built in my mind shattered. He wasn't doting. He wasn't nice.

He was unstable, insane.

And every small kindness he'd shown me had been a lie, a manipulation.

"What did I do wrong?" I heaved out on a sob as terror took hold of my mind. He'd been harsh with me, but he'd always been fair, in his own way. "I didn't do anything. I didn't. Please."

Once I was fully bound beneath him, he paused and finally looked down into my eyes. His face was drawn, his scar puckered and twisted as he clenched his jaw tightly. He stared down at me for several agonizing seconds, then he drew in a deep, shuddering breath. He trailed his fingers over the leather restraints that held my body at his mercy, and his fierce expression eased. He reached out and brushed at the wetness on my cheeks. I tried to cringe away, but there was nowhere to go.

"Please," I whispered brokenly. "I promise I didn't do anything wrong. Don't hurt me."

"I'm not going to hurt you," he promised, his accent thick. "Much," he amended. "Hush now," he said in his usual soothing tones as he stroked my trembling body. "This isn't a punishment."

"But you're angry," I said tremulously. "You're going to hurt me."

"I'm not angry with you," he replied, calm settling over him as he continued to pet me. "My brother..." His fingers firmed on my skin, pressing too hard. He drew another deep breath and resumed stroking me, concentrating his attentions around the leather straps that held me down, as though seeing me helpless and at his mercy comforted him in some perverted way. "I need to accelerate your training," he said. "My brother is not a patient man."

I tensed. Andrés continued stroking me, his focus shifting to my hair.

"I'll protect you," he promised. "But I've been too indulgent with you. You must learn your place."

"So you're going to beat me," I said in soft accusation.

"I'm going to train you," he countered. "You will experience a little pain, but you will enjoy it. I know you will. You like your spankings. You'll like this, too."

"I don't want you to flog me again," I whispered.

"I don't want you to be scared of me, *cosita*," he said instead of responding directly.

"I thought you like it when I'm frightened," I said bitterly, remembering all the fucked up things he'd said about my lovely eyes when I was crying from fear.

His lips firmed, and he cut his gaze away from mine. "That doesn't mean I want you to fear *me*. But yes, a part of me likes your fear."

"Please let me up," I begged. "You don't have to do this."

His gaze snapped back to mine, hard with determination. "Yes, I do. It's for your own good."

I didn't dare say how crazy that statement was. I was too intimidated, and he held all the power. He could do anything he wanted to me, and there would be nothing I could do to stop him.

He placed his hand on the back of my neck, lightly squeezing. In his messed-up world, this was a comforting gesture. At least, it seemed to comfort him. It was a demonstration of control, of ownership.

"You'll like this," he said. "You'll see. You have to trust me."

I bit back the retort that I'd never trust him. He might be calmer, but his mood was precarious, violence lurking just under his skin. No matter what he said about me enjoying whatever he was about to do, he needed to hurt me. I could see it in his eyes; I could see the all dark things that stirred in their black depths: desire, anger, pain.

Something about what had happened with his brother had triggered him, and he needed me to soothe him. If he were a normal man and we were in a normal relationship, I'd hold him and kiss him and tell him everything was okay.

But this wasn't normal. He was my captor, and right now, he was on the edge of sanity. There was only one way the madness inside him would be soothed: my complete subjugation. Already, just having me bound and crying beneath him seemed to have quieted his more volatile emotions. Next, he'd extract pleasure from my screams.

I shuddered, my teeth chattering as cold terror settled into my bones.

He dropped to his knees beside me, his face leveling with mine. Through my watery vision, I saw his brow furrow with concern.

"Samantha," he said my name almost hoarsely. "You're okay. You're safe with me."

"I'm not," I said, my voice hitching. "I'm scared. You're scaring me. And you like it."

"I don't. Not like this. Please. Don't be afraid."

Please. I'd never heard him utter the word.

"I don't want to be in here," I whispered.

"All right, *cosita*. It's all right. You're safe." He

started murmuring to me in a stream of soothing Spanish, running his fingers along my chilled skin as he released me from the cuffs that trapped me against the spanking bench.

A relieved sob heaved from my chest when he lifted me in his arms and cuddled me close. My hand fisted in his shirt, and I turned my face against him as I wept and shook.

He carried me back into the bedroom and settled me on his lap when he sat on the edge of the bed. He held me while I cried, all the fear and pain that lingered inside me from the night he'd flogged me spilling out to soak his chest with my tears.

"*Lo siento.*" I caught the words several times as he continued to speak to me in low, calming tones.

I'm sorry. I knew what it meant.

That helped bring me back to my senses more than anything. My big, scary captor was apologizing. Blinking up at him, I studied his taut features. He seemed truly distressed, and when my sobs finally quieted, he pressed a tender kiss against my forehead.

"I was worried about you," he rumbled, his arms tightening around me to pull me closer to his warmth. "I didn't mean to upset you."

"You did," I countered quietly. "You wanted to see me cry. You wanted to hear me scream."

His eyes flicked away from mine, and he tensed beneath me. "I do want those things from you,

Samantha," he admitted, his voice strained. "But not like this. I won't break you. I won't." He still wasn't looking at me, and he seemed to be speaking to himself as much as he was reassuring me.

"I don't want this," I said, my voice small. "I don't want to be here. I don't want to be tamed. I don't want to work for your brother."

"You don't have a choice in that. Neither of us do."

"What do you mean?" I didn't understand. Of course Andrés had a choice. He could hurt me, he could beat me, he could savor my pain. He could choose to do anything he wanted with me.

But he chose to cuddle me close and run his hands over my cool skin, imbuing my body with his steady warmth.

He didn't answer my question. Instead, he suddenly crushed his lips to mine in a fierce, hungry kiss. Every stroke of his tongue dominated my own, his mouth caressing mine hard enough to leave my lips swollen and tingling. I finally softened against him as my body warmed, the last of the chill of terror leaving my system as I found comfort in my captor's desperate kiss.

CHAPTER 15

Andrés stayed with me for the rest of the day, holding me until Lauren brought lunch. She seemed surprised to see us together, and she had to come back a second time with more food for him. I wondered what had happened with Cristian to drive Andrés back to me in such a black mood, but I didn't dare press him on the subject. I didn't want the scary, violent man to resurface. I much preferred the sweet, caring man who petted me and draped my body across his chest while he leaned back against the headboard and read *Watchmen* with me.

I went back to the beginning of the story since Andrés had never read it before, and I found a strange joy in sharing it with him, almost as though I were able to experience it again for the first time myself. Only better than that, because he wasn't jaded by years of warring fandoms. There was a weird innocence in watching him begin to enjoy the story, his lips curving with satisfaction as he turned the pages faster and faster.

He glanced down and noticed me watching him.

"Am I more interesting than your superheroes?" he asked, ruffling my hair.

"Anti-heroes," I corrected him. "Well, some of them, anyway. That's what makes them interesting."

"Then why are you looking at me?"

I shrugged. "I already read it. I know the story."

He set the book aside. "Then I'll get you a different one. I don't want you to be bored."

"I'm not," I answered honestly. "You can keep reading it."

His smile twisted. "I don't want to read right now. Not when you're watching me like that, my curious *gatita*." He took my hand and pressed it against his growing erection. His suit was rumpled from laying on the bed with me for hours, but he still looked powerful. Magnetic. The feel of his desire for me through his slacks made power pulse through my veins. This was for *me*. I wasn't scared of him when he was like this, even though a part of my brain acknowledged the fact that my captor's arousal should definitely terrify me.

But he'd never used me against my will. He'd never forced me to take his cock. He might have conditioned me to like it, but the knowledge that

I'd been conditioned didn't make his training any less effective.

My core fluttered and heated, my lower lips growing slick with my own arousal.

His hands closed around my waist, and he shifted my body off his. "On your hands and knees," he ordered, his voice dropping deeper with desire.

I got into position without argument. After the intense fear and vulnerability of our scene in the playroom that morning, I was feeling particularly clingy. I wanted to be close to him, for him to touch me and tell me I was safe. Even though he had been the one to scare me in the first place. It was fucked up, but I ached to please him, to make him laugh and look at me with pleasure in his dark eyes.

I told myself that my weird feelings were a survival imperative; if my captor was happy with me, he wouldn't hurt me.

But I'd seen the pain that lurked alongside the rage when he'd strapped me down to the spanking bench. I'd seen the calm that came over him once he had me bound, unable to escape him. He needed this from me.

"You are so beautiful," he murmured as he traced the line of my spine. "Stay."

He left me briefly to retrieve a few items from the chest of drawers where he seemed to stash a multitude of kinky toys. I waited, trying to remain calm without his touch to ground me. It was unnerving, this... *need*. I craved physical contact with Andrés, and even in those few seconds of separation, a hollow sensation began gnawing at my gut.

Subdrop. I'd read about it online. Submissives could go into a depressive state after an intense BDSM scene, and they needed to be cuddled by their Doms until the feeling passed.

Only, Andrés wasn't some dreamy Dominant partner I'd willingly gifted with my submission.

My animal brain warred with my rational mind.

Rational mind: *resist, fight, escape.*

Animal brain: *pet me, hold me, kiss me.*

"Settle, *cosita*," he ordered, smoothing a hand down my back when he returned to my side. He'd read the mounting tension in my body, and it was soothed away as soon as he touched me.

My animal brain won. With Andrés so close, it was impossible to cling to rationality. I was too fragile from my breakdown a few hours ago, and neediness obliterated my brittle willpower to maintain emotional distance from him.

"I'm not going to restrain you, so you're going to have to be very good for me," he said, continuing to pet me. I sighed and relaxed under his hand, enjoying the sensation of his skin on mine. "Just like that," he approved. My heart squeezed at the pleasure evident in his twisted smile.

"I want you to trust me," he said. "So I'm going

218

to trust you, too. I'm going to trust you to stay in position for me. I wanted to tie you down so you wouldn't be able to move away from me. It's safer for you if you stay still. That way, I won't inflict pain unintentionally." He shushed me before I could question him about *inflicting pain*. "You'll like this," he continued. "I'll make sure you do, I promise. But you have to trust me. Can you do that for me?"

Fine lines of strain appeared around his eyes. He was asking for my trust, not demanding it. He was leaving me free to resist, to fight. It was my choice to submit or not.

And the fact that he gave me a choice made the decision for me.

"Yes," I said softly. "I can trust you."

His grin dazzled me, knocking the air from my lungs. There was no dark satisfaction in it, no triumph at my defeat; only pure joy at my willing surrender.

His touch eased down my back, over the curve of my bottom, before tracing the line of my soft folds. I moaned and pushed back into him, welcoming him to press inside me. Two fingers entered me, slowly penetrating my tight channel. I'd adjusted to taking him like this, so there was no pain as he stretched me, sliding his fingers in and out as I rocked my body in a rhythm to match.

I stilled with a soft whine when something hard

and wet touched my asshole. I craned my head back to find him watching me carefully. He captured me in his warm gaze.

"Trust me," he urged. "This will feel good."

His fingers withdrew from my sheath to play with my clit, and he increased the pressure of the small red anal plug against my tight ring of muscles. It glistened with lubricant, and I knew he was going slowly so he wouldn't hurt me. As his calloused fingertips traced teasing circles around my clit, my muscles relaxed. The tip of the plug slipped inside me, reminding me of how he'd penetrated my ass with his finger for the first time in the shower. That seemed so long ago now. It had been scary, and he'd done it to demonstrate his complete ownership of my body.

This was different. It wasn't a power play, even though the power dynamic was definitely shifting between us. The farther he pressed the plug in, the more I submitted. He made it pleasurable for me, taking care to ensure that I enjoyed every deliciously deviant second of my virgin hole being stretched. I surrendered to the pleasure, surrendered to *him*. Dark bliss sizzled through forbidden places, lighting up my body in ways I'd never imagined I'd accept. Anal play had always seemed too taboo, too humiliating to contemplate.

With Andrés staring down at me with such intensity, I certainly didn't feel humiliated. I felt precious. Revered. His hands might be masterful, knowing exactly how to make my body flower open for him, but there was also something worshipful in his touch.

A light burning sensation threatened to erode my pleasure, but he rubbed my clit more firmly, giving me a hit of ecstasy to mitigate the discomfort.

"Almost there," he assured me. "You're doing so well. You're going to love taking my cock in your ass, once you're properly prepared."

The widest part of the plug sank past my tight ring, and my muscles closed around the slender base as it settled deep inside me. I drew in short, panting breaths, struggling to adjust to the sensation of being filled.

His thumb stayed at my clit, and his forefinger returned to my sheath, sliding inside with aching care. I cried out, and my fingers clawed at the sheets beneath me as twisted pleasure washed over me. I could feel him stroking along the length of the plug through the thin barrier inside me. Although I'd learned to accommodate two fingers inside me, I felt almost unbearably full with the added pressure of the toy in my bottom.

"Come for me," he urged, increasing the pressure on my clit as his forefinger found my g-spot. At the same time, he gently tugged on the plug. All my pleasure centers lit up at once, and I screamed as my orgasm claimed me. I felt my body clamping down on his finger and on the plug, and the sensations of my inner walls undulating around them heightened my release. I couldn't push him out, could only submit to being penetrated and played with as he wrung the final drops of bliss from my shuddering system.

I gasped against the sheets, breathing hard. He finally pulled his hand away, but he didn't remove the plug.

"Stay just like that," he ordered, his voice thick with his own desire. "Don't move."

Before I could turn my head to see what he had planned, a small *pop* reached my ears and fresh sensation assailed me. A light sting bloomed on my bottom, and my inner muscles tightened and danced around the plug. I looked back at him as I cried out at the shock of pleasure.

I groaned at the sight of Andrés towering over me, dressed in his suit, a crop in his big hand. It was like something out of one of my dirtiest dreams. I'd never before envisioned a man like him—dark and unquestionably dangerous—but desire flooded my entire being as he smirked down at me.

He touched the tongue of the crop beneath my chin, letting me feel the buttery soft leather as he lifted my face. "I like when you look at me like this," he said, his accented voice lilting with his own pleasure. "My kinky virgin."

He slid the crop up to my lips, and the rich, slightly salty scent of leather intoxicated me. Without thinking, I kissed it, the same way I'd worship his cock.

A low growl left his chest, the sound rumbling through me to heat my core.

"You please me, Samantha. Very much."

I hummed in response and licked at the length of the crop, words escaping me. My rational mind had utterly receded, leaving my base instincts to rule me.

"You like the crop?" he asked, the question light with arrogant amusement. "You're not scared of it? You're not scared of me?"

"No," I moaned, lifting my ass in wanton invitation. "Please."

"All right, greedy *gatita*," he chuckled. "Don't move."

He tapped my bottom with the crop. My flesh jiggled slightly, making my asshole contract around the plug. More sparks of pleasure crackled inside me, heating my empty pussy. I let out a long sigh, and my head dropped forward as I submitted fully, waiting for more.

He struck me again on the opposite cheek, a little harder. The sting of the leather hitting my flesh made my skin heat with pleasant warmth. When I didn't protest or move away, he increased the intensity of the next blow, then then next. I groaned as my entire body relaxed. Everything tingled, and I started to float. It felt like he'd suspended me, but no ropes held me aloft. The harder the crop landed, the higher I flew. The world was beautiful and dark and warm, and all that existed were the sensations being inflicted upon my body and the man who was inflicting them.

"Andrés," I moaned his name, needing... more.

The hits stopped, and his heat washed over me. "I could fuck you right now, couldn't I, kinky virgin?" he asked, his silky voice threading through my mind. "Your tight little pussy would welcome my cock."

"Andrés, please..." I wasn't sure what I was begging for. Just... *more*. More pleasure; more connection; more of his power washing over me, taking me high and setting me free.

"You shouldn't say my name like that, *sirenita*. You really shouldn't." He sounded breathless, hoarse.

He bit out a curse. "Open your mouth."

My lips parted, and my eyes fluttered open just in time to watch his cock surge between them. I whimpered around him as he slid all the way to the back of my throat, but I accepted all of him. His fingers tightened in my hair, and he held himself deep for a few seconds before easing almost all the way out.

"I'm going to fuck your mouth," he told me

roughly, surging forward again. "The way I want to fuck your little pussy. But not today. Not when you're like this."

I didn't understand what he meant, and I was too high to care, anyway. I didn't have to think when he was in control. I didn't have to worry.

He held my face and worked his cock in and out of my mouth as I sucked and swirled my tongue around him, lost in a sensual haze. All I wanted was to connect with him, to bring him the same bliss he'd given me.

He kept one hand in my hair and picked up the crop from the bed beside me. He tapped it against the plug in my ass, sending vibrations rumbling through my core. I came apart, my scream of release muffled around his thick cock. He followed me, throwing his head back on a rough shout as his cum coated my mouth. I swallowed it all down, just as he'd trained me to do.

He withdrew, and he caught me as my trembling limbs gave out, no longer able to support my weight. The mattress dipped as he collapsed beside me. He pulled my body tightly against his, kissing the top of my head as his hands roved over my sweat-slicked skin.

I remained cocooned in warm darkness, reveling in the blissful headspace I'd found in finally, fully submitting to Andrés.

CHAPTER 16

Andrés stayed with me late into the following morning. The sun was already high when I finally awoke. The last few nights, I'd been getting the deepest, most peaceful sleep of my life with Andrés' corded arm draped over me, his hard body shaped around mine. I wasn't accustomed to sleeping so many hours, or to feeling so well rested. It helped calm my buzzing brain.

Trapped in my captor's strong arms was probably the last place in the world I should get a good night's sleep. That definitely would have been my attitude when he'd first captured me. He'd been huge and scarred and scary, and his claims that I belonged to him had terrified me.

I was still being kept here against my will, but I was coming to understand Andrés a little better. He might be violent and mercurial, but he'd always been completely honest with me. He planned to train me to accept his touch and even come to crave it—something he'd managed with almost laughable ease.

But he'd also promised never to harm me, and I was coming to truly believe that. I was starting to trust him, despite everything. He might be harsh, but he had his own code. There were lines he wouldn't cross, and he'd proven that to me when he'd freed me from the spanking bench and taken me into the safe haven of his arms, holding me and apologizing for scaring me.

He'd wanted to hurt me. He'd needed it. I'd seen it in the wildness of his eyes.

But he'd held himself back. He'd put my needs before his own. And considering he could do absolutely anything he wanted to me as his helpless captive, that meant more to me than was probably healthy.

I mulled all this over while I went through my morning routine, separated from my captor by the flimsy barrier of the bathroom door. Since he was still in the suite with me, I was allowed to leave the bed and see to my needs.

Andrés hadn't yet collared me for the day, and I found myself touching my fingers to my bare throat. It was a little weird, not feeling the soft leather there. I was becoming accustomed to it, and its absence made me feel...

I shook my head sharply, deciding to stop contemplating it. I should definitely resent the collar, even if I couldn't bring myself to hate Andrés the way I should. He'd taken my freedom from me. And no matter how kind and caring he might seem at times, he still wanted to keep me as his pet, his plaything. He didn't respect me as a woman, as a fully-functioning human being with a mind of her own.

"*Sirenita*," he called out, his stern voice emanating through the bathroom door. "Your breakfast is getting cold. Come."

I blew out a long breath and tried to quiet my whirring thoughts. Like a puppy being called to heel, I had to go back into the bedroom. If I didn't, he'd just come in here and retrieve me. And then he'd probably punish me for defying him.

I was feeling particularly brittle after the intensity what had passed between us last night, and I didn't think I could handle his rebuke at the moment. Even though part of me got turned on by his discipline, I much preferred when he praised me and cuddled me. My nightmare scenario of being held captive was so much easier to bear when he was being nice.

Nice.

God, I am turning into Lauren, I thought bitterly,

but I made my way back into the bedroom without complaint.

Andrés was seated on the edge of the bed, fully dressed. That meant he was going to leave soon. A pang shot through my chest, and the irrational reaction only darkened my mood further.

"What's wrong?" he asked as I walked toward the bed, going to him without thought of resistance.

"Nothing." I waved him off, not willing to further examine my conflicted feelings, especially not with my captor.

His brows drew together. "Don't lie to me," he warned

He reached for me, grasping my waist and positioning my body so I was seated in his lap, the way we usually shared meals. He didn't bother trying to keep the cutlery from me anymore. I eyed the knife and fork where they sat on the tray beside my huge plate of bacon. I could just grab the knife and...

My stomach turned before I could even begin to visualize Andrés' blood spilling onto my hand.

"*Cosita?*" he prompted, waiting for my honest response.

I tore my eyes from the knife and focused my gaze on him. "I am a little upset this morning," I admitted. "But I don't want to talk about it."

He cupped my cheek in his big hand, his dark

eyes studying mine intently, as though he could see straight into my soul.

"You don't have any secrets from me," he said, but his tone held a note of strain. He wanted me to share with him, even though he was trying to command me to open myself up and give him everything.

I was starting to understand him, but it seemed he might be coming to some revelations of his own. He was beginning to realize he couldn't force my devotion, even if he could condition my obedience.

"Please," I whispered. "I don't want to think about it right now."

That was the truth. When I saw pain stir in his eyes, an illogical yearning to erase it rose up within me. Laying all my tangled emotions bare for both of us to see would only cause more hurt and confusion.

"You do have a very busy brain," he said, pressing a tender kiss against my forehead. "If your thoughts bother you, let me put them at ease."

I knew Andrés was capable of making my mind go quiet. I'd found peace in his ropes, under his masterful hands.

And that power he held over me scared me, even as his touch aroused me.

He leaned in to capture my lips with his.

I turned my face away. "Wait."

He frowned and lightly gripped my jaw to hold

me in place. "No. I know what's best for you. You're upset. I'm going to make you feel better."

"You can't just kiss me and make everything okay," I told him, even as my head tipped back slightly, my body already surrendering despite my protest.

"I can. But I don't have to. I can distract you from your thoughts in other ways, if you don't want me to kiss you."

He shifted my body in his lap, turning me so my back pressed against his chest. He hooked my ankles around his calves and spread his legs, opening my thighs wide. One hand tangled in my hair and tugged to the side, exposing my neck. His teeth sank into my sensitive flesh, the flare of pain making my sex clench. He held me trapped in his harsh bite as his free hand skimmed over my breasts, his palm teasing my peaked nipples.

I cried out as sensation assailed me, my entire body lighting up with awareness. He growled his approval against me, and the sound rumbled over my skin, making it pebble and dance.

He finally released me from his bite, running his hot tongue over the little indentations his teeth had left in my skin. I moaned and tipped my head farther to the side, offering him better access to my neck. He pressed feather-light kisses along my throat, up to my ear before nipping at my lobe. His hand left my hair to trail down my waist, over my hip, moving down between my legs. He suddenly slapped my exposed pussy.

I shrieked at the sting that bloomed on my flesh, and I tried to close my legs. He bit down on my neck again and kept me spread wide, his legs keeping mine splayed apart.

I writhed, my ass grinding against his thick erection. He spanked my pussy a second time, and I whimpered, accepting that I couldn't fight him.

His bite eased, and he resumed kissing my neck sweetly, even as his harsh hand smacked my tender labia. I groaned as dark pleasure settled over me, my thoughts floating away as I became lost to sensation. I was powerless to escape him, and bliss began to pulse through me as I slipped into submission.

"Are you still upset?" he murmured, his lips teasing the shell of my ear.

"What?" I struggled to gather my wits and focus on forming a coherent response. "No. I'm not upset. I'm..." I trailed off on a low moan when he traced around my clit in a little circular pattern.

"Horny?" he finished for me. "Does your wet little pussy want to be filled after being spanked?"

"Yes," I begged on a ragged whisper. "Please."

Suddenly, the world spun as his strong hands maneuvered my body. When everything settled into place, I found myself lying back on the mattress, staring up at him. The sight of him towering over me in his suit made lust pulse through my system. I remembered how alluring he'd been when he'd stood over me last night, wielding a crop.

He grinned down at me with savage pleasure. "I do like when you look at me like that, *sirenita*." He reached for his zipper and freed himself from his slacks. I licked my lips, and he growled in satisfaction. "Are you as hungry for my cock as you were last night?"

I nodded, my mouth watering for him.

"But what about your pussy?" he asked, his voice dropping deeper, rougher. "I could have fucked you last night. But you weren't aware enough to know what you would be agreeing to. You weren't capable of knowing what you were begging for." He began to stroke his shaft. "*This* is what you're begging for. I'm going to fuck you, Samantha."

Some of my euphoria ebbed, trepidation burning into my bliss. My body might be aching for him, but I wasn't ready for this.

Was I?

"You have to beg me," he said, his black eyes boring into mine as he imposed his will. "Beg me to fuck you."

"Andrés..."

Please teased at the tip of my tongue, but I swallowed it back. I didn't want to lose my virginity like this: begging my captor to fuck me. It was twisted and wrong, and it felt like defeat. My arousal soured

233

as I was reminded of the early days of my captivity, when he'd told me how he'd subjugate me.

"I can't," I said, my voice small. "I don't want to. Not like this."

He stared down at me, his jaw working. His dark eyes shuttered, and he abruptly tucked himself back into his slacks. I could still see his cock straining against the expensive material, but he turned sharply and started walking away from me.

"Wait," I called out. "I didn't mean..."

I wasn't sure what to say. I hadn't meant it when I said *no*?

That wasn't right. I'd definitely meant to refuse.

What I hadn't meant was to hurt him.

"I'm sorry," I whispered, my eyes burning.

My mind registered that it was fucked up that I was apologizing to my captor for preventing him from taking advantage of me. But that didn't make my sense of guilt abate.

He stopped in his tracks and stiffly turned back to me. For a moment, my heart leapt. I thought he was coming to kiss me, to hold me and tell me he'd never ask me to debase myself for him again.

Instead, he picked up my collar where it already lay on the mattress, chained to the bed and waiting for me. Without a word, he locked it around my neck.

He turned to leave, but I caught his wrist in the strongest grip I could manage.

"Wait," I asked again. "Don't leave like this. I didn't want to upset you. I just... I can't give you what you want."

He turned back to face me, his face carefully blank. "I won't force myself on you," he said, his voice rough.

"Thank you," I whispered. I pulled his hand toward me and pressed my lips against it, softly communicating everything I didn't know how to put into words. I wasn't sure how to express what I was feeling, but I knew I didn't want to hurt him.

He blew out a shuddering breath, and the tension melted from his powerful body. He leaned down and brushed a kiss across my lips, a silent apology.

"I'll see you tonight," he promised.

He pulled his wrist free from my grip and walked out of the bedroom, leaving my body and my heart aching for him.

CHAPTER 17

"A board game?" I asked, nonplussed. "You want to play a game that involves an actual board?"

Andrés' dark brows rose as he set the chess pieces out between us, white for me, black for him. "Is there some other kind?"

"You're kidding, right? How about *World of Warcraft*? You know, something with multi-layered storytelling, cool effects, and kick-ass heroes?" I gestured at the board. "Who's the hero in this game? What's the story? There isn't one. It's just us, staring at some funny pieces that don't have any special abilities at all."

"Chess is a battle of wits. It's just you, against me. But you can be the hero in this scenario, if you want." One corner of his lips tipped up in an indulgent smile.

I considered making a quip about him being the perfect real-life villain, but I held it back. Mostly because it hit too close to home, and I didn't want to hurt him. He might be my captor, but I was coming to see him as more than that. Andrés wasn't an evil man, even if he was holding me against my will. He put my needs first, in his own weird way. Even when he was obviously desperate to fuck me, he held back. After I'd refused to give him my virginity a few days ago, he hadn't pressed me for it again. Instead, we split our time between reading comic books and playing kinky games.

Tonight, he had a much more vanilla, much more boring game in mind.

Chess. Ugh. So analog.

"You don't have to look so disdainful," he said, still smiling. "I'll teach you how to play. If you really hate it after a few games, we can stop. I'll warn you now, I will win. So don't let that deter you from enjoying the game."

"You're a little cocky," I remarked drily, reaching for my queen to examine the exquisitely-carved pieces. They were worn from age and use, but the quality of craftsmanship was still discernable.

"I've been playing for years, and it's an impossibility for a new player to beat someone with my kind of experience."

"Who says I don't know how to play? They do

have online chess, you know. I've dabbled. I know the rules, even if I do find it boring."

He grinned. "Knowing the rules won't prepare you for playing against me, but it will certainly make these first few games more interesting. How advanced are you? Who taught you how to play?"

"An online tutorial taught me how to play. I get the rules and know some trickier strategies. I pick things up quickly."

He shook his head. "A tutorial isn't going to prepare you for playing against me, but show me what you know, and we'll go from there."

I was starting to get irritated. Didn't he value my intellect at all?

"Why bother playing chess with someone when you think they won't be able to beat you?"

"Because I believe you will be able to challenge me, just not in the first few games. Or even the first dozen."

I eyed him, considering. His response allayed my irritation. Just a little. I still wasn't sure if I wanted to play a game that Andrés would certainly win. He already won all of our kinkier games.

Didn't he?

If attaining multiple orgasms is me losing, I guess I don't mind.

I shook it off, focusing in on the current challenge.

"How long have you been playing?" He'd assessed my skill level. It was only fair that I do the same.

He picked up one of his knights, stroking the edges of the piece. It was a familiar touch, something he seemed to be doing without realizing. "This was my first chess set. I got it for my tenth birthday. That's when *Abuela* taught me how to play."

"*Abuela?*"

The ghost of a smile flickered around his lips before giving way to something harder. "My grandmother."

"Oh." I could tell from his suddenly tense demeanor that she'd passed away. I hadn't meant to pry into painful topics.

He placed the knight back on the board, and his dark gaze focused on me again. "White goes first," he prompted me.

"I know." He'd given me the slight advantage, presumably because he thought he'd defeat me so easily.

Well, too bad for him, I'd picked up some pretty sweet strategies, even in my dabbling. I wasn't being overly-proud when I said I was a quick study. It was just the way my brain worked. A little bit of internet research had told me some of the strongest opening moves.

Since he'd made the mistake of letting me play white, I'd checkmate him in six moves.

I moved my pawn from E2 to E4.

Andrés studied the board, then made his countermove. It didn't affect my strategy at all.

Okay, maybe this was going to be fun, after all. He'd been so cocky with all that talk about how I didn't have a chance at beating him. I was really looking forward to seeing his crestfallen expression when I made him my bitch.

This felt almost as good as winning a battle in *World of Warcraft*. Maybe even better, because this was *Andrés* I was defeating, not some anonymous person online.

I took a minute to pretend to consider my next move, even though I was about to win. It would be even more satisfying to take him by surprise.

I moved slowly as I placed my bishop on C4, trying to make it look like I was hesitant about my choice.

Andrés' face remained impassive. He sat for a full two minutes of silence before making his next move.

Usually, I would have found such a long wait boring, but anticipation sizzled through me.

I didn't bother to hold back when I maneuvered my queen to attack his pawn. I clicked it down on the board decisively.

Andrés grinned, and my heart did a funny flip.

That sharp, arrogant smile made something flutter low in my belly.

He knew.

"Scholar's Mate," he observed. "I'm impressed. You did study properly, *cosita*."

He moved his knight to F6, blocking me.

His black eyes glinted as he captured me in his steady stare. "Now, we can play."

"When did you realize my strategy?" I asked.

"I suspected on your first move. I knew by the second."

"But you didn't try to stop me."

"You were so cute, trying to fool me. I thought I'd let it play out for a few moves. You're not capable of lying to me, Samantha. You can't play dumb with me, either. I know you better than that."

I flushed with pleasure. Did Andrés really respect my intellect? He'd proven he cherished me in his own way, but I'd never thought he might care about my mind. So far, he'd seemed more interested in my body. Even though he'd expressed that he wanted me to be happy, that wasn't the same as respecting me.

"Who do you play with?" I wondered who usually was capable of challenging him.

"Believe it or not, I do play online mostly. There's not anyone here I'm interested in playing against. It doesn't compare to sitting across from your opponent, though. Studying you is part of the game."

"You play online? I thought you only got on your laptop to work. There's like, no technology in this penthouse. I never even see you with a phone."

"I don't like to be easily reached once I come home. This is my space. And if you're worrying that I'm wasting my time playing chess while you're tied up, don't. I'd much rather play games with you. I really am taking care of my business in the evenings. This is the first time I've played a game in weeks."

My mind chose to skip over the topic of his *business*. Instead, I focused in on the fact that he'd chosen to play chess with *me*. He could just tie me up and toy with me. He could fuck my mouth and take his pleasure from my body, even without taking my virginity.

But he was choosing to play chess with me instead. What had seemed ridiculous and boring at first now made my chest warm.

Andrés valued me as more than his plaything.

"Don't be too disappointed when I win this game," he continued. "I really am impressed with your knowledge of chess. But I've known Scholar's Mate for years. Valentina beat me with it half a dozen times before I caught on."

"Who's Valentina?" Something ugly stirred in

my gut at the thought of him playing with another woman.

His face hardened again, the same way it had when he'd mentioned his grandmother. "My sister."

I'd managed to pry into some secret pain again. "I'm sorry." Guilt nipped at me, even though I wasn't sure exactly what I was apologizing for. "You lost her?" I asked quietly.

"Yes," he bit out. "I lost her."

"How—"

"It's your move," he said tersely, a clear warning not to press him on this topic.

I nodded and moved a pawn, not really focusing on my choice. I was so caught up worrying over the fact that I'd upset him that he managed to beat me in five more moves.

He barely took the time to say "checkmate" before putting the board away.

"Can we play again?" I asked timidly.

He blinked and focused on me for the first time since I'd asked about Valentina's fate. "You want to?"

"Yes. I'll do better next time. I know I can beat you."

A half-smile tilted his lips, and my heart squeezed. "Tomorrow," he promised. "I have another game I want to play with my clever *gatita*."

He hurt me that night. He made sure I enjoyed the experience, but he still left marks on my skin.

My tears seemed to calm the dark mood that had settled over him.

I gave him my tears willingly, hoping that by shedding them for him, I could ease some of the pain that he kept locked inside.

CHAPTER 18

A ndrés kept beating me at chess. But I persevered, if for no other reason than the fact that I liked watching his brow furrow in intense concentration when I actually managed to outmaneuver him. He was clearly a master strategist, which shouldn't have surprised me, given the way he'd handled me over the last few weeks. He seemed to anticipate my every move—in chess and in the kinkier games we played.

I should have been scared at how complacent I'd become, but I couldn't help finding moments of joy when we were together. I'd never shared this kind of intimacy with anyone, and it felt good to be so connected. It made me ache for more, and sometimes I almost broke down and begged him to fuck me.

I couldn't quite bring myself to do it. I didn't

want to beg him for it. That reminded me of our first few days together, when he'd been demanding and scary. I enjoyed the fantasy of our relationship too much to face the reality that he was still demanding. And even if I no longer found him scary, he could definitely be intimidating. He touched me however he wanted, whenever he wanted. Just because I liked it didn't mean my consent was necessary.

Was it? He still hadn't taken me against my will. He held himself back, even though I could tell it caused him almost physical pain to deny himself what he wanted: me.

He wants me to beg, I often reminded myself. *I won't beg.*

I might beg him to touch me on a daily basis, but I wouldn't beg him to take my virginity. It was my last shred of dignity, of control over my own body and my own life. I couldn't surrender it. No matter how badly my body ached for him to fill me, to connect with him in the most intimate way possible.

After years of fear and isolation, his touch was like a drug. I doubted even Bliss would have been more effective at keeping me wet and needy for him as soon as he walked into the bedroom in the evening. He'd been right from the very beginning: he didn't need drugs to make me compliant.

At times, dark thoughts plagued me. Despite

our chess games, it occurred to me that perhaps I was nothing more than his plaything, his pet. That made my chest ache, a sensation I didn't fully want to contemplate.

So I'd ignore it and concentrate on potential opportunities to escape. Even if that made the ache persist.

But it wasn't like he ever afforded me an opportunity to escape. He still kept me collared and chained to the bed in his absence, and I was completely reliant on him to see to all my needs. It should have made me resentful. I should have hated him.

But the way he held me so tenderly when he cared for me made me feel cherished. Even the pain he gave me was a form of caretaking; he brought me transcendent bliss with his deviant toys. I wasn't scared of the playroom anymore. I wasn't even scared of the flogger. He'd shown me how good it could feel when applied with my pleasure in mind rather than wielding it to punish.

When I did think about escape, it was to plan for the day when Andrés would give me access to a computer. The day he decided I was ready to work for his brother. It was the only opportunity I could see available to me.

And it was coming soon. Some of my days were hazy, but I thought my assessment of three weeks in captivity was about accurate. That was the deadline Cristian had given Andrés. I'd been so well behaved, surely my captor would think I was ready to be trusted with access to the internet.

Then I could finally get away from him and make my way back to the Bureau. Back to my friends. Back to Dex.

I rubbed at the dull throb in the center of my chest and turned my attention back to my comic book.

I'd only been reading for a few minutes when the bedroom door banged open and Andrés stormed in. It was the middle of the afternoon. He shouldn't be back yet. And the fire in his eyes and furious twist of his scar mirrored his expression on the day he'd dragged me to the spanking bench and threatened to hurt me while he was angry.

I scooted back on the bed and held up my hands to stall him.

"Wait!" I gasped out. "Andrés, wait. Please."

He stiffened and stopped in his tracks, only three steps away from grabbing me.

"You're upset," I said quickly. "I don't like it when you're like this. You scare me. Please, don't... Don't hurt me." My heart twisted as the words left my lips. He might give me pain sometimes, but never more than I could handle. He was always fully in control, carefully administering how much pain he was inflicting. But he wasn't in control right now. I hadn't begged him not to hurt me in... How long?

Long enough that I'd forgotten how terrifying he could be when he was in a truly black mood.

A low, feral sound rumbled from his chest, and his fists clenched at his sides.

"Please. Talk to me. Tell me what's wrong. What happened. Is it your brother? Did he—?"

"Of course it's my brother!" he shouted, and I cringed away as his rage slammed into me. He closed the distance between us and grabbed my upper arms, pulling my body up against his. I struggled, but he snarled down at me. "He wants to see you. He expects you to be ready by now. But you're not. I've been too soft with you."

"You haven't," I insisted, desperate. "You don't have to hurt me."

"I don't want to hurt you," he bellowed. "He does. Why can't you understand that? I'm not the one who wants to break you. I want to save you. I want to protect you. I can't do that if you continue to defy me."

"I haven't defied you," I gasped out, my fear rising. "I've done everything you've asked."

"No," he railed, shaking me. "I've given you everything *you've* asked. I've tried to make you happy here with me. I've indulged you and played with you when I was supposed to be training you. And now he wants to see you, and you're not ready."

"I am," I squeaked out, needing him to believe

he could trust me with a computer. Terror rode me hard, and in that moment, I wanted to escape him more desperately than I had since the day I'd first been captured.

"Don't lie to me, Samantha," he warned on a growl. "You think you can manipulate me with your pretty tears? You think I'll do anything you ask if you smile for me? I won't allow you to play games with me. I'm in control. You belong to *me*."

His eyes took on a feverish light as he spoke.

"You're not in control," I said, trying to blink back the tears that burned at the corners of my eyes. "You're scaring me. You're hurting me." His fingers were digging into my arms hard enough to bruise, but that ache was nothing compared to the horrible sinking sensation in my chest.

Fighting him would get me nowhere. He wasn't rational at the moment. He was in pain. I could see it in the wildness of his black eyes, the deep furrow of his twisted scar. With trembling fingers, I reached up and tentatively touched his cheek. He flinched away. I tried again, pressing my palm against his scar.

"Talk to me," I begged. "Tell me what happened."

"What happened is my brother takes everything from me," he said on a harsh whisper. "*Abuela*, Valentina. Now he wants to take you." He pulled me impossibly closer. "He can't have you. You're mine."

"Yes," I agreed, trying to soothe him. "I'm yours. I'm not going anywhere. You won't let Cristian take me away. I... I trust you." Despite his bruising grip on me, I knew the truth deep in my soul. Andrés would do anything to protect me from his sadistic brother.

I traced the line of his scar with my fingertips. I'd never touched it before. I'd never touched his face with tenderness. We came together in carnal need, but I never initiated intimate contact.

He shuddered, but he leaned into my hand. His hold on my arms eased, and he embraced me, cradling my body carefully against his.

"*Sirenita*," he said, his voice strained. "*Lo siento*." He turned his face into my palm, kissing my hand.

"What happened to them?" I asked softly. "The people your brother took from you. Your grandmother and sister." I didn't really want to hear the horror of it, but Andrés needed to purge some of the pain from his soul. It was eating at him, driving him to the edge of sanity. I'd known he'd lost them, but it wasn't until just now that he'd revealed Cristian's role in that loss.

He grimaced, but he kissed my palm again, and his arms didn't tense around me with renewed aggression. He was so big, and I felt tiny in his embrace. But he held me carefully, as though I was something precious and fragile.

"Valentina..." His voice hitched on her name. "My sister. Half-sister. Cristian and I share the same father as Valentina. Our father kept her mother as his mistress after our mother passed away, but she died giving birth to Valentina. Father let Valentina's grandmother live on our estate, so she could care for her. Valentina was my best friend. Her grandmother became *mi abuela*. I spent more time in their home than my own. Cristian was always jealous of our friendship, our little family. As the oldest, father was harder on him. He had more responsibilities, a legacy resting on his shoulders."

He paused, his eyes sliding out of focus as he fell into memory.

"Your father dealt in cocaine," I prompted, knowing their family's criminal history. "He wanted Cristian to take over the business?"

"Yes. But then father died when I was sixteen. Heart attack."

"I'm sorry," I said softly.

His jaw firmed. "He was not a nice man. But I had a home with *Abuela* and Valentina. Until Cristian took over father's organization. He resented us, our family. Maybe if I hadn't left him alone with father, things would have been different. But he always had a sadistic streak, even as a child. I wanted nothing to do with him. He scared me, so I stayed away."

"What did he do?" I asked, softly prodding. This was the most personal information Andrés had ever shared with me, and I was beginning to understand his warped relationship with his brother. Andrés was bigger than Cristian. Scarier. Smarter. It didn't make sense that he worked for him when he so obviously hated him. Unless the emotional scars went deeper than the ones carved into his flesh.

"He sold Valentina," he whispered, his gaze dark with pain. "She was fourteen. He traded her for money, for bribes to secure his place as father's successor. Well, he said it was for money. He did it to punish me. To punish both of us for our happy childhood. One that had been denied him."

My stomach churned, and my heart ached for the innocent, teenage Andrés who'd lost his sister and best friend in such a horrible way.

"*Abuela* died nine months later," he said bitterly. "Breast cancer. She didn't even try to fight to survive it. Not after losing Valentina. She left me alone. With Cristian."

I suddenly understood Andrés' fierce desire to *keep* me. He didn't want to lock me in a cage like an animal, to keep me as a pet. He just wanted someone who was his, someone to care for and protect. Like he hadn't been able to protect his grandmother and sister.

Lauren had been right when she'd said Andrés needed me to be good for him. He needed my submission, my willing surrender to his control. He needed to see me restrained, because it reassured him that I couldn't leave him. He needed to see me cry, because he couldn't shed the tears himself. He wanted to care for me, but more than that, he craved my devotion in return.

Cupping his scarred cheek in my hand, I leaned up into him and lightly pressed my lips to his. For a moment, his mouth was tense beneath mine; a hard, anguished slash. Then he groaned, a long sound of pained release, and he opened for me. His fingers threaded in my hair, pulling me closer as his tongue swept into my mouth, devouring me like a starving man.

Hunger rose within me, more than physical need. I craved his closeness, skin-to-skin. He'd just dropped so many barriers between us, letting me see into his tormented soul. I wanted to offer him something in return, something I'd never offered to anyone.

But I didn't want to beg. I didn't want to prostrate myself before him and cheapen our connection to nothing more than his victory and my subjugation. I wanted *him*. All of him, good and bad, ugly and beautiful. And I'd give myself to him, willingly, eagerly.

My hands went to his shirt, tearing at the buttons in my haste to feel his hard chest, the thick ridges of the scars that were physical marks of his inner pain. I wanted to touch them, to explore every lash that had been inflicted on his soul and heal them.

He growled against my mouth, kissing me harder as he shrugged out of his shirt and helped me remove the rest of his clothes. When we were both naked, he gripped my waist and guided me down onto the bed, his weight settling over me. His hard cock pressed against my inner thigh, straining toward my virgin channel.

"I want you, Andrés," I gasped when he broke our kiss so we could both draw in much-needed air. "Don't make me beg. I want to give this to you. I want to give myself to you."

He pressed his forehead to mine, so we exchanged each ragged breath. "You don't have to beg, *sirenita*. You just have to say *yes*. I need to know that you want me. Let me in."

The tears that spilled from my eyes welled up from a place deep inside as emotion flooded free. "Yes," I whispered. "Please, Andrés."

I begged because I chose to. Because he didn't demand my surrender. I gave it willingly.

"Samantha," he groaned my name and lined up

with my slick opening. I was wet and ready for him, my core throbbing with need. "Do you feel what you do to me? You are so perfect."

His swollen cockhead pressed at my entrance, parting my pussy lips as he eased inside. I whimpered at the burning stretch of him pushing in, but he didn't stop at the sound of my discomfort. He stroked my cheek with one hand and reached between us with the other, playing with my nipples, giving me the little bites of pain that always drove me wild. My whimper turned to a high whine, and my inner muscles relaxed as my arousal grew, easing his progress as he penetrated me slowly.

Once he was fully seated inside me, he paused. My core contracted, struggling between pushing him out and welcoming him in. His jaw was clenched, his scar drawn deep and fierce. But the sight didn't scare me. I touched the mark again, tracing the furrow across his handsome face. He closed his eyes, a shiver running through his entire body as his cock jerked inside me.

He withdrew slowly, using aching care with my untried body. His cockhead dragged across my g-spot, and pleasure lit up my system, burning away the discomfort. My core heated and relaxed, opening for him. I wrapped my legs around his hips and dug my heels into his sculpted ass, pulling him back inside me.

A rumbling shout left his lips at my bold movement, and he grasped my wrists, pinning them over my head with one hand while his other played with my breasts more harshly. He pinched and pulled at my nipples. Each little hit of pain went straight to my pussy, making it flutter around him.

He began to move, pumping his hips faster and harder as he clung to his control by a thread. I knew he was holding back so he wouldn't hurt me, but I didn't want that. I didn't care if it hurt. I welcomed the burn of his huge cock filling and stretching me. It made me hyperaware of our intense connection, bound together by pleasure and pain. This was how it was meant to be between us: our bond so tight that it was nearly too much to bear.

"More," I begged, rocking my hips up to meet his thrusts. "Please, Andrés..."

My pleading triggered him. With a snarl, his control snapped, and he started fucking me in harsh, possessive strokes. His hand tightened around my wrists, and his weight pressed me deeper into the mattress, pinning me down so there was no escape from his onslaught.

I cried out, welcoming more. I didn't want to escape. I wanted to stay right here, in Andrés' brutal hold.

He hit my g-spot over and over again, making pleasure build deep inside. My entire body tensed, my toes curling and my legs shaking around him.

"Come for me, *sirenita*," he ground out, the order barely intelligible.

My body conditioned to come on his command, I let go. My orgasm claimed me with shocking force, ripping through my system in a vicious rush of ecstasy. My scream mingled with his wild roar, and his scorching seed pumped into my pussy, branding me with heat.

He drove deep one last time, holding himself inside me as he emptied his cum into me. Primal chemicals mingled in my body, easing my harsh rush of pleasure to something softer, cocooning me in tingly bliss.

Our shaking and spent bodies remained locked together as his lips crashed down on mine in a soul-searing kiss, marking me as his.

CHAPTER 19

Andrés was gone when I awoke the next morning. The warm glow that filled my chest dimmed as soon as I opened my eyes to find myself alone in his bed. My fingers searched the cool sheets, as though I could summon up his warmth somehow.

He'd held me all night after our mind-blowing first time together. He'd petted me and told me how beautiful and perfect I was. It had felt real. I'd felt... whole.

I didn't like waking up without him beside me. I needed his touch, needed to be cuddled close after the intensity of what had passed between us.

I sat up and crossed my arms over my chest to ward off the sudden chill that clung to my skin.

Something was different. When I moved, the familiar sound of metallic clanking didn't reach my ears. I lifted my fingers to my throat. The collar wasn't there. I wasn't chained to the bed.

Tears pooled in my eyes as an irrational sense of loss knifed through my chest.

Why hadn't he put it back on this morning? Didn't he want me to bear the mark of his ownership? The symbol of my devotion to him?

I took several deep breaths, telling myself that I was being unreasonable. My emotions were raw and exposed, and I didn't like not having Andrés' strong arms to cling to when I was feeling so vulnerable.

The bedroom door opened. My heart leapt, then sank to my stomach.

It was only Lauren, bringing my breakfast.

"Where's Andrés?" I asked.

She shrugged. "Master Andrés doesn't tell me about his business."

Something ugly stirred in my gut when she called him *Master* Andrés. I'd never liked it, but this time it stung. I tried my best to ignore it and act rational.

"He instructed me to give you this." She held out a large white pill and offered me a glass of water.

"What is it?"

"The morning after pill."

A block of ice formed in my stomach. "Oh." The sound left my chest along with all the air from my lungs, as though someone had punched me.

"He wants me to give you a birth control shot, too." She gestured at the waiting syringe on the cart.

My fingers went numb, and the glass of water dropped from my hands, soaking the carpet.

Lauren was saying something in a harsh tone, but I couldn't listen. I couldn't focus on her. All I could do was feel the pain my heart ripping open. I gasped for breath, pressing a hand against my aching chest.

I had unprotected sex with my captor. I could have gotten pregnant. And I begged for it.

A maddened laugh bubbled from my throat. Of course I couldn't have gotten pregnant. Andrés had made provisions to ensure his fucktoy didn't inconvenience him with a pregnancy. He'd sent his mindless slave to give me the morning after pill and a birth control shot.

Stupid. So fucking stupid.

I'd Stockholm-Syndromed the shit out of myself. I'd been scared of him in the beginning of my captivity. How could I have forgotten that was exactly what I was: his captive?

He'd told me so many times that I was his fucktoy, his pet. But my brain had reasoned its way around that horrible reality and presented me with a pretty fantasy that he actually had secret feelings for me.

He'd never lied about the fact that he was a

master manipulator. And I'd fallen for it. I'd let him shape me into his willing, eager plaything.

I had to get out, before I lost my mind completely.

My training kicked in, and Lauren wasn't at all prepared for the half-crazy FBI field agent who launched herself at her. I tackled her to the floor, pinning her on her front. I wrapped my arm around her throat and squeezed, putting pressure on her artery.

"I'm sorry," I whispered, tears almost blinding me as she went limp beneath me, slipping into unconsciousness. I released her immediately, not wanting to cause her any lasting damage. Lauren might be loyal to Andrés, but she was still a victim.

I pushed up off her still form and raced to Andrés' wardrobe. I slipped on one of his huge dress shirts, only taking the time to secure three buttons with shaking fingers, just enough to cover myself.

Lauren groaned, and I hurried back to her. I braced my arm around her waist and dragged her upright. She stumbled along beside me, somewhere partway to consciousness. I pulled her through the bedroom, into the sitting room, and straight to the elevator. I pressed her thumb against the call button.

The door slid open without a sound. No angry buzz. Nothing to alert anyone that I was escaping.

I shoved Lauren back into the sitting room and jammed the button for the door to close before she could come back to her senses. She was still blinking up at me from where she was sprawled on the floor when the silver doors slid closed. I pressed the button for the ground floor, praying no one else had access to this elevator except for those Andrés trusted. I couldn't afford to be stopped on my way down.

Adrenaline coursed through my system, my body preparing for a fight. If I did meet anyone, I'd remember my training for once.

I have to get out. I have to.

The elevator glided all the way down to the ground floor without stopping. When the doors opened, I found myself at the end of a long corridor. I could see light at the end of it, streaming through a glass door.

I started moving before I fully thought it through, my feet racing toward freedom. If I could just get outside—

A hulking body blocked the light in front of me, blotting it out as he ran straight for me.

"Hey!" he shouted. "Stop right there."

I didn't stop. I launched myself at the man, my fist connecting with his jaw. He reeled back, and I darted past him. His fingers tangled in my hair, and a defiant shriek left my lips as he dragged me back, away from the light. Using his leverage on my hair, he jerked me toward him so he could grab my upper arms. Before I could get my hands up, he slammed me back against the wall. My head cracked against it, pain lancing through my skull. The world flickered around me, and I lost control of my limbs.

"How did you get out?" he asked, his voice rough with anger. "I saw you running down here on the security feed. You whores are supposed to be locked up on the third floor."

Blinking hard, I willed the world to stop spinning. As soon as his furious, red face came into focus, I slammed my forehead into his nose.

He dropped me with a curse, and I stumbled forward. My head ached, and my vision swam.

I struggled to right myself, to run. I made it two fumbling steps before his weight barreled into me, taking me down to the hard marble floor.

"Bitch," he snarled. "You almost broke my fucking nose. You'll pay for that, dirty little whore."

I felt something hard pressing against my ass where Andrés' shirt had ridden up, leaving me exposed. I screamed and scrambled against the marble, my hands slipping uselessly against the smooth surface.

Dirty little whore.

Dirty little girl.

You want me to touch your secret place again, don't you, dirty little girl?

Dirty. Wrong.

Pure, icy terror seized my lungs as I heard his zipper lowering, heard the dreaded sound of his fist pumping his shaft.

I didn't want this. I didn't. It was dirty and wrong. It felt good for a little while when he touched my secret place, but then it hurt.

I beat my fists against the marble as I thrashed and screamed. All my training left my head as my mind receded to a long-forgotten, long-buried place.

I don't want this.

I don't want this, Uncle Robert. Please...

I couldn't breathe. I gasped for air, but nothing filled my lungs. He was on top of me, his breath hot on my neck as he pinned my tiny body down...

His weight was lifted off me, and a furious roar reverberated through my skull. I curled my knees up to my chest and hugged them tight, trying to protect myself in the only way I knew how. I heard a horrible, wet sound; a man screaming; bone crunching; silence.

"Samantha." Red-painted hands reached for me, and I flinched away, curling more tightly into myself.

"*Cosita*, it's okay. You're safe now."

"Andrés?" My voice was soft and strangely high, like a child. Past and present mingled, toxic fear clouding my brain. "I don't want him to touch my... I don't want this. I don't... I don't..." I started hyperventilating, my chest convulsing as hysteria overwhelmed me.

Strong arms closed around me, but they didn't frighten me. They were warm, powerful enough to protect me.

I turned my face into his chest and sobbed, my fingers fisting in his shirt as I struggled to get closer. A soothing stream of Spanish rumbled over me. Even though I couldn't understand the words, I focused on the lilting cadence, allowing it to fill my mind and blot out all the awful things.

But now that the memories had finally been unearthed, I couldn't bury them again. They played out in my head in horrible, vivid detail. Every muffled cry, every shameful gasp. The wrenching pain between my legs as Uncle Robert violated my small body.

Big hands stroked my back, my hair, my cheeks. They were warm. Familiar. I leaned into them, seeking more heat. I was so cold, frigid down to my bones. My entire body shook, except for my fingers, which were fisted so tightly in his shirt that my knuckles were white.

I didn't want to remember. I didn't want...

"Where is your uncle now?" he asked in English. His soothing voice roughened, and his arms were tight around me.

"What?" I asked, struggling to move from memory to reality.

"You said..." He trailed off on a growl. "You mentioned *Uncle Robert*. Where can I find him?"

I shuddered at his name. "Why?"

"I'm going to kill him for you, Samantha," he swore, his hand firming on my head where he'd been stroking my hair. I realized I wasn't the only one shaking. Andrés' strong body practically vibrated with barely-restrained violence.

"He's dead," I said hollowly, remembering the day I'd watched his casket being lowered into the ground. I'd been fifteen then, when his alcoholism had sent him to an early grave. Six years after my parents had left me alone with him so they could go on a week-long vacation. They hadn't known about his drinking at the time. They hadn't known about *him*. About what he wanted to do to me.

"I cried at his funeral," I whispered, anguished. "I didn't know why I was so upset. I fucking cried over him."

"How old were you?" Andrés asked. "How old were you when he—?" His teeth snapped closed, as though he couldn't let the words leave his tongue.

"Nine," I said softly. "But I forgot. How could I forget?"

Everything made so much sense now: my nervous tics, why I was so uncomfortable around men. I'd always been awkward and shy, even as a child. Before. But I'd had friends at school. People I wanted to play with.

After, I stopped going to my classmates' birthday parties. The idea of a slumber party, especially, gave me crippling anxiety. I didn't want to leave my parents.

So I'd stayed at home. I'd found solace in my computer games. I hid behind a screen, isolated from everyone. No one could touch me.

Until Andrés. He hadn't let me hide from him. He'd pushed past my barriers and demanded that I let him in. It might have been fucked up, but he'd been right: I never would have found intimacy with another man like what I shared with him. Not even Dex. My gentle giant of a friend might be a Dominant, but he was far too sweet to have given me what I truly needed.

I needed ruthlessness. I needed darkness. I needed Andrés.

"I'm sorry," I choked out. "I'm sorry I tried to leave. I thought you didn't care about me. I thought—"

"You thought I didn't care?" he demanded, his muscles tensing and rippling around me. "Do you know what it did to me, seeing another man hurting you, touching you? Seeing you broken and crying when you remembered what—?" He cut himself off again before he fully verbalized what Uncle Robert did to me.

His black eyes bored into me. They sparked with fury, but lines of anxiety tightened around them. "Did I hurt you?" he asked, his voice strangely thick. "Last night. Did I hurt you?"

He thought he'd hurt me during sex?

"No," I reassured him, touching my fingertips to his cheek, tracing the line of his scar just as I'd done when he'd been buried deep inside me.

"Then why? Why would you leave me?"

Shame heated my cheeks at the hurt in his voice. "I woke up, and you were gone," I said, my voice small. "I didn't have my collar. Then Lauren brought me the pill and the shot, and I thought I must have imagined... I thought you didn't care."

His face shifted to a carefully blank mask, but something stirred in his dark eyes. "Do you want to get pregnant?"

"I... No. Not... Not right now."

The thought of having a child with Andrés—of having a family again after losing my parents—made something tug in my chest.

He started petting me again. "That's for the best," he said, sounding as though he was talking to himself as much as to me. "You need to take the pill."

"I... okay." It was the rational thing to do.

But then why were my eyes stinging?

"You were upset because I was gone?" he asked, cuddling me close. "Then I'll stay. Do you want your collar back on? I thought you resented it."

"I, um, I got used to it. I like it," I amended

truthfully. "It makes me feel safe. Like you're with me, even when you're not here. But I'd rather not be chained to the bed," I added. It would be nice to be able to take care of myself during the day, instead of relying on Lauren for everything. In a weird way, part of me would miss it, knowing Andrés was thinking about me waiting in his bed. It seemed I'd developed a kink to match his.

He traced the line of my jaw, rubbed his thumb along my lower lip. "You can have your collar, but I'm not going anywhere. I left this morning to see my brother. I was convincing him to give me more time with you."

"Oh. Thank you." I'd thought he'd been playing me this whole time, but he'd been honest with me from the beginning. Yes, his kinky games were meant to train me in how to please him, but everything he did was ultimately meant to protect me. He wanted me to cooperate for his brother so Cristian wouldn't hurt me.

"I still don't want to work for him," I said quietly. "It goes against everything I believe in."

"I know. I've read enough about your superheroes to see that."

"Then what are we going to do?"

He sighed, his eyes clouding with anxiety. "I don't know yet. I'll figure something out."

"*We'll* figure something out," I told him. I was no longer willing to sit around and wait for rescue.

Cristian was the one threatening me, not Andrés. He wasn't my captor, he was my protector.

He stared at me with something like awe, cupping my cheeks in his hands before pressing his lips to mine.

Despite the horrible memories that had just resurfaced, I didn't flinch away from his masculine touch. I leaned into him and parted my lips, offering myself to him. I wanted him to claim me. I wanted to be his.

CHAPTER 20

A ndrés held the final bite of bacon to my lips, and I playfully nipped at his fingers as I took it. His lips curved up in a doting smile. There was no sharp warning in his eyes, no rebuke. Just pleasure.

He'd held me all day after my ordeal and cuddled me close through two nightmares involving my uncle. It had been a difficult night, but he'd comforted me and kissed me back to sleep.

This morning, he was staying late again. I worried about our timeline with Cristian, but Andrés didn't seem to want to leave me.

That suited me just fine, because I didn't want him to leave, either. Until we figured out how to deal with Cristian, I didn't want him to face his cruel older brother.

"Yesterday, you said you wanted your collar,"

Andrés murmured, trailing his fingers along my bare neck. "Do you still want it?"

"Yes," I said immediately, leaning into his touch.

He beamed at me. "Then you'll have it."

He lifted me off his lap where we'd been cuddled on the bed and went to the chest of drawers. When he turned back to me, he held the thin strip of black leather in both hands, touching it with careful reverence.

"Kneel for me." It was an order, but there was a hint of trepidation in his tone that made it clear that I could refuse. He wanted me to choose to obey. He wanted me to choose *him*.

I got up off the bed and sank to my knees before him, moving more gracefully than I ever would have imagined I was capable of. He'd never asked me to kneel for him before, but I knew how to present myself from what I'd seen online. I spread my thighs so my pussy was open to him, and I pulled my arms behind my back, placing my hands on the opposite elbows. The position made my back arch, offering my small breasts to him. Keeping my spine straight, I bowed my head and waited to feel the leather kiss my throat.

He was silent for a long moment. Then his fingers brushed over the top of my head, trailing down through my hair before exploring the line of my jaw. His forefinger curled beneath my chin, and he lifted my face so I looked up into his dark gaze.

The light flashed against his eyes, making them shine brighter than I'd ever seen.

"You are so beautiful," he said hoarsely. "So perfect. *Mí sirenita*."

I flushed with pleasure. "So are you."

I still saw his scars clearly, but they weren't repulsive. They were physical reminders of his vulnerability. They were slices in his armor, and he'd allowed me to open them up and look inside to the man underneath the monster.

He stared down at me in awe. "You're not scared of me? I don't frighten you?"

"No," I promised. "I'm not scared of you, Andrés."

His lips parted, as though he was about to speak. Then he closed them and swallowed hard. His eyes shone with a worshipful light as he brought the collar up to my throat and wrapped the leather around my neck.

I heaved out a sigh of relief at the familiar, reassuring feel of it encircling my throat, a physical reminder of our connection.

"Mine," he said, tracing the line of the collar.

"Yours," I replied with fervor.

He bent down and gripped my waist, lifting me up and guiding me back down onto the bed.

"Are you ready for me?" he asked, his voice strained with need.

He was asking my permission. He didn't want to

push me after the dark memories that had risen up to torment me.

But those memories couldn't destroy my desire for Andrés. He'd taken me in his harsh hands and ripped down all my barriers, helping me conquer my fears, even when I didn't understand them.

"Always," I promised, taking his hand and moving it between my legs so he could feel my desire for him. "I want you."

He groaned and grasped my ankles, pulling my ass to the edge of the bed before resting my calves against his shoulders. Still standing while I lay on my back, he gripped my hips and entered me in one hard thrust.

I cried out as he stretched me, my lingering soreness from our first time making me hyperaware of his size.

He paused, his brow furrowing. His dark eyes studied me, tight with concern.

I placed my hands atop his, curling his fingers deeper into my hips. "Please, Andrés..."

A low sound of longing left his chest, and he withdrew from me before slowly pushing all the way back in. He claimed me in long, careful strokes, playing with my clit and lighting my body up with pleasure.

He fucked me until I saw stars, and we both came undone.

No. Deep in my soul, I knew that wasn't right. He didn't fuck me.

We made love.

LOVE.

I was still contemplating my feelings hours later, as Andrés and I lay tangled in the sheets. He'd dozed off for a while after we'd had sex, but I'd been wide awake, my brain buzzing.

I had feelings for him. On a rational level, I had to acknowledge that they'd been building within me for weeks.

But *love?*

It was insane. He was a dangerous drug lord. How could I share a life with a man like him?

I hadn't thought about a future with him before. I'd just been living day to day, vaguely planning my escape with waning enthusiasm.

I didn't see how I could be with him in any real way.

And that made my heart twist in my chest.

There was one obvious way out of this that I could see, but it put him at risk: I could pretend to work for Cristian, and I'd get a message back to my friends at the Bureau. They'd come in to rescue me, and they'd arrest Cristian for abducting me.

They'd also want to arrest Andrés.

I couldn't let that happen. I might be able to arrange immunity for him if he turned on his brother, but that wasn't a guarantee.

I could also try convincing Andrés to give me access to a phone, so I could call my friends. That way, I wouldn't have to face Cristian at all.

It still wouldn't guarantee his safety, though. I couldn't see how to get back to my life without betraying Andrés.

But the idea of going back to my life without him in it made my chest ache. I wasn't ready for my time with him to end, even if I didn't want to stay locked in this penthouse forever.

"What are you thinking about?" he asked, his fingertips brushing over the furrow in my brow.

I blinked and propped up from where I'd been resting against his chest.

"I thought you were asleep," I said instead of answering.

"I was, but I could hear you thinking." He gave me a languorous smile and stroked my hair back from my cheek. "You do have a very busy mind."

"Let me guess. You're going to help me make it go all quiet and blissful?" I was only half-teasing. That sounded kind of nice right now. It would free me from my inner turmoil.

"I can, if that's what you need," he said. "But I like your clever brain."

"You do?" He'd never openly expressed admiration for my intellect before. After our games of chess, I'd come to suspect it, but he'd never said it outright. It made my heart do a funny flip. I'd worried so many times that he saw me as nothing more than a pet, but actually respected me as an intelligent woman.

"Of course," he replied. "You challenge me. I find you fascinating. Did you not know?"

"I..." I swallowed down the lump in my throat. "No. I guess I didn't know that. Not for sure."

"I should tell you more often, then."

He was being so sweet. I just wanted to melt into him, to feel his weight settle over me as he drove deep inside me, connecting us intimately.

His fingers curled beneath my chin, lifting my face so he could study my expression. "Did I make you sad?"

"No," I said, my voice catching. "That... means a lot to me."

"Then why are you crying?"

"Because I don't want to leave," I whispered. "I don't want to leave you, but I should."

His jaw firmed, his eyes flaring. "You're still thinking about how to escape?"

"No," I said quickly. "I mean, yes. I mean, I want to get out of working for Cristian. I don't want to spend my days locked in this penthouse, fearing the day your brother comes for me. And if you really value my mind like you say you do, you won't want that for me, either."

He scowled. "This is the safest place for you. You should fear Cristian. This is the only way I know how to protect you."

"This isn't the life I want," I said, desperate. "I can't stay trapped in a cage forever. I need to do something meaningful. I need to help people."

"You've been reading too many comic books. You can't be a superhero, Samantha. You're far too breakable, and I won't put you at risk."

"I can be a hero," I informed him, anger rising. "I used to do it every day, before you took me. I had a life. I had purpose."

He wrapped his arms around me and rolled, settling his heavy weight on me so I was pinned beneath him. "Your life is with me now," he said, his voice rough. "And my purpose is to protect you."

"You won't be able to keep me from Cristian forever," I tried to reason with him. "Let me call my friends at the Bureau. If you go into hiding before they come for Cristian, I can cover your tracks. They won't find you. You'll be safe."

"And what about you?" His black eyes burned into me. "Where will you be while I'm in hiding? Will you go back to your friends? To your Dex?"

"I... I don't know," I whispered, torn. I didn't want to go back to my life without Andrés.

"You're *mine*," he snarled. His cock was hard

against me, pressing at the entrance to my sex. "And you're not going anywhere. Not back to your Dex. And not to my brother. You belong to me."

"I'm yours," I agreed. "But I can't—"

He crushed his lips to mine, silencing me on a warning growl. My body heated for him, and I softened under his onslaught. My pussy grew slick with arousal. As soon as I moaned against his mouth, he thrust into me in one brutal, possessive stroke.

He fucked me hard, claiming me in deep, merciless thrusts. My body welcomed his ferocity. Because I didn't want him to let me go. I didn't want to return to my old life and have Andrés disappear forever.

I couldn't yet see a clear path to a future with him, but I knew I didn't want to lose him. I wrapped my legs around him and pulled him impossibly deeper, welcoming his harsh claim over me.

CHAPTER 21

Andrés woke me early the next morning with a soft kiss against my neck. I turned my head, offering him better access. He rumbled his approval, the sound humming against my sensitive skin as he nipped at me. I pressed my ass back against his erection in wanton invitation, my body awakening for him before my mind was fully aware.

"It's time for your punishment," he murmured against my neck.

"Punishment?" I asked sleepily, not at all alarmed by the threat. "Why?"

"You tried to escape," he reminded me, but he sounded more aroused than upset. "That was very naughty, *gatita*. I've owed you a punishment for days."

"Oh. Okay," I agreed, knowing he needed this

from me. After almost losing me, he needed to see me bound and begging for him. And I needed it, too. I felt guilty and foolish for thinking he didn't care about me, especially after our last few days of intense intimacy. A little pain and his forgiveness would absolve me.

He kissed the tender spot he'd bitten. "Good girl."

He gave me a few minutes for my morning routine, and I emerged from the bathroom with my teeth brushed and face freshly washed. He was waiting for me, his powerful body on full display where he stood at the threshold to the sitting room. He held out his hand, beckoning me toward him.

"Come."

I crossed the bedroom and placed my hand in his, allowing him to lead me to the playroom. I knew pain was coming, but my body heated at the prospect. He'd conditioned me to enjoy a little pain. Or maybe I'd always been built this way. I'd gotten aroused when he'd spanked me the first time, on the day I woke up in his bed after my capture, scared and confused.

I wasn't scared anymore. Not of the pain, and not of Andrés.

I followed where he led, trusting him implicitly even as we entered the room that had once terrified me. We came to a stop at the far wall, where he kept a multitude of implements designed for my torment hanging in neat, orderly rows.

He selected a length of crimson rope, and I shivered in anticipation. I'd come to love rope: the slightly earthy smell of hemp, the rough fibers that stimulated my sensitive skin. I felt secure when he bound me so thoroughly. He often used leather cuffs to strap me down, but rope was more intimate, methodical. Almost artistic. I was his to mold and shape, to bend and stretch into whatever position he desired, making me into something beautiful to be admired.

I took a deep breath and released it on a long, shuddering sigh as he began to wind the rope around me, forming a familiar harness around my chest. He took extra time and care to create a pretty lattice pattern above my breasts, turning my body into his work of art.

When he was finished tightening the rope around my chest, he drew my arms behind my back, binding them together from shoulder to wrist, until my back arched and my breasts stood out proudly, my nipples peaked and throbbing for his attention.

He tied off his work and took another length of rope, feeding it through the large metal ring bolted into the thick wooden beam above my head. He then looped it through the bindings on my arms, pulling them up behind me so I was forced to bend at the waist. My breaths came faster, shallower as carnal need began to take hold of all my senses. I spread my legs without him having to issue a command, wantonly offering my wet pussy to him.

Satisfied with my helpless state, he knotted the ropes in place and stepped back. He took a long minute to admire me, but he didn't touch me. I whined for his attention, but he returned to the wall to select the next item for my punishment.

He held up the shiny set of rubber-tipped nipple clamps so I could see them clearly. A chain dangled between them, decorated with little red gemstones. It was pretty and perverted and perfect. I wanted the pinch of the clamps, the pull of the swaying chain as he toyed with it. I wanted him to take full control of my body; my pain, my pleasure.

He came back to me and lightly cupped my breasts, his calloused fingertips barely skimming my flesh as his palms kissed my tight, aching nipples. I tried to lean into him, but the ropes kept me trapped. The sense of helplessness I had once feared now sent me soaring, granting me the sweetest release. I put myself fully in Andrés' domineering hands. I was his to play with, his to punish, his to cherish.

He began to roll my nipples between his fingers, preparing me for the harsher bite of the clamps. When I whimpered and wiggled, torn between wanting relief and craving more, he caught my tight peaks in the clamps. I cried out as he turned the screws on the sides, slowly increasing the pressure to ensure they'd stay firmly in place when he tugged on the chain that connected them. I hissed out a breath and struggled to adjust to the pinch.

As I settled into acceptance, euphoria flooded my mind. He flicked the gems that dangled from the chain, and it swayed beneath me, tormenting me sweetly. I moaned, and my eyes slid closed as my head dropped forward, my weight sagging into the ropes that held me so securely. They shifted around me, tightening and caressing, embracing me.

I felt his heat recede, but my eyes remained closed as I drew in short, panting breaths. As my chest rose and fell, the chain tugged at my nipples. Every little hit of pain sizzled through me, sending scorching lines of pleasure straight to my clit. My inner thighs grew slick with my arousal, and my core contracted, eager for him to fill me.

I sighed in bliss when I felt the snap of the crop against my ass. He started slow, peppering my flesh with little sharp slaps, the smooth leather tongue leaving bright patches of heat everywhere it landed. My skin warmed and tingled. Little sparks danced over my flesh, crackling up my spine to flood my mind with bliss.

Suddenly, he cracked the crop hard against my upper thigh, a harsh, punitive stroke. I cried out at the rush of pain, but I didn't try to move away. I welcomed it, craving the absolution he offered.

"Never leave me again," he said, his voice rough with emotion.

Another blow cracked across my thigh, stinging and burning.

"You don't get to leave me. Never leave me." There was something desperate in his harsh tone, yearning mingling with command.

"I won't," I promised, tears of release spilling down my cheeks. "I won't leave you. I love you."

The blows stopped, and the crop clattered to the ground. Both of his big hands curled into my ass, spreading my cheeks wide.

"Say it again," he ground out.

"I love you." The soul-deep truth left me on a sob. "Please, Andrés."

He snarled and slammed into me, his cock thrusting deep into my wet channel. "Tell me," he demanded, driving into me with ruthless, branding strokes. "Tell me again. Don't stop."

"I love you!" I cried out as he thrust into me mercilessly. "I love you, I love you..." The words left me in a litany, over and over again as his cock dragged across my g-spot, driving me higher. He reached beneath me and pinched my clit.

"Andrés!" I screamed out his name as I shattered. His raw shout echoed around us, and his cum filled me, marking me as his. He kept pounding into me, riding out the last of our pleasure with brutal force. I welcomed his claim over me.

Finally, he stopped, completely spent. He withdrew from me and carefully removed the clamps from my nipples. I whimpered when blood rushed back to the abused buds, but he soothed the sting away with gentle fingers, morphing the pain into pleasure.

He cut me down, severing the ropes that bound me. He supported my limp body and eased us down to the cool tiled floor, holding me tight.

"Mine," he murmured, tracing the contours of my body as though seeking to memorize every inch of me. "All mine."

I kissed his neck, tasting my tears on his skin. The salt mingling with his unique flavor was intoxicating. Better than any drug. I licked at it, craving more. A low, rumbling sound left his chest, vibrating against me. The sensation rolled through my body, making its way to my core. Despite the rough way he'd fucked me, my pussy wept for him, wanting him again.

I shifted in his hold, straddling him. He stiffened for me, needing me as desperately as I needed him. I boldly lowered myself onto him and captured his lips, welcoming him to claim my mouth the way he'd claimed my pussy. I moved against him, slowly sliding up and down on his shaft. His hands captured my waist, guiding me to take him faster, deeper. We found our bliss together, our sweat-slicked bodies entwined as closely as possible.

I screamed out his name, my fingernails scoring his back. I gave him everything, but at the same time, I claimed him as well, marking him.

I loved Andrés, and he was all mine.

CHAPTER 22

A ndrés left me with a promise to return in a few hours. He was going to see Cristian to convince him to give me more time. Despite my devotion to Andrés, I couldn't bring myself to help with his business. And he wouldn't ask me to. In the beginning, he'd been determined to make me cooperate in order to protect me, but we were past that now. He promised he wouldn't force me to do anything that went against who I was.

Because he cared. He cared about *me*, not some version of me that did exactly as he said. I wasn't his doll. I wasn't his pet. I wasn't his fucktoy.

He might not have told me he loved me, but I could feel it in the reverent way he held me, the way he called me *his*. I knew he'd lost the people he loved in the past. He wasn't ready to say the words aloud, because he was afraid he'd lose me, too. I was still targeted in Cristian's crosshairs, and I didn't expect Andrés to admit his feelings for me until I was safe. Until he was certain his sadistic brother wouldn't take me away like he'd taken Andrés' beloved sister and grandmother.

So for now, I was content with his branding kiss, with his harsh claiming of my body. His possessive touch communicated all the things he wasn't ready to say to me.

I still didn't understand how we could have a future together, but I resolved to come up with a solution. I needed to push aside my worry and focus on formulating my plan.

Not worrying was difficult when I knew Andrés was facing his brother right now, defying him in an effort to protect me. I didn't particularly enjoy feeling like a damsel locked in a tower for safe-keeping while my dark knight fought my battles. But without a computer, I really wouldn't have been much help in a fight.

I resolved to ask Andrés about that when he returned. Now that there was trust between us, he might allow me access to his laptop. I could take down Cristian's organization piece by piece, destroying his financials and leaving him utterly ruined.

But it was Andrés' livelihood, too. And although I knew he didn't approve of the Bliss and human trafficking, that didn't mean his hands were clean. I'd become convinced that he had a good heart, but he'd never known anything but a life of violence and crime. Circumstance had twisted him into a cruel monster on the surface, but I'd seen the damaged man at his core, the boy who had lost everything. His scars ran deep, and although he wouldn't like to admit it, he feared his brother. He was as much a captive in his dark life as I was in this suite.

I just had to convince him that I could help set him free, if he'd let me. He might not be able to take on Cristian, but I could do it for both of us. A few clever keystrokes would bring his entire empire crashing down.

I was only idly turning the pages of my comic book out of habit as my mind was absorbed in plotting Cristian's downfall. I wasn't sure how long I'd been skimming through the story without reading when Lauren arrived with my lunch.

I sat up in bed, covering myself with the sheet. I still wasn't comfortable with anyone but Andrés seeing me naked, even though Lauren had seen everything already.

She didn't even look me in the eye today. I suspected her jealousy of my relationship with *Master* Andrés might be growing into resentment. Not to mention the fact that I'd recently attacked her.

Without a word, she handed me the morning after pill and a glass of orange juice. I'd taken the birth control shot a few days ago, but it wasn't guaranteed to be effective immediately, and Andrés hadn't been using condoms with me. I didn't want him to, anyway, so I'd accept the slight nausea that came along with the pill. I really wasn't ready to get pregnant.

I drained the glass of juice and handed it back to Lauren. She finally looked me in the eye. Her lovely face was drawn with anguish.

"I'm sorry," she whispered.

I blinked at her. "Why? Because of Andrés? I know you care about him. That's okay." I didn't begrudge the woman her admiration of my captor any longer. I understood everything she'd claimed about him. He *was* kind. He was a good man, deep in his soul.

"No," she said softly. "Master Andrés is going to be so angry with me."

"What are you talking about?" I asked, more sharply. Fear for Andrés flooded my chest, pressing against my heart.

"Cristian made me," she said, wringing her hands. "You have to come with me now."

I shook my head. It felt lighter than it should, but I couldn't focus on that. "I'm not going anywhere without Andrés."

"You will in a minute." Her eyes filled with tears. "He's going to hate me."

My body heated with anger. Or was it just hot? No. I was very aware of the cool air caressing my skin, making it pebble. I shivered, feeling as though Andrés was running his fingers down my spine. My core warmed and pulsed, need blossoming low in my belly.

"What did you do?" I asked, even as a pleasant, floaty sensation settled over me. It felt almost as good as being suspended in Andrés' ropes.

"Cristian made me put Bliss in your drink. He wants you to be with the other girls, since you won't work for him. You have to come with me."

"I don't..." The refusal died on my tongue, and a soft moan left my chest as my clit began to pulse.

"I'll try to keep the worst ones away from you," Lauren sniffled. "Come on. We have to go."

I got to my feet, shuddering as the sheet slid down my sensitized body. My rational mind receded as desire swelled. My feet followed where Lauren led, with no thought of resistance. There was no thought at all. Just need.

I needed to be touched, to be kissed, to be fucked.

I needed Andrés.

We arrived at the elevator, and the silver doors opened for Lauren. She took my hand, and I gasped as my fingers tingled with awareness. She started to cry as she pulled me into the elevator with her, but I didn't understand why. How could she be sad when everything felt so *good?*

I was warm. So warm. I leaned back against the cold mirrored wall, and a whine eased up my throat. My eyes slid closed as my inner walls began to contract, aching for Andrés to fill me.

"Andrés," I groaned his name.

"You'll see him later," Lauren promised, her voice hitching. "After."

The elevator stopped, and the doors slid open. Lauren was still holding my hand, and she tugged me out into the long corridor. I followed without question, without concern. All I could focus on was the lust coursing through my system, the need building deep inside me.

She led me a few steps down the hall and stopped at a closed door. She retrieved a key from her dress pocket and turned the lock before ushering me inside. The door closed behind me with a sharp *click*, but I barely registered it.

The room was huge, yellow lights filling the decadent space. Everything was red velvet and gold gilding. It was warm, soft, sensual. Couches lined the walls, and a massive circular bed dominated the center of the room. People lounged on the couches in varying states of undress. One particularly voluptuous woman was dancing to a heavy, hypnotic beat, her naked body undulating around a silver pole. A musky scent filled the space. It made my pussy clench and my blood race.

Several sets of eyes turned on me, male and female. I heard deep, masculine voices rumbling beneath the music, a harsh laugh punctuating the sensuous beat.

A man approached me slowly. I recognized him. It was the boy who'd come to clean Andrés' suite, the one who'd threatened me. His eyes flicked past me to focus on Lauren.

"What's she doing here?" he asked. "She's supposed to be upstairs. Do you know what Andrés will do to us if he finds her in here?"

"Cristian wants her down here," Lauren said, her voice still trembling with tears. "He said he'd deal with Master Andrés."

Something stirred at the edges of my mind.

Andrés. He was with Cristian. And he...

God, I needed him. My body was on fire, my pussy throbbing to the point of discomfort. I needed relief, release.

Not caring that I was naked in front of a room full of strangers, I closed my eyes and cupped my breasts, squeezing them to make the tingling in my nipples abate. My firm touch only made my desire grow, and my wet arousal slipped down my thighs.

"If you're sure..." I heard the boy's voice getting closer, but I didn't care about him.

I cared about getting back to Andrés, so he

could help me ease this craving that was gnawing at my insides.

Long, masculine fingers closed around my wrists, directing my hands to my sides. Warm flesh touched mine, and I cried out at the shock of sensation as he caressed my breasts. My nipples were hard peaks against his soft palms.

Soft. Not calloused.

This was wrong. It felt wrong. But *so good...*

A loud *bang* sounded behind me, accompanied by the *snap* of splintering wood. My eyes flew open when the hands were jerked away from my breasts. Andrés' savage snarl filled my senses, and a pleasurable shudder ran through my body at the sight of his scarred face. It was twisted with maddened fury. He held the boy's face in both hands and twisted sharply. Bone cracked, and the boy's body fell to the floor, his neck at an odd angle.

Andrés positioned his body in front of mine, his fists curled tight at his sides.

"Who else touched her?" he roared. "Who?"

"N-no one." Lauren's voice was a high squeak. "I'm sorry, Master Andrés. I'm so sorry."

"Do not speak to me." He bit out each word. "You're lucky I don't snap your neck, too."

I heard her heave out a despairing sob, heard her soft footsteps whispering across the carpet as she fled.

"*Master* Andrés," I said. "I don't like that she calls you *Master*."

He turned to me, his black eyes burning with rage. Despite his fury, he handled me as though I were a fragile doll as he lifted me up in his strong arms and carried me out into the hallway. I moaned and rubbed my face against him, like the needy kitten he'd always claimed I was.

"You're not hers," I murmured, snuggling into his heat, loving the feel of his corded muscles rippling beneath me. "You're mine. My Master." I giggled. "Isn't that funny? I always wanted a Master. And you're mine."

The elevator took us up to his penthouse, and he carried me to the bed. He tried to set me down and pull away, but I locked my arms around his neck, keeping him close.

"Touch me, Master," I breathed. "Please. I need you."

My pussy ached, and my desire for him coated my thighs.

He grasped my arms and pried them away from him. His hands slid up to my wrists, and he pressed them into the pillows above my head. I whimpered and arched my back, lust pulsing through me as he dominated my body.

"I can't," he rasped. His lips were twisted downward, pulling his scar to a deep slash. "I can't be with you like this."

Holding my wrists in place with one hand, he brushed my hair back from my face with the other. I hummed my pleasure and nuzzled into him.

"My Master," I sighed. "Mine."

"You don't know what you're saying," he said tightly. "I'm sorry," he continued, his voice breaking in a way I didn't understand. "I'm so sorry. I wasn't here. I didn't know. When Cristian told me..." He gnashed his teeth. "I should have killed him. I should have fucking killed him."

I wasn't used to hearing Andrés curse in English.

"You're upset," I observed. "Don't be upset. Make love to me, Master."

"Don't call me that," he growled, his eyes tightening with anguish.

"But you are," I said. "I love you, my Master. My Andrés."

He cupped my cheek in his hand. "Please, don't say that. Don't."

I wasn't used to hearing him beg, either.

"Don't be sad," I said, dimly noting the wetness pooling at the corners of his black eyes.

He blinked hard, and some of the wetness fell to splash against my cheek.

"Make love to me," I urged again, arching my back, lifting my tingling breasts in wanton invitation. My entire body was *alive*, my nerve endings crackling and popping. Heat was building inside me. I was going to burn up if he didn't touch me where I craved it most. "I need you."

He pressed a tender kiss against my forehead. "All right, *cosita*," he murmured. "I'll help you. I know you must be aching."

"I am. My pussy hurts."

"I'll kiss it better," he promised.

"Thank you," I sighed in relief. He was going to touch me. He was going to kiss me. I lifted my face to his, but he turned away.

"Not your lips," he said, still sounding oddly pained. "I can't when you're like this."

"But you said you'd kiss me," I whined. "You said— Oh!"

Ecstasy lashed through me when he lowered his mouth to my tight nipple, flicking the tip with his tongue before sucking the peak into his mouth. He didn't use his teeth, and I was grateful. Just the heat of his mouth was intense enough to bring tears to my eyes.

"Please," I begged, lifting my hips. I needed him to touch my pussy. It was starting to throb to the point of pain.

He shushed me gently, pressing his palm against my stomach to pin me down. He moved onto the bed with me, but his body didn't settle atop mine. I wanted his comforting weight holding me down, but he positioned himself between my quivering thighs.

I watched in rapt fascination as he lowered his head to my pussy and touched my wet folds with his tongue. His hungry groan mingled with my harsh cry. He'd never kissed me there before. And it felt...

"So good," I panted, my fingers spearing in his thick hair as I pulled him closer. "More."

He traced the line of my opening, teasing the little patch of skin between my pussy and my asshole before licking all the way up to my pulsing clit. I thrashed as stars burst across my vision, bliss singing through my veins. He growled against me, and his hands locked around my thighs, forcing me wide open. His tongue circled my clit, applying firm, hot pressure. My inner walls contracted and clenched, yearning to be filled. He licked and sucked at my pussy lips, tormenting me with ruthless pleasure.

It wasn't enough. I needed him inside me, needed him to mark me with his cum.

Tears leaked from the corners of my eyes as pleasure turned to a deep, knifing pain between my legs. The building pressure had to release, or it would destroy me.

"Please," I choked on a sob. "I need you inside me. It hurts. Please, Master..."

He pressed one final kiss against my clit before his body covered mine. He freed his hard cock from his slacks and lined up with my soaked pussy.

His eyes searched mine, dark with hunger and yearning. "You shouldn't call me that," he ground out, hesitating at my opening. "You shouldn't."

I wrapped my legs around him and drew him into me. "My Master," I moaned in relief when he filled me to the hilt.

A deep, pained sound slipped between his clenched teeth. He braced his arms on either side of my head and started to move within me, thrusting hard and deep. His forehead dropped to rest on mine, and he stared down into my eyes, his face drawn tight in an expression I didn't understand.

"Forgive me," he whispered. "Forgive me, *sirenita*."

I didn't know what he was talking about, and I couldn't focus on his words. All I could think about was how good his big cock felt stretching my tight sheath, how perfectly we fit together. The ruthless pleasure that had been building inside me crested, and I shattered on a scream.

My fingers fisted in his hair again, and I pulled his face down to mine so I could revel in his exquisite taste while my orgasm rolled through me. I caught his rough shout on my tongue, felt more wetness on my cheeks as his hot cum lashed into me, soothing the need that had consumed me. I shuddered beneath him as bliss flooded my body, making me light and tingly. My numb fingers fell from his hair, finally releasing him as all my muscles turned to jelly.

I closed my eyes and slipped into velvety darkness, his softly-spoken words following me down into sleep: "Forgive me."

CHAPTER 23

I stirred, slowly coming back to awareness. My body felt strangely heavy, and I was sore between my legs. I opened my eyes to find the shades drawn, with only the soft glow of city lights peeking around the edges. Night had fallen, but I was just waking up. Everything started to come back to me in pieces: Lauren, dosing me with Bliss; the red and gold room; the boy touching me; and Andrés, coming to my rescue like some dark avenging angel.

I sat up, searching for him. He sat on the edge of the bed, watching me with bloodshot eyes. His posture was stiff, his face a blank mask. He was fully dressed in his sharp suit, but his hair was wet, as though he'd just taken a shower.

"Thank you," I murmured, reaching for him.

He shifted away, grimacing. "Don't thank me. I

fucked you while you were high out of your mind. I violated you."

"No," I said fiercely, grabbing his hand before he could retreat farther. "I begged you to." Even though I hadn't been able to control myself while under the influence, I remembered everything clearly now. "I needed you to. I was hurting. You helped me."

He turned his face away from me, but he didn't pull his hand from my grip. "You shouldn't have called me Master," he said hollowly. "You shouldn't have done that. I couldn't—" He pressed his lips to a thin slash, holding in whatever he was going to say. "I'm not blaming you. You didn't know what you were saying. It's not your fault. None of this is your fault. You didn't ask to be trapped with me. You didn't ask to be beaten and raped."

"You didn't rape me. Don't you dare call it that. Don't you dare." Angry tears made my vision swim, and I swiped them away from my cheeks. "You were helping me. I trusted you to help me. I love you, Andrés. And I meant what I said. You're my Master."

He rounded on me, his eyes blazing. "Don't call me that," he barked, his hand tightening around mine in a vice-like grip.

I moved toward him, scooting across the bed so I could get in his face. "You did nothing wrong," I said, imbuing the words with as much fervor as I possessed. "You saved me. You've been saving me this whole time. You've been protecting me from Cristian. He would have—"

"He would have what?" he shouted over me. "Ordered Lauren to slip you Bliss and whore you out? That's what he wanted, Samantha. He wanted you to scream in pleasure while they violated you. He wanted them to send you back to me, broken and used. He wanted to punish me for my failure. I should have killed him," he hissed, his gaze turning feverish. "But I didn't. I ran back to you as soon as he told me. He fucking laughed while I ran away from him."

"You got back to me in time." I cupped his face in my hands, trying to get him to focus on me. "You saved me. You protected me."

He grabbed my wrists, squeezing to the point of pain. But he didn't move my hands away from his face.

"I can't protect you," he rasped. "I'm a coward. You deserve better than me."

"I don't, and you're not," I asserted. "I want to be with you, Andrés. You're not a coward."

"I'm afraid of him," he admitted on a bitter whisper.

"I know," I said softly. "And I understand."

"You don't. My face..." He trailed off with a shudder and cut his eyes away.

I touched his scar, applying enough pressure to

guide his face back to mine. "Tell me what he did to you." It was a steady command. Andrés needed to purge this from his soul. It was the only way he'd be able to free himself from the power his brother held over him.

"It was three years ago," he began, the words bleeding out of him. "Cristian made a deal with some Russians. He started dealing in Bliss. I'd never dared to challenge him, but I hated it. It was too far, too much. He was selling women, just like he sold my sister. So I decided to stage a coup and take over the organization myself. I'd always been the one to keep the business running. I could do it without him. My life would be better without him."

He paused, his eyes sliding out of focus as he fell into memory.

"He found out," I surmised, quietly urging him to continue.

His jaw tightened beneath my hands. "One of my men betrayed me. Cristian came for me before I made a move against him. He strung me up in front of all of our people—the ones he hadn't killed for following me. He cut me. He made me scream. He humiliated me. Then he stitched me up himself to make sure the marks lasted."

My stomach churned, nausea rising in my throat. "Andrés..." I said his name shakily, struggling to get my tears under control. I wanted to weep for him, but that wasn't what he needed from me. He needed me to be strong. He needed me to show him that his scars only made him more beautiful in my eyes. They were marks of his defiance, of his goodness. He bore them because he'd tried to put a stop to his brother's evil.

I leaned in and brushed my lips across the deep furrow in his cheek. "I love you," I said with the weight of an oath. "We're going to get away from your brother. Together."

His brows drew together, his face twisting in lines of anguish. "I have something for you," he said instead of responding to my fervent declaration. I didn't like that he was avoiding what I'd said, but he pulled me into his lap, cuddling me close.

I sighed and pressed my cheek into the crook of his neck, relief washing through me at the feel of his strong arms around me.

He shifted slightly, reaching for something on the cart beside the bed. Confusion threaded through me as he uncapped the syringe.

"Lauren already gave me the birth control shot," I told him.

One corded arm wrapped around me, pinning me against his hard body as he carefully slid the needle into my upper arm.

"It's not birth control. I should have sent you away hours ago, but I had to see your lovely eyes one last time."

"What are you...?" My tongue grew heavy in my

mouth, and lethargy rolled over me as my eyes drooped closed.

"I can't protect you," he said, pressing a kiss against my motionless lips. "Goodbye, *sirenita*. *Te amo*."

I knew what it meant. *I love you.*

CHAPTER 24

I awoke to the sound of someone's fist pounding on wood. Forcing open my sandpaper eyelids, I struggled to assess my surroundings. In my gut, I knew something was wrong. The bed beneath me, the too-rough sheets that covered me, the slacks I wore.

Wrong.

I could still smell Andrés' unique, masculine scent. But that was because I was covered by one of his huge shirts.

The pounding increased in volume, escalating to banging. The sound reverberated in my skull, and I winced, my aching brain working overtime to process everything.

"Sam!" A familiar voice bellowed. I glanced toward the locked hotel room door that separated me from my friend.

JULIA SYKES

"Dex?" I rasped, my throat too dry.

Wood splintered, and the door burst open. My best friend rushed toward me.

"No," I breathed.

Dex couldn't be here. That meant...

"No!" Anguish wrapped around my heart.

Andrés had sent me back to my friends, back to safety. And he'd left himself at his brother's mercy. Cristian would punish him for letting me go.

"It's okay, Sam. It's me." Dex stopped a few feet away from me, keeping the same careful, respectful distance he always did.

"Are you hurt?" Jason asked. He stood even farther away, barely inside the broken doorway. Tension gripped his body, and his dark green eyes studied me intently. His lips twisted in disgust when his gaze fell on Andrés' shirt covering me. It obviously belonged to a man; it nearly swallowed my much smaller frame. "Who did this to you?" he ground out, clearly putting two and two together. He saw my state of dress and assumed I'd been violated by my captors.

"Where is he?" I asked thickly, struggling to control my tongue. The drugs lingered in my system, sapping my strength and dulling my mind. All I knew was I had to get back to Andrés before Cristian hurt him.

"Who?" Dex asked, kneeling beside the bed so he could study my face. "Who were you with? We

310

got an anonymous call saying you'd be here. Are you..." He eyed Andrés' shirt, his pale blue gaze igniting with rage. His jaw clenched, and he took a deep breath. "Are you hurt?"

"I'm fine." I slurred. "I have to go."

"Go? Sam, you've been missing for almost a month. You're not going anywhere."

I tried to sit up, but the world wavered around me, and I dropped back onto the pillows.

"I have a bus on the way," Jason said.

I didn't want an ambulance. I didn't want to go to the hospital. I wanted to get back to Andrés before something terrible happened to him.

But I couldn't seem to move. I could barely think. I heard Dex talking, but I couldn't quite focus on what he was saying. The room kept sliding into darkness. Every time the world disappeared, I tried to force my eyes back open.

I was fighting a losing battle. Everything dissolved around me, until all I had left was fear for Andrés.

WHEN I FINALLY CAME BACK TO FULL AWARENESS, I found myself in a hospital bed. Dex was standing at the threshold to the room, his massive body blocked by a short nurse who was clearly struggling to hold her ground.

I heard her murmur the words *rape kit* as she tried to shoo Dex away, and my stomach dropped.

I couldn't let them run a rape kit. I'd had sex with Andrés a few hours ago while under the influence of Bliss, and he'd come inside me. I doubted his DNA was on file anywhere, but I couldn't allow them to collect that kind of evidence against him.

"I want to talk to Dex," I said loudly, alerting them both to the fact that I was awake.

His blue eyes blazed when they focused on me, his tanned face oddly pale. He evidently hadn't liked the words *rape kit*, either. Although, he was disturbed for entirely different reasons. He thought I'd been used against my will, violated.

"I need to talk to you," I said, more softly. "Please."

My mind whirred to life. I had to figure out a way to save Andrés before Cristian realized I was missing. I'd start by questioning Dex. I needed to know what the FBI suspected about my abduction and what was being done to try to find the people who'd taken me.

The nurse finally stepped aside and allowed Dex to enter. He approached me carefully, moving slowly so he wouldn't spook me. He reached for me, almost touching my shoulder. Then his hand clenched to a fist, and he pulled away. He never had been willing to push past my barriers and touch me.

We were buddies, and he respected my personal space issues.

Once, I'd longed for him to look at me with desire, with love. Now, he was watching me with concern.

And all I wanted was for him to get out of my way so I could get back to the man I loved before something terrible happened to him. I knew where Andrés' building was located. I'd spent enough time staring down at the cross streets below his penthouse windows to know exactly how to find my way back to him.

Andrés obviously thought I'd accept the sanctuary offered by the Bureau. He thought he could send my friends to retrieve me, and I'd quietly go back to my life with the FBI, kept safe by my fellow agents.

He was wrong. I was going straight back to him.

Te amo.

He loved me. He loved me, so he'd let me go. He didn't believe he was strong enough to fight his brother.

But he hadn't counted on having me by his side. He'd only seen me in my weak attempts to fight as a field agent. He'd never seen me in hacker-geek-goddess mode. If I could get back to him, I could show him how easy it would be for the two of us to take Cristian down.

I just needed his laptop, and I'd be able to

JULIA SYKES

destroy Cristian financially, backing him into a corner before sending the full power of the FBI after him. I'd send all the incriminating evidence straight to Jason and Dex, and they'd handle the arrest.

Especially if they knew Cristian was the one responsible for my abduction.

"It was Cristian Moreno," I said quietly, looking straight into Dex's eyes. "He kidnapped me."

His jaw clenched. He knew about the Bliss and human trafficking. He'd seen me in Andrés' shirt, and he was clearly coming to some dark conclusions.

"Jason thought Division 9-C had you. We looked into Moreno, but there was no evidence. We didn't think you were on his radar. We were looking in the wrong place. Fuck, I'm sorry. I'm so sorry, Sam. Did he... Were you hurt?"

I cut my eyes away from his, even though I didn't feel any particular compulsion to do so. My nervous tic seemed to have been eradicated, but I didn't want him to see the truth in my eyes. I hadn't been hurt. Not really.

But it was to my advantage if Dex thought I had been. I needed him to think I was weak, shaken. Not fully mentally sharp and calculating the best way to get Andrés away from both his brother and the FBI.

"Where's Jason?" I asked instead of answering him.

"He's out looking for the people who did this to you. I'll call him and tell him it was Moreno."

"What about you?" I pressed quietly. "Will you go after Cristian?"

"No. I'm staying right here with you."

Crap.

I needed him to leave. I had to get back to Andrés, especially while the FBI was distracted with tracking Cristian. I'd been running through all the potential ways to save Andrés, and one had become clear to me: I had to get him and his laptop from his penthouse and go into hiding.

I didn't know how to get in touch with Andrés directly. I'd never seen him with a phone, and while I knew he must have one, I didn't know how often he kept it on him. Certainly not when he was in his penthouse. That was a mostly technology-free zone, except for his laptop. Even if I was able to find his number somehow—and I'd need access to a computer for that—it would take too long to track down.

I wasn't sure how long I'd been out of it, but Cristian could find out I was missing at any time and decide to hurt Andrés for letting me go.

So the time factor ruled out trying to communicate with Andrés remotely. That meant I'd need to go to him in person. Which was an impossibility as long as Dex was hovering over me. He'd follow me. Or worse, prevent me from leaving the hospital.

I couldn't risk telling him about Andrés, because then the Bureau would know exactly where to find the man who'd been holding me captive. They wouldn't treat him gently if they knew his role in my abduction, no matter what I said to defend him.

Once I got away from Dex and back to Andrés, we'd leave Chicago. I wasn't sure what kind of private transportation Andrés had at his disposal, but I was fairly certain he'd have something we could use to leave the city. A car would do. A jet would be awesome.

I'd never cared for his drug money, but in that moment, I hoped to hell Andrés had a private jet. If he didn't, I'd have to get us fake passports, and that would be a snag I wasn't quite ready to deal with. Maybe he'd have a connection somewhere that could help. What good was being in love with a master criminal if he didn't have some useful seedy connections?

Somehow, we'd get out of the country. I'd move all his money to an offshore account—at least, as much as we needed to survive. And then we'd ride off into the sunset together.

Now that I was faced with the prospect of being returned to my old life, I realized I didn't want it. I'd spent years hiding behind my computer.

I was ready to live my life, and I wanted to share it with Andrés. I didn't care where we went, as long as we were together and he was safe from Cristian.

But I had to get past Dex first. My eyes searched the room. He'd left his keys and phone on the table in the corner, beside a chair where he must have been sitting while I slept.

I needed those keys.

Not the phone, because that could be tracked. I didn't know how to call Andrés, anyway. Access to the internet from the smart phone would have been nice, but I didn't have time to do any hacking, especially not from a phone. I could do much more significant damage to Cristian once I had access to the raw data on Andrés' laptop.

"Um, can you do something for me?" I asked, still not meeting Dex's eye. He wouldn't think anything of it; I rarely looked directly at him.

"Anything," he said hoarsely.

"Can you get me some real clothes?" I wore a hospital gown, which wasn't ideal for escape.

"I got Chloe to bring you some," he said, gesturing at a pile of neatly-folded clothes on the table beside my hospital bed.

"Oh. Thanks. Could you, um, get me something else?"

My mind raced, trying to think of some errand I could send him on to make him leave me alone for a few minutes.

"Coffee," I said quickly. "I haven't had coffee in weeks."

It was true, but I hadn't needed it, so I hadn't really missed it. I'd slept so soundly with Andrés that I hadn't required my usual two cups a day.

"I don't want to leave you," Dex said. "I can wait until another agent comes to relieve me, and then I'll get you anything you want."

"Please," I begged, letting my real desperation shine in my eyes as I finally looked up at him. "I miss it. Coffee is normal. And I haven't... I couldn't..." I trailed off, letting Dex read whatever dark things he wanted into my unfinished sentences.

His jaw worked as he ground his teeth together, and he nodded tightly. "Okay, Sam. I'll get you coffee."

"Is there a Starbucks here? You know what I like. Quad venti iced Americano with two pumps of mocha syrup. Please," I added again when he looked hesitant.

"That's all the way downstairs," he said gently. "It will take a few minutes. I don't want to leave you here by yourself."

"I'll be fine," I said, feigning a yawn. "I'm still so tired. I'll nap while you're gone."

"Okay," he said reluctantly. "There's a CPD officer just outside the door. She'll keep you safe while I'm gone. You don't have anything to worry about."

"Thank you," I forced myself to say.

Shit. Now, I had to talk my way past a police officer, too.

I set about formulating another plan as I watched Dex leave my hospital room. A small pang speared my heart as he walked away. This would be the last time I saw him. In person, anyway. I fully intended to keep in touch online, if he was willing.

As soon as the door closed behind Dex, I got out of bed and quickly pulled on the clothes Chloe had brought for me: a pair of yoga pants made for a woman with a much more toned butt than me, and a soft black t-shirt. It felt weird wearing clothes after spending so much time naked in Andrés' bed, but they were comfortable enough.

I picked up Dex's car keys and made my way to the door, opening it with purpose.

"Excuse me," the officer said as soon as I stepped into the hall. "Where are you going?"

"I need to find a nurse," I said. "My call button isn't working, and I need some painkillers."

The woman eyed me, assessing. "You don't look injured to me."

I dropped my eyes again to hide my lie, hoping it made me appear frail and damaged. "Um, you can't really see where I'm hurting."

"Oh. I'm... I'm sorry. I'll go find someone for you."

"Thank you," I murmured. I watched her walk down the hall through lowered lashes. As soon as she rounded a corner, I took off in the opposite direction. I wasn't familiar with the hospital's layout, but it wasn't difficult to find my way to the elevators and ride down to the parking garage. Once I was there, I hit the panic button on Dex's keys so I could locate his car.

I raced across the garage, sprinting toward the sound of shrill beeping. As soon as I got to his black sedan, I turned off the panic signal and got into the driver's seat. I was careful to leave the garage at a normal speed, even though I wanted to tear across town to get to Andrés. I couldn't get a cop tailing me for speeding right now.

I was only a few blocks away from the hospital when a phone started ringing in the glove compartment. Sighing, I retrieved Dex's personal phone and noted his work phone number on the caller ID. I also noted that he had a spare SIG stashed in there.

Good. I could use a weapon, just in case.

"Don't be mad," I requested as I answered the call.

"Where are you?" he growled. "You took my keys. The officer said you were wearing Chloe's clothes. Do you know what I thought when I came back and you were gone? I thought he'd come back for you. I thought—"

"I'm fine," I promised, cutting off his tirade.

"Why?" he demanded. "Why would you leave? And where the hell are you going?"

"Back to him," I said truthfully. "I have to save him, Dex."

"You're going back to Moreno? Are you crazy?"

Dex probably thought I was unhinged, warped by my time in captivity.

I hadn't been warped, but I had been changed. Maybe I was a little darker than I had been, a little less pure. Maybe some of my light had spilled into Andrés, just as some of his darkness had seeped into me.

I had to get back to him, to grab him and his laptop and get the hell out of Chicago before Cristian realized I'd been freed. Once we were off the map, we could take Cristian down. I wasn't exactly sure where we'd go, but I'd make sure to set enough of Andrés' money aside in an offshore account to establish a safety net for the two of us. The rest could be donated to various charities, to start to set right some of the evil Cristian had brought into the world. Evil that Andrés had facilitated, even if he hadn't wanted to do it.

I'd help him atone.

I'd have some atoning of my own to do. After

all, I was stealing Dex's car and going on the run with a notorious criminal.

I grinned to myself. Maybe I was a bit of an anti-hero.

Cool.

"Sam, come back to the hospital. Please."

"I can't. Sorry, Dex."

"Do you know what it did to me when you went missing? I can't lose you again. Come back to me."

I didn't like the anguish in his voice. I didn't want to hurt my best friend. I owed him an explanation.

"I'm going back to Andrés," I told Dex. "I love him."

"Andrés Moreno? No, you don't. You're confused."

"I'm not confused," I said calmly. "Not anymore. I used to think I was in love with you. Did you know that?"

"What?" His breathless tone let me know he'd had no idea.

"It's okay. I'm supposed to be with Andrés. Just like you're supposed to be with Chloe. If she were in danger, you'd do anything to save her, wouldn't you?"

"Of course, but—"

"That's what I'm doing right now. I'm saving the man I love. I'll send you all the dirt you'll need to arrest Cristian in a few hours. Call Jason and tell him to start getting ready to move in on Cristian. I need you to find him fast, Dex. I'll do what I can to drive him out into the open."

"Don't do this, Sam," Dex pleaded. "Let me help you. I know I failed you, but let me help. I can't make it right, but—"

"I made my own choices," I said firmly. "And I'm making my own choices right now. You didn't do anything wrong, Dex. I'm happier than I've ever been in my life. Well, I will be," I amended.

I just had to go save my man.

"Don't try to look for me," I warned. "I'll see you online, if you're ever up for a game."

"I'm going to find you, Sam," he promised. "Whatever's happened to you, I'm going to help you."

"I don't need your help. You need mine. I'm going to keep tracking Division 9-C for Jason. I'm going to make sure Natalie is safe for good. I'll email him. But don't bother trying to trace it, because you'll just be wasting the tech analysists' time. I mean, I know you'll make them try, but don't be too mean to them when they fail."

I was in full-on hero mode, and it felt damn good. I was armed with a weapon and my wits, more powerful than I'd been in weeks. Possibly ever. Now, I just needed to get back to Andrés, log on to his laptop, and proceed to destroy his sadistic brother for good.

"Sam. Come back. Please."

"I really do hope I'll see you online," I said, softening. "Don't shut me out. You're my best friend."

"I'll see you in person," he said firmly.

"Webcams have been around for like, a quarter of a century, Dex. And I'm going to have a really great internet connection, so you'll be able to see me crystal-clear. Tell Chloe she'd better take good care of you. I'll be checking in."

I ended the call and dumped the phone out the car window so Dex couldn't use it to track me. I'd leave his car in the garage for Andrés' building. By the time he traced it there on traffic cams, we'd be long gone.

It took me precisely twelve minutes to get to Andrés' building. I relished knowing exactly how long it had taken me down to the minute. I really had missed everyday conveniences like digital clocks. Wherever Andrés and I ended up, we would have one in every room. I'd insist.

I diverted myself from my little fantasy of our home together and pulled into the garage. Well, I tried to pull in. The barrier didn't open for me.

Fuck.

I put the car in park and hurried out of it, grabbing up Dex's SIG on my way. I'd have to go in through the front. Which was a shitty non-plan, but I couldn't linger here, either. If someone noticed Dex's unauthorized sedan blocking the entrance to the garage, I'd be a sitting duck.

I needed to get up to the penthouse, get Andrés and his laptop, and get out.

Mustering up all the new-found confidence as I possessed, I strode through the glass front doors. The atrium was surprisingly bland, like any nondescript office building. But I supposed it wasn't in Andrés' best interests to be ostentatious about where he lived.

A man in a security uniform looked up from a row of computer screens as soon as I stepped through the door. He stood quickly, pushing out of his chair where he'd been lounging behind the front desk.

I pointed my weapon at him and shook my head before he could reach for his own gun.

"Don't even think about it," I warned. "I'm taking the elevator up to the penthouse. Do you have access?"

"No," he said quickly, shaking his head and holding his hands up high to prove he wasn't a threat.

"Okay, then. I'm going to the third floor. Is there another elevator?"

"Yeah. That way." He pointed toward a darkened corner, and I saw little glowing circles that indicated call buttons for a set of elevators.

"You're coming with me," I told him, gesturing

for him to come out from behind the desk. "Keep your hands where I can see them."

He moved where I'd instructed, and I closed the distance between us to take his gun from its holster.

"Let's go." I ordered, and he began walking toward the elevators, his hands still held high.

I just needed to get to the third floor and find Lauren. She had access to the penthouse. Well, she did as of yesterday. I hoped Andrés hadn't had time to revoke her clearance.

I shook my mounting worry from my mind. If she couldn't take me upstairs, she'd know how to contact Andrés. I'd never seen him with a phone, but he must have one he used when he left his suite. I considered asking the guard if he was able to call Andrés, but I had to guarantee that he'd bring his laptop down with him. His most likely reaction to finding out I'd returned to his building would be to storm downstairs and try to make me leave. He'd be too enraged to think to bring his laptop, even if I asked.

No, I needed to personally get up there and get both my man and the computer. The guard and I were only three yards away from the elevators when something sharp pierced my lower back. Pain lanced through me as electricity jolted my system. I lost control of my limbs, and I dropped to the hard marble floor, my guns slipping from my hands as I went down.

Fuck!

I knew what a Taser felt like. I also knew I wouldn't be able to move for another minute or so.

The guard I'd taken as my hostage bent down and scooped up my weapons, training one on my heart.

"Wait," a new, unfamiliar voice said. "We need to call this in and see what the boss wants us to do with her."

A second man appeared over me, holding the Taser that had taken me down.

Yes, I wanted to say. *Call Andrés.*

The words were an unintelligible groan.

"Took you long enough to get here," the guard complained. "She could have fucking shot me."

"You're lucky I came back from my break early, then," the second man said coolly. "Cuff her," he advised.

The guard nodded and grabbed the handcuffs attached to his belt. He quickly secured my wrists at the small of my back while the second man pulled out his phone and placed a call. He spoke into the receiver in rapid-fire Spanish that I couldn't follow.

I'd been disarmed and restrained in a matter of seconds.

I really sucked at being a field agent. As soon as

Andrés got me out of this mess, I promised myself I'd never fight crime in person again. I could work far more effectively from the comfort of my ergonomic chair behind my computer screen.

"Moreno wants to see her," the second man said, ending his call. "Get her downstairs."

Downstairs? Not up?

The two men gripped my upper arms and wrenched me to my feet. I couldn't support my own weight, so they started dragging me the short distance to the elevators. Once we were inside and the guard had pressed the button for the basement, I started to regain some control over my muscles.

I'd only just managed to get my legs to support me when the doors slid open, and my knees gave out.

Andrés wasn't waiting for me. Cristian was.

CHAPTER 25

"Samantha," his accented voice caressed my name. "I thought you were gone." His sharp smile flashed in the dim light of the spare bulb overhead. I recognized this as the same room where he'd brought me when he'd initially captured me. The day he'd given me to Andrés.

I didn't respond. What was I going to say? The phantom chill of his knife on my skin made me tremble as fear pulsed inside me.

Andrés will come, I told myself. *He'll find me.* He always did. He'd come charging in and kill everyone who threatened me.

Wouldn't he?

Did that vicious protective streak extend to his brother? I wasn't certain Andrés would be able to challenge him.

He will. For me, he will.

I hoped I wasn't lying to myself. My own fear of Cristian was enough to blow all the wits right out of my mind. I couldn't imagine the clawing, instinctive panic Andrés must lock inside every time he faced his brother.

The men holding me upright dragged me forward. I tried to dig in my heels, but my feet stumbled uselessly as they closed the distance between me and Cristian. His black eyes—so like Andrés'—studied my face, searching.

"You came back," he said, his head canting to the side as his eyes narrowed at me. "Why? My men say you were armed. Were you going to kill Andrés?"

"No!" The word popped out before I could hold it back.

"Then why return, when my brother set you free?"

"I..." I swallowed hard and braced myself for the lie, drawing on a defiant mask. "I came to kill *you*. I was trying to find you. I was going to deal with him after." I couldn't tell him about my feelings for Andrés. If I did, he might hurt him again.

Andrés had warned me about Cristian, even in our early days together. The sadistic bastard liked to force you to watch while he hurt the person you loved most. When Andrés had first told me about his brother's sick proclivities, I'd feared for Dex's safety. Now, I feared for Andrés. I had to make Cristian believe I saw Andrés as my cruel captor, and that I was coming for revenge on the Moreno brothers.

Cristian laughed, the sound rich with genuine delight. "You do want to kill him? He'll be so devastated. He does tend to get a soft spot for his pets. You, especially. I thought he was actually going to try to attack me when I told him I'd ordered Lauren to dose you with Bliss. He didn't like the idea of other men fucking you."

I remained silent, willing my brain to start figuring a way out of this.

"How about we make a deal?" Cristian continued before I could gather my thoughts. "I can't let you kill Andrés. He's the only family I have left, and he's very good at running my business. But I'll let you cut him up a little. I was about to do the same, myself. He really shouldn't have let you go back to the feds. That puts my entire organization at risk."

My stomach turned. I couldn't hurt Andrés. But if Cristian was offering to hand me a knife...

No. That would be suicidal. There were still two armed guards in the room with us. If I tried to stab their boss, they'd shoot me.

"Take off the cuffs," he ordered his men, but he didn't take his eyes off me. "I'm going to need to make this look right to keep Andrés in line. I'm sure you understand."

The handcuffs fell from my wrists, but I didn't have a chance to think about defending myself. Cristian's fist slammed into my jaw. Pain cracked through my skull, and I tasted blood in my mouth as my cheek cut against my teeth. The basement flickered out of existence.

When I started to come back around, I became aware of the familiar feel of leather cuffs around my wrists. My arms were being pulled above my head, and my weight started to fall on my wrists. I scrambled to get my feet under me, but the tension on my arms increased, forcing me up onto my toes.

I blinked hard, fear helping clear away the throbbing pain in my skull. It receded to a dull ache as adrenaline kicked in.

Cristian came into focus, his handsome face filling my vision. He touched his long fingers to my injured jaw, and I hissed as pain spiked.

"This will do," he said, studying me as though I were an object instead of a person. Worse than that: a tool he was going to use to hurt Andrés. "I had this set up for my little brother," he explained, gesturing at the restraints that stretched my body taut. "He screamed so much the last time I did this to him. I didn't think he'd ever want to repeat the experience, but then he let you go. Imagine how upset he'll be when he sees you here instead, after he tried to save you from me." He grinned. "He'll be absolutely destroyed once you start to work on him. Don't worry. I'll let you down so you can get your revenge, once I have him where I want him. Then, the offer to work for me still stands." He gabbed my jaw hard, making me cry out. "If you refuse, I'll find another use for you. Did you enjoy your time in my brothel?"

"I'll work for you," I forced out, struggling to speak when pain lanced through my jaw. I'd say anything to buy some time.

I'll get us out of this, I promised myself. *I will.*

"Good." He released my jaw, and I sagged forward, my weight falling onto my wrists before I caught myself on my tiptoes. "My brother might be obsessed with you, but you're too skinny to earn me much as a whore. No matter how pretty your skin is. I knew Andrés would enjoy marking it up."

He reached around me, and his fingertips trailed over my bare thigh, tracing the line of one of the faint bruises Andrés' crop had left when he was punishing me for trying to escape. I gasped and tried to move away from his hand, but there was nowhere for me to go. His touch on my exposed skin made me look down to assess my body. I'd been stripped again. But in this horrible place, it didn't feel normal to be completely bare. Cold air teased across my skin, making me very aware of how vulnerable I was.

"*Mí hermanito* is on his way down," he told me. "Should we put on a little show for him?"

He reached for his belt, where he kept the wicked hunting knife close to his side.

"Don't," I begged, remembering the grating agony of the blade scraping across my collarbone.

"I need to make a point," he told me, waving off my plea as though it was nothing to be concerned about.

He stepped behind me and touched the knife to my throat, the cold steel barely kissing my skin. My breath stuttered. I knew how easily it could part my skin, carving me up the way he'd tortured Andrés.

The soft *thump* of the elevator arriving sounded just before the doors slid open. I had a moment to register Andrés' face fixed in a carefully blank mask before his features twisted with rage.

"Samantha," he snarled out my name and launched himself out of the elevator.

"Stay right there," Cristian commanded.

The knife sliced a stinging line into my throat, and Andrés stopped in his tracks, his entire body vibrating with barely-suppressed violence.

"Be a good boy and have a seat, or I'll cut her open right now. Do you want your pet returned to you scarred or dead?"

"Let her go," Andrés ground out. "I know I'm the one you want to punish. Just let her go."

"And send her back to the feds, like you did? I

don't think so. Samantha has agreed to work for me, once we're finished here. Sit down, *hermanito*. Or I'll slit her open and let you watch her pretty insides spill all over the floor."

I gagged, my body's nauseated reaction to the horrific mental image.

Andrés' dark eyes were drawn tight with anguish, his scar twisting deep into his cheek. A growl slipped between his clenched teeth, but he began to move stiffly toward the spare metal chair that had been positioned a few feet in front of me. The two guards flanked him, pushing his shoulders down so he dropped onto the chair before securing his wrists behind him with a length of rope. Once his arms were bound, they trained their guns on the back of his skull.

"That's better," Cristian said with satisfaction.

The knife left my throat, and I heaved in a gasping breath.

"How should we punish my little brother for his transgressions?" he mused, as though he didn't already have his twisted plan in place. He suddenly cupped my breast with his free hand, squeezing hard. I bit back a whimper, but my eyes began to burn. He tutted at me and twisted my nipple. I cried out at the bite of pain, and wetness slipped down my cheeks.

Andrés' nostrils flared, his eyes blazing. He tried

to push up onto his feet, but the guards held him down with a firm grip on his shoulders.

"He doesn't like that," Cristian observed. "I thought you enjoyed when she cried, Andrés. Or are you the only one who's allowed to enjoy her tears?" He leaned around me, so his chest pressed against my back as he brought his face close to mine. His hot tongue touched my face, tasting my tears.

I shuddered and flinched away.

"I should fuck her raw while you watch," he continued, his tone conversational.

"You said..." I gasped for breath, desperate to get away, to save Andrés before Cristian could use me to destroy him. "You said this was for show," I managed on a ragged whisper. "You promised I could hurt him if I worked for you."

I had to get down and get my hands on that knife. It no longer mattered to me if I got shot. It was the only opening I'd get, and I had to take the risk.

Cristian laughed, running his hand along the curve of my hip.

"She's a vicious little thing," he said. "No wonder you couldn't manage to break her. Is that why you're so obsessed with her? All of your other pets were very obedient by the time you handed them over to me."

My gut churned at this horrible revelation.

Andrés had trained other women before me. Of course he had. I'd always known, even if I didn't want to dwell on it. Why else would he have kinky toys stashed all over his penthouse, with a built-in playroom?

But the knowledge that Cristian had taken them for himself once they were trained made nausea creep up my throat. No wonder Andrés had been so possessive of me from the very beginning. I remembered Cristian promising that he'd be allowed to keep me. I was the only woman his brother had ever allowed him to keep, and now, he was trying to take me away from Andrés, too.

I wouldn't allow him to take anything else from Andrés. He'd taken his family, his innocence, his pride. He'd stripped him of everything and everyone he cared about, leaving him scarred and cold.

"Let me down," I demanded with as much vindictive fervor as I could manage. I drew on my hatred of Cristian to channel righteous rage into my features. He had to believe I'd hurt Andrés for him. "Give me what I want, and I'll give you what you want."

"Savage," Cristian remarked with approval. "Your little pet is going to cut you up for me," he told Andrés. "You risked your life to set her free, and she came back here to kill you. But don't worry. I won't let her take things that far. You'll survive this, and I'll patch you up again after. I'll always take care of my baby brother."

Andrés had gone pale, and his body shook with something other than rage. He stared at me, his eyes wide with disbelief. Then his jaw firmed, and he nodded.

More tears flowed down my cheeks. I wasn't sure if he thought he deserved for me to hurt him, or if he was trying to tell me it was okay to do what I had to in order to survive. Either way, his response was unacceptable. I wanted to scream at him that I loved him and I'd never hurt him.

But I had to get the knife first.

Cristian reached up and finally unbuckled the cuffs around my wrists. My body dropped, and I barely caught my hands on the concrete floor before my face smashed into it.

"Get up," Cristian said coldly. "You have work to do."

I pushed up onto my feet and turned to face him. He held out the knife, offering it to me hilt-first.

I drew a deep breath and then sprang into action. I grabbed the knife at the same time as I jammed my forefingers into his throat. He clutched at his neck, dropping to his knees. Gunshots rang out. Pain seared through my right hip, but adrenaline coursed through me, keeping my body going. I ducked behind Cristian for cover and pressed the knife to his carotid artery while my other hand fisted in his thick hair, yanking his head back to expose his throat.

I could have killed him in that moment. I would have killed him for everything he'd done to the man I loved, but the guards were still armed, and Andrés was still bound and at risk of being shot.

"Drop your weapons," I ordered. "Do it, or I'll kill your boss."

The guards slowly lowered their guns to the ground, their eyes fixed on the knife I held to Cristian's throat. He was still making horrible choking sounds as he struggled to draw in air.

"Untie Andrés," I barked the command.

They hesitated, so I increased the pressure of the knife just enough to make a drop of blood bead on Cristian's skin.

They hastened to comply, sealing their fates.

As soon as Andrés was free, he attacked. He was breathtaking in fluid, violent motion. My dark avenging angel. I watched with detached interest as he snapped their necks. The world was going hazy, surreal, but I kept my hold on Cristian as he continued choking beneath the knife.

Andrés turned to me as the second guard's lifeless body hit the floor. He closed the distance between us and went down on one knee so he was eye level with me.

JULIA SYKES

"Hand me the knife, *cosita*," he ordered, his voice oddly smooth and calm.

My fingers were going numb around the hilt, anyway, so he easily plucked it from my hand.

His gaze left me to focus on his brother. A vicious snarl twisted his scar deep into his perfect face, and he lashed out. Cristian screamed as the blade sliced through his cheek, deep enough that I caught a flash of teeth and bone. Andrés closed his eyes and took a deep breath, savoring the sound. Then his gaze found Cristian again, piercing him with a wickedly sharp black stare.

He drew the knife back and slammed it into the center of his brother's chest. He growled as he twisted the blade. Cristian's entire body shuddered, then sagged back against me where I was still crouched behind him.

His dead weight fell on me, and I couldn't seem to get my hands up to push him away. The room was growing darker, the spare lightbulb dimming.

Andrés heaved his brother's body off me, his expression twisted with some emotion I didn't understand.

"*Sirenita*," he said, strained. "Stay with me."

"I came back for you. I'll never leave you," I promised, my voice strangely faint. I tried to reach up to touch his face, but my arms wouldn't work. "I love you."

He scooped me up against his chest, and agony

lanced through my hip. A strangled cry ripped its way up my throat as he rushed me to the elevator. As it slowly ascended, Andrés started murmuring to me in Spanish in the soothing way I loved so much. I sighed and pressed my face into his chest, the pain receding as I slipped into warm darkness.

CHAPTER 26

ONE MONTH LATER

"Seriously, Dex, I'm fine," I told him for the thousandth time. My webcam specs and internet connection were flash enough that I could see the little furrows in his brow where his face filled my laptop screen. "Are we going to play a game, or what?"

"Where are you?" he asked. "Come home. Please."

I shook my head and lounged back against my headboard, glancing down to make sure Andrés' shirt wasn't gaping open. I didn't want to accidentally flash my best friend. I'd only covered myself with the shirt so I could video chat with him. Otherwise, I wasn't really allowed clothes these days.

I didn't mind at all. I liked being naked here. It

was warm and humid on our little private island, far too hot to bother with clothes.

"I *am* home," I told him firmly. "Andrés and I are perfectly happy and settled here."

He scowled. "You shouldn't be with him. He's a criminal."

"Not anymore," I told him, repeating something I'd said another thousand times. "I'm starting to regret telling you we're together. I want to share things with you. I don't want to lose you as a friend. But if you keep interrogating me every time we talk, I can't keep doing this. You already know you won't find me. I've made sure of that. If I worked so hard to cover my tracks, do you really think I'm just going to tell you if you pester me often enough?"

He blew out a long sigh. "No, I don't expect you to tell me. Even though I wish you would. I worry about you."

"Don't," I insisted. "I've never been happier. Really. Now, if we're not going to play a game, fill me in on what's going on. Did you get all the dirt I sent you on Cristian Moreno? I want to make sure all his people get rounded up and the people they've hurt are saved." I thought about Lauren, my heart squeezing. Dex had told me they'd recovered her and the other girls from Andrés' building weeks ago. I hoped she was okay and able to get the help she needed to heal.

"Yes," Dex confirmed, his lips still thin with disapproval. "Although there seems to be a key player missing in everything you've sent us. You know, the man who was actually running the organization."

I waved him off. "Andrés was acting under duress. He's squeaky clean now. And he'll never hurt anyone else."

Well, he might still whip me occasionally, but that was just for fun. And Dex definitely didn't need to know about it.

"Tell Jason I haven't given up on helping him, either," I shifted topics. "I'm still trying to track Division 9-C for him. We'll find them and trace them back to whatever organization they represent."

I was in full-on hero mode these days, kicking ass and taking names. From behind the safety of my screen, of course. I was working on ensuring all Cristian's people were arrested, tracking Division 9-C for Jason, and—although I hadn't told Andrés— looking for any whispers that Valentina was still alive. I didn't want to open up old wounds, only to let him down if I found something horrible about his sister's fate.

"I'll tell Jason," Dex promised. "But I wish you weren't going all vigilante on me. I can't keep you safe if I don't know where you are."

"That's not your job," I told him. "Andrés is here to protect me. Trust me, he's way scarier than you. He'll keep me safe."

"Always," he swore, his accented voice rumbling over me. Even after spending nearly every waking moment with him for a month, I still got all shivery and blissed out in his presence. I didn't think that would ever fade.

He crossed our bedroom, closing the distance between us. He took a moment to glance at my screen, shooting a warning glare at Dex before he tangled his fingers in my hair and crushed his lips to mine. It was an obvious display of ownership. He still wasn't entirely happy that I'd maintained contact with Dex, even though I'd managed to convince him I only saw Dex as a friend.

He deepened the kiss, claiming my mouth in firm, dominant strokes of his tongue against mine. I moaned and brought my hands up to capture his face, pulling him closer.

Dex cleared his throat pointedly.

Refusing to break our kiss, Andrés reached out with his free hand and snapped the laptop closed. I giggled against him, giddy at his possessive instincts when it came to me. He loved me fiercely, to the point of obsession.

I was equally obsessed, so I didn't mind at all. I couldn't get enough of him, and I never would.

His hands fisted in the shirt that covered me, and the buttons popped free with a powerful jerk of his arms. He wore only a towel, his hair still wet from a shower. I tugged the soft fabric from his hips, revealing his hard desire for me.

His weight settled over me, pinning me down against the massive bed we shared. Andrés had spared no expense in selecting a home for us and furnishing it with all his favorite kinky gear. Other than three members of staff, we lived alone on our private little slice of paradise. No one was around to complain about my screams of tormented ecstasy that floated through the humid air.

I felt a little guilty at the extravagance, but after looking at Andrés' financials, I decided we could keep a small piece for ourselves to ensure our safety and comfort. No one would find us here. I'd donated the rest of the money from his drug empire to various charities, mostly organizations that supported women who'd suffered abuse. Andrés had approved, wanting to do what he could to atone for Cristian's Bliss trafficking.

He was so good at his core, so kind and caring. He'd carry guilt for what he'd helped his brother do for the rest of his life, but I'd be here to help purge him of the dark moods that claimed him.

He wasn't in a particularly dark mood at the moment, just possessive. Hungry.

He kissed his way down my neck, between my

breasts, pausing to press his lips against the raised pink scar on my hip where the bullet had ripped through me. He'd managed to get his private physician to arrive at his penthouse in time to stop me from bleeding out. One of my ovaries had been damaged, but the doctor said I'd still be able to have children. My birth control shot would be effective for another three months, but I didn't think Andrés was going to provide me with another one when it wore off.

I didn't want him to, anyway. I wanted a child with him. Our lives would be unconventional, but we'd be a family.

He finished lavishing attention on the mark I'd gotten when I'd saved us, my wet pussy distracting him. He gripped my thighs with harsh hands and pinned them down, spreading me wide for him. My eyes closed on a groan when he licked me, his clever tongue knowing just how to caress and play to drive me wild. My fingers speared into his hair, pulling him closer. He growled against me and nipped at my clit. I shrieked as my pleasure spiked in response.

"Please, Master," I panted, loving the feel of his title on my tongue. "Please fuck me."

As much as I reveled in his hot mouth on my pussy, it couldn't compare to the feel of him filling me, marking me.

He pressed one last kiss on my clit before

pulling away. Shifting his grip from my thighs to my hips, he flipped me over onto my front.

A delighted laugh bubbled up my throat as giddiness soared through me. The strong, assured way he so easily handled my body send bliss pulsing through my veins. When he was in control, I could let go and relax. I didn't have to worry about being a hero or think about the weight of everyone who was counting on me to save them. I could just be *me*. I could be vulnerable with him, because I knew in my heart I could trust him to take care of me. I hadn't withered in his captivity; I'd become stronger than ever. He'd torn me down to my basest self and built me back up again, making me whole for the first time in years.

He made me whole. And I'd made him whole, in return. He still bore the marks of his brother's torment, but they didn't go deeper than his skin anymore. He'd escaped. We'd both escaped. In so many ways, we'd freed each other.

"I need you," I moaned as he pulled me up onto my knees, positioning my pussy where he wanted it. "I need you inside me." I needed to feel him penetrating me deep, for him to complete me.

He entered me in one hard thrust, stretching me ruthlessly. "Mine," he snarled, driving into me in harsh, fast strokes. This wasn't slow seduction, but it was our own particularly dark brand of lovemaking. My pleasure crested as his cockhead dragged across my g-spot, delicious tension coiling low in my belly. His hand fisted in my hair at my nape, pulling my head back sharply so I was forced to arch into him. At the same time, he pinched my clit.

I screamed and shattered, my inner walls fluttering around him as he roared out his own release. His cum branded me with the heat I loved so much.

He held me in place as he emptied his seed deep inside me, keeping our bodies locked together as we both rode out the last of our ecstasy.

When he finally pulled out, he collapsed onto the bed and draped me over his chest so he could cuddle me and pet me. He needed to touch me as badly as I needed to be touched.

We lay there for several minutes, catching our breath while our fingers explored the lines of each other's bodies. After a while, I trailed my hand down his abs, making my way to his cock. It jerked beneath my soft touch, his desire for me rising to meet my own craving for him.

He sat up, propping his back against the pillows as I straddled his hips and guided him inside me once again. He hissed out a long breath as I slowly lowered myself onto him.

"*Te amo, mí sirenita,*" he said on a rough whisper. "*Te amo.*"

"I love you, my Master. My Andrés."

I leaned into him and captured his lips, claiming him as he'd claimed me. Andrés was mine, and I would never let him go.

EPILOGUE
ONE MONTH LATER

Andrés

"I have something for you, *gatita*." I leaned over Samantha from behind, wrapping my arms around her. She jolted, shocked out of her focused state. Then, she shivered and sighed as I kissed her neck.

"Put your work away," I commanded.

"But I'm super busy," she protested.

We might have made our home on our little slice of paradise over the last two months, but my clever Samantha hadn't been wasting her time lounging on the beach. She'd insisted on shifting back into hero mode, taking down bad guys from the safety of her ergonomic chair.

After sending all the information on my laptop to the FBI, she'd ensured that her friends at the

JULIA SYKES

Bureau cleaned up what was left of my former criminal organization.

That hadn't been enough for her. She attained a sense of purpose and satisfaction out of helping others, and she insisted on continuing to fight crime. I allowed it, as long as she did it under my watchful eye.

Her hacking skills really had been wasted in her brief time serving as a field agent. My Samantha was brilliant and as fierce as ever. She could do far more damage from behind her screen than she could with her fists.

I also allowed her to keep in touch with her former co-workers, even though I didn't care for her continued interaction with her male friends. Knowing that she'd safeguarded our location and it was untraceable eased some of my worry. And knowing that an ocean separated the men from my pretty pet helped suppress my violent impulses when it came to asserting my ownership.

I nipped at the shell of her ear. "You can go back to your work tomorrow. I have plans for you tonight."

She drew in a shuddering breath, but she didn't put her laptop away. "I thought you were working on a project today."

"I was," I allowed.

She thought I'd been working on our new home. I derived calm satisfaction from making custom

352

additions to the house that had already existed on our private island. I was crafting kinky furniture for one particular room in our own personal, depraved haven. I'd never had the opportunity to build something with my own hands. Although my efforts were slow as I learned, it felt good to create rather than destroy.

"Close the laptop," I ordered, dropping my tone with warning. "Now, *cosita*."

She huffed out an exasperated breath, but her little tremor let me know she was as responsive to my dominance as ever. She saved her work and closed the laptop.

"Good girl." I kissed the top of her head. "Come. I got you a present."

I took her hand, and she followed me into our bedroom without question. The large windows were open, gauzy white curtains swaying in the warm breeze. Brilliant pink and orange painted the sky, giving us a picturesque view of the sunset over the water.

It was beautiful, but not nearly as breathtaking as the perfect woman by my side. She wore a silky black robe—one of the only items of clothing I allowed her. She preferred to be covered while she was in "work mode," so I'd bought her some pretty lingerie. Otherwise, I kept her stripped, so I could admire her at my leisure.

Tonight, I did have something for her to wear. I

released her hand and gestured to the large white box on our bed. It was wrapped in a pale blue ribbon, which I'd thought was appropriate for the occasion.

"Open it," I ordered.

She hastened to comply, a delighted grin illuminating her delicate features. Samantha loved presents, and I relished showering her with gifts. I'd give her anything she desired, just to see her heart-stopping smile.

"What's this?" she asked as she pulled the white dress from the box. It was long enough to cover her entire body down to her toes, and the high neck and long sleeves appeared demure. When she held it up in both hands, her eyes widened. The garment was crafted of delicate lace, without any lining beneath. It wouldn't hide her from my covetous eyes.

"It's your wedding dress," I told her, my voice rough with something more than carnal hunger.

Her pale eyes lit up, but her jaw was slack when she turned to face me. "What?" she asked faintly.

I traced the curve of her cheek and rubbed my thumb over her parted lips. "We can't make it official legally, but we're going to have a ceremony."

"Andrés, I..." She swallowed and trailed off.

I couldn't read her reaction, so I issued a command. "You're going to be my wife."

She placed her hand over mine where it rested

against her cheek, leaning into my touch. "Yes," she answered, even though I hadn't asked a question.

Samantha was mine, and I'd tie her to me in every way possible.

I brushed a kiss over her lips. "Good girl. Get dressed and meet me outside."

I already wore my slacks and crisp white shirt. In the last two months, I'd become accustomed to more casual clothes—it was far too hot on the island to wear my customary suits. Besides, there was no one here I needed to intimidate by enhancing my aura of power. The only person I craved to control was Samantha, and she ceded to my power willingly, giving herself to me completely.

In a few short minutes, I'd possess her in a new way. I didn't need a legal document to tell me that Samantha belonged to me, but I wanted to vow to her that I'd always keep and protect her.

I stepped onto our porch, which extended out to the edge of the beach. I'd lit torches and driven them into the sand, adding soft illumination in the waning light of the setting sun. Flowers were scattered along the wooden floorboards, waiting to cushion Samantha's bare feet as she processed the short distance toward me.

There would be no witnesses to our union, but we didn't need any. I wouldn't allow anyone to look at Samantha in her pretty wedding dress. This moment was just for me. For us.

When she stepped into the open doorway, my breath stuck in my lungs. The white lace hugged her body, covering her completely while revealing everything to my hungry gaze. I could clearly see the curve of her breasts, her tight pink nipples peeking through the sheer fabric. Her pussy was a little more concealed, but the teasing glimpses of her pale flesh made my mouth water.

Her copper hair shined as it caught the light from the torches, reflecting their fiery glow. The pretty flush on her freckled cheeks reminded me of her innocence. Somehow, she'd managed to maintain it despite the perverted things I did to her body.

I held out my hand, beckoning. She closed the distance between us, moving gracefully as she glided toward me. Her glowing aquamarine eyes filled my world when she stood before me and took both my hands in hers.

"I love you, Andrés," she murmured, going up onto her toes to press a sweet kiss against my scarred cheek. "This is perfect."

"You're perfect. *Te amo, mí sirenita*," I swore.

A melodic giggle bubbled from her throat. "So, what are we going to do?" she asked, curious rather than teasing. "Is there a cake to cut or something?"

"What we're going to do is say our vows," I told her. "Then, I'm going to rip this dress off you and fuck you senseless, until you scream for mercy."

She shivered, but her delighted smile didn't falter. She didn't fear me in the slightest. I still gave her pain with her pleasure, still demanded her tears when I needed to soothe the darkness inside me. But she wasn't afraid of me. By some miracle, this perfect creature desired me, almost as desperately as I needed her.

"I guess I'll go first," she offered.

I nodded, giving her permission to continue. My heart squeezed, then beat faster in anticipation of her declaration of devotion.

She stared up at me, her eyes shining. "I need you, Andrés. I mean, I know we had a weird start and all, but that doesn't change how I feel. I didn't know what it meant to really be happy before you. I was always anxious and—let's be honest—pretty awkward. I guess I'm still kind of awkward. But you make me better. I'm not anxious when I'm around you. I'm not scared. You make me feel safe. You make me feel loved and cherished. I love you, and I'm never going to leave you. I won't let anything separate us. I'm yours."

By the time the rapid-fire words stopped spilling from her lips, a wide grin twisted my scar deep into my face. She wasn't repulsed at the sight of me. She looked at me like I was her world.

I cupped her cheek in my hand, threading my fingers through her silky hair. "Samantha," her name came out on a rasp. I took a breath and tried again, getting my surge of emotion under control. "I don't know how to exist without you. I'm going to keep you with me always, no matter what. You're mine, but I belong to you, too. Body, heart, and soul. I'm yours."

My vows were more concise than hers, but I mirrored her final words, promising her a lifetime of love and protection.

She beamed up at me. "Are we married now?"

"Now and forever, my sweet Samantha."

My fingers tightened in her hair, trapping her in place so I could claim her lips with mine. She opened for me, her low moan rolling into my mouth. The needy sound made my own arousal stir, and my cock stiffened against her hip.

Wasting no time on following through with my wicked promise, I fisted her lace dress in both hands and ripped it apart. The delicate material shredded, fully exposing her breasts and pussy. I palmed her cunt, running my fingers through the wetness that soaked her labia.

She gasped and shuddered, and I growled against her lips.

Unwilling to wait a second longer, I tossed her over my shoulder and carried her into the bedroom. A giggle burst from her chest as her body draped docilely against my much larger frame. She didn't fight or shriek for me to release her.

But she would be screaming my name in a few minutes.

I dropped her on the bed, the soft mattress cushioning her fall. She laughed, thrilled at my harsh treatment. The tattered remnants of her dress pooled on the sheets at her sides, framing her lithe body like an offering. My pretty, perverted, perfect bride.

I quickly stripped off my clothes and settled my weight over her, lining my cock up with her slick opening.

"My birth control shot might not be effective anymore, you know." Her voice was breathy, and I wasn't certain if she was warning me not to come inside her.

"I know," I replied evenly.

She blinked. "You haven't given me another one."

"I haven't."

Her eyes widened, and she sucked in a small gasp. "You're not going to, are you?"

"No," I growled, thrusting into her.

She cried out and wrapped her legs around my waist, digging her heels into my ass to pull me deeper. "Good," she panted. "I don't want you to."

I pulled back and slammed into her again, taking her with brutal force. She wanted me. She wanted to have a child with me.

Possessive hunger surged through me, and I

fucked her with primal, ruthless strokes. She rocked her hips against me, welcoming my claim.

"Andrés!" she screamed my name, her inner muscles contracting around me as she came undone. I followed her on a rough shout, my heat lashing into her.

I spilled my seed deep inside her, sealing our fate, our future.

My Samantha.

My baby.

My family.

All mine.

The End

ALSO BY JULIA SYKES

The Captive Series

Sweet Captivity

Claiming My Sweet Captive

Stealing Beauty

Captive Ever After

Pretty Hostage

Wicked King

Ruthless Savior

Eternally His

The Impossible Series

Impossible

Savior

Rogue

Knight

Mentor

Master

King

A Decadent Christmas (An Impossible Series Christmas Special)

Czar

Crusader

Prey (An Impossible Series Short Story)

Highlander

Decadent Knights (An Impossible Series Short Story)

Centurion

Dex

Hero

Wedding Knight (An Impossible Series Short Story)

Valentines at Dusk (An Impossible Series Short Story)

Nice & Naughty (An Impossible Series Christmas Special)

Dark Lessons

Mafia Ménage Trilogy

Mafia Captive

The Daddy and The Dom

Theirs to Protect

RENEGADE: The Complete Series

The Dark Grove Plantation Series

Holden

Brandon

Damien